Haunted Steel Adventures

(Love Among The I-Beams)

E. Scott Spencer

ISBN-10: 0-9785587-1-5
ISBN-13: 978-0-9785587-1-0

Published By Horsington Press
Martindale, Texas

For further information, please visit
www.escottspencer.com

AUTHOR'S NOTE: This book, its characters and actions, are fictitious: locations and names, if real, are used fictitiously. Layout: InDesign, type Adobe Garramond Pro, LITHOS PRO. Printed by Lightning Source.

Chapter One
A Surprising Trip

Stanford University, Summer Quarter, August first: Matthew and Sally were together in the dark on his squeaky narrow dorm-room bed in Stern Hall. They were enjoying one of the great benefits of co-ed dorms, making-out after studying together. Matthew had been chasing Sally since April, and finally, for the first time, had her full attention for the night. He was just about to ease down her running shorts when the phone rang. He ignored it until it rang for the third time in succession. Matthew glanced up at the caller ID screen and mumbled, "It's someone in Chicago: must be a wrong number."

"Especially at ten P.M.," she whispered back, moving her tongue along his earlobe. As her lips covered his, the phone started ringing again. Sally sighed, then gently moved his right hand, "Something could be wrong with your uncle. You'd better answer it." The phone was only a foot from their heads. Matthew picked it up with a mixture of annoyance and curiosity.

A distant upper-class female British voice came across the line, "Matthew, Matthew George Atkinson, have I reached you? I am sorry that I am calling late at night, but this cannot wait."

Matthew was puzzled. He had no idea who this was, but she knew his full name, "Yes, er, no, I mean, yes, this is Matthew, and no, it's not too late. I'm studying with a friend." He had just studied Sally's lips and planned to do a systematic appraisal of her left breast next.

Sally's ear was up against the phone too, as her body gently moved against his, keeping up his interest in their studying. The distant voice answered, "I wish that this were not such short notice, but I will be at your door at five in the morning to take you to England. There is someone you must meet on the Dorset coast. Her name is Marti Sedgeford."

He was shocked and for a minute didn't know what to say.

The voice continued, "Her funeral is not for several days, but you must come immediately so that you can talk with Marti before she dies. I cannot over-emphasize the importance of your visit."

Matthew vaguely recalled hearing the name, because the first time he heard it he thought Marti was a man. Was it his mother, who had been dead for sixteen years, who had mentioned the him who turned out to be a her? "Wait a minute, Who's Marti? I've heard of her somewhere. Is she an old relative or something?" Sally unbuckled his belt and slowly unzipped Matthew's pants. The call had gone on long enough for her. Matthew wanted desperately to hang up.

The voice replied, "Not a relative exactly, but she was your maternal grandmother's best friend, and your mother's guardian. It is critical that she talk with you now. She is ninety or ninety-one ears old, but sharp as a tack. Don't worry about the travel arrangements, I have the tickets and will be at your door at five A.M. sharp: we must catch a seven o'clock plane. Please pack appropriate clothing for a funeral. Any questions?" Sally was pulling his pants off, as Matthew tried to focus on the telephone call.

Matthew thought to himself, "Questions! There must be a zillion, but not now!" He confined himself to only one, "Who are you?"

The voice replied, "Forgive me, my name is Azur, or more formally, Azur-Elita Lowther, and I am Marti's second cousin, twice removed. See you in seven hours. Cheerio."

With that, the phone went dead, and fell quickly to the floor along with the rest of their clothes. As Matthew caressed Sally's soft snowy body, he forgot about second cousins. Probably just a crank call and unlikely that Azur Elita Lowther would actually show up as early as she had promised. Sally was playing with his left foot, the one that had been damaged in the car accident that had killed his parents. He hadn't realized how sensitive the mangled foot was to a girl's touch. He writhed in ecstasy. It was almost the first time since he had started at Stanford that Matthew had let another person see his foot, and nobody had ever touched it, let alone in such an interesting way. In the accident that had killed his parents on the Mass Pike sixteen years ago, he had barely survived. Seven operations had been done on his foot but it was still misshapen, scarred and somewhat smaller than his right foot. Sally's gentle caresses and tiny kisses on his toes made him feel a bit better about being a crip. After the car accident, Matthew, only five years old, had spent two very sad months in Massachusetts General Hospital, missing his beautiful mother, Georgiana, and his fast-talking cheerful father. When his foot had healed enough for him to get around, he went to stay with his Uncle John in Cambridge. John was a music Professor at Harvard, and his wife was a very good pianist. Matthew had learned to play the piano from her, surrounding his wounded heart with music, distracting him from his sadness at the loss of his parents.

An hour later, Sally's head was quietly resting on Matthew's shoulder, as he slowly ran his fingers through her hair, massaging her head gently. Matthew couldn't believe his good fortune, finally being in bed with Sally, and had almost forgotten the phone call. Quietly, she hugged him, "I'm going to miss you every minute you're away."

Matt had been so distracted by Sally that he had forgotten. He didn't want to go to England with this stranger, Azur, he wanted to stay here with Sally. "What, oh, damn, maybe I can cancel the trip or get out of it, or you could come along?"

"Not with my schedule. I've got a three-hour Midterm in the genetics lab tomorrow, and a disaster in organic chem next week, but I'll be thinking of you, especially at night. What could be so important that you have to rush to Marti's bedside?"

"I'll check with Uncle John to see who this Marti person is. He always took a dim view of my mother's family since they were theater people. Someone even suggested that Mother was illegitimate. That's probably why nobody ever mentioned her guardian. Azur didn't sound like she's ninety years old like Marti, must be younger, maybe fifty or sixty? That's about how old my mother would be now. I wonder if Azur knew my mother."

"If Marti was your mother's guardian, she might know some secret about your mother that she needs to tell you before she dies."

"Or maybe there is an inheritance that is coming because Marti is dying. Wish it could wait a while: I don't want to leave you,"

Matthew said as he hugged her tightly.

"You never told me your mother was British. Do you remember much about her?"

"I scarcely remember Mom, I think of Aunt Phillipa as my mother. But Georgiana, my real mother, was an actress before Dad rescued her from England and brought her to Manhattan. They died just before my fifth birthday. Since my parents died in such a gruesome way far from home, there wasn't even a funeral. Nobody from her family in England would think of coming to America. They regarded it as a barbaric place, or at least that's what I was told. The family had disowned her when she married an American stockbroker and settled in as a rich housewife. I've seen photos of Mom in her heyday, and her mother, Floris The Magnificent, was even more famous. A magician, as I recall."

Sally started rubbing against Matthew, "Speaking of acting, think you can get it up for a repeat performance? I'm ready for an encore." This was much more fun than working in the lab with Sally. She was an outstanding Bio-Chemistry student and everyone on campus knew that she was going to win a Nobel Prize some day. But Matthew had sensed from their first meeting in the lab that Sally was more than a geek. They had become steadily more interested in each other as the months went by and perhaps now they were beginning to make the transition from friendship to a romance that could last the rest of their lives.

A loud knocking on the door roused Matthew almost as soon as he put his head on the pillow. The digital clock said five. Then he remembered the call. "Matthew, Matthew," the proper British voice called from the other side of the door. "Are you ready? Open up! It is time to leave for the airport."

He was shocked, and for a minute, didn't know what to say. He stumbled out of bed, completely naked, wrapped himself in a towel and opened the door a crack. "What's going on?" Sally asked sleepily.

"We have a visitor," Matthew said, opening the door. Once he opened the door he was no longer able to speak. So this was Azur. The visitor wasn't sixty as he had expected from the formal voice on the phone, she was more like twenty, remarkably pretty, and dressed in expensive clothes. Her beautiful blue eyes glanced at her gold Piaget watch in obvious annoyance as he stared in disbelief.

"You must be Matthew. I am Azur-Alita Lowther. You do not seem to be ready and the car is waiting."

Matthew was astonished and mortified with embarrassment, both for himself and for Sally. "Geez, you only called last night. I'm not some nitwit you can boss around." Matthew fumbled with his towel and noticed the unusual scent of her perfume.

"Have you packed? Do you have you proper clothes for a funeral?"

Azur was at least as surprised at the situation as Matthew, but she was intensely focused on the trip. Without waiting for an invitation, she entered his messy nine-by-twelve dorm room and switched on the light, revealing books, clothes, and papers everywhere. Azur was startled by the mess and by Matthew's lack of preparation; she didn't realize that the rumpled pile of covers on the bed included Sally. "You are hardly awake. I will pack while you dress quickly. We cannot miss the plane, this is very important."

She saw that the walls were covered with pictures and blueprints of bridges and raw steel structures, as well as unusual buildings. The desk was overflowing with papers and a large Sun Unix workstation as well as a small computer. An 88 key Roland Digital Piano occupied much of the remaining space. Azur opened his closet, found an old suitcase, and started throwing things into it as she commanded, "Don't just stand there, get moving".

Azur found a white turtleneck, black slacks, and an old herringbone sport coat. "Put these on, hurry up."

Matthew realized that protesting would be no use, so after a brief hesitation he dropped his towel on the floor and began to dress his naked body. Azur was startled and looked the other way, but he saw her checking him out in the mirror and laughed to himself: he was beyond embarrassment now and was beginning to almost enjoy this odd experience. His encounter with Sally had made him feel supple and strong, but he hated having Azur see his mangled foot. As he dressed, Azur rushed through his drawers, selecting what he would take, shaking her head, and once commenting, "Do you really wear these?"

For the first time in his life, Matthew was ashamed of his collection of student clothing. "What's the big hurry? I don't even know this old lady who is dying."

"We can discuss that on the plane. Who is that, in the picture with the piano?" Azur had noticed that the one non-engineering picture on the thoroughly-covered walls was a poster advertising a charity concert. It showed a beautiful woman in a glass conservatory, next to a large piano.

"That's my aunt, Phillipa, who raised me after my parents died. She's very good, but doesn't play professionally."

Sally, still half-asleep, sat up angrily to vent her fury at Azur's high-handed style. She blinked and stared at the elegant young Englishwoman. "Who the hell do you think you are?"

Azur hadn't realized that there was a girl in the bed and not just a girl, but a naked girl. Azur almost lost her composure, but then regained her stiff upper lip, and replied, "I am here at the request of Matthew's mother's family. May I suggest that my right to be here is somewhat greater than your own. I will take this young man from your bedroom in just a few minutes."

"Can't you let him pack his own suitcase? You're not his mother for chrisake."

"As you may know, she passed away sixteen years ago, but he could certainly use some maternal help with clothing and personal grooming." Matthew was reassured that Azur knew this about his mother, but was annoyed that she was rude to Sally.

"Watch it, sister, or you're going out the door with that suitcase smashed over your head," Sally muttered, fuming, instinctively jealous of the well-dressed confident girl who was bustling about.

Matthew crossed the small room and put his arm around Sally, sitting on the bed beside her. "Calm down, it's just a quick round trip. I'll be back in a few days."

"I strongly doubt it. You have no idea of the importance of this trip," Azur said.

"What? I thought this was just a funeral," Matthew said as he turned to Azur.

Sally just had time to ask, "What about the dance next week?"

Matthew kissed her tenderly, "I'll be back soon, don't worry."

Azur snapped the suitcase shut, "Hurry up! You can buy proper clothes after we arrive in England. Move!" To Sally, Azur commented over her shoulder as she switched off the lights, "Perhaps he will call you later, after his situation becomes clear."

Matthew stopped suddenly, opened his closet, grabbed three pairs of shoes and stuffed them into his backpack: he was just awake enough to remember that all his shoes were custom-made to fit his damaged foot: Azur hadn't thought to pack any of them. He cast a last longing glance at Sally then limped out the door after Azur. He had trouble keeping up, as he lugged the heavy old suitcase with a book bag over his shoulder. They rushed toward a Mercedes limo that was waiting on Escondito Road with its trunk open, the uniformed driver standing nearby. Matthew was embarrassed to hand over his old suitcase and bag of books and shoes.

The limo headed quickly up Bayshore to the San Francisco airport as the sky slowly brightened in the pre-dawn light of early August. Inside, Matthew looked at Azur as she checked her tickets and papers. Azur was so different from anyone on campus: so much more refined. From head to toe, she exuded class. Simple pearl earrings, a matching pearl necklace, a beautiful Hermes silk scarf with a plain gold ring holding two corners together, a soft, almost translucent peach-colored silk blouse, under a cashmere blazer, followed by a comfortable black travel skirt and practical, but delicate, shoes. He caught a glimpse of a small gold watch and a few thin gold bracelets. And her manner, upper-class accent and absolutely correct speech: it was a bit too much to take all at once.

He thought of the contrast to his own impoverished student appearance. Matthew was blond, reasonably tall and athletic, yet he walked with a pronounced limp. He was very self-conscious about his foot, even though Sally had said many times that it didn't matter in the least to her. Azur, with her perfect body and formal clothes, exuded confidence, walking wherever she wanted, literally and figuratively, expecting others to move out of the way. Quiet, shy, Matthew found himself following behind, cooperating with her every request.

Matthew had no way of knowing that Azur's commanding and posh exterior was only a thin shell covering a very nervous and worried young woman. Azur hadn't slept since hearing from Marti and was wrapped in worries about Matthew and how inferior she felt toward him. Azur's PhD dissertation concerned his grandfather Rick, whom she had been studying, but had never seen. In Azur's world, Rick was extremely important so she had wanted to make a good impression on Matthew, but everything had gone the wrong way. He was probably furious with her rushed approach, but she hadn't known what else to do. Azur had rehearsed several speeches and conversational gambits to explain the situation in England, but she had been so rattled by her entrance into a bedroom shared by Matt and Sally that she had forgotten her plans. She had expected Matt to be dressed and packed, waiting for her by the door, just like her proper English friends would have been in similar circumstances. And the sight of his naked body almost completely un-nerved her: she now wondered if Matthew strongly resembled grandfather Rick. What a coup if Matt could be tricked into letting her study him as well.

To Matthew's surprise, they went to the first class cabin. How different from his student trips back to Massachusetts in the tail of the plane. As they settled into the large seats, Matthew could see that Azur belonged here, while he felt very much out of place. He didn't know what to say, there were so many questions: he decided to start with flattery, hoping that it might melt the ice a little. "What kind of perfume are you wearing? I don't think I've ever noticed a scent as nice as yours."

"I have it made in Paris by a small shop on Rue Michel: it's probably unique."

"There must be so many different ingredients and an impossible number of blends. How did you ever choose one to call your own?"

"Just so, you have hit upon the most difficult part. After being in the shop for a few minutes, my nose is almost anesthetized and I can hardly tell what is what. I started with the perfume that my mother wears, and asked the shop to make variations. They put each variation in a numbered bottle. Then I wore each for a week to discover the combination I liked best."

"Do you ever change, or wear something different for special occasions?"

"Not yet. I just started wearing this a year ago. I do have two strengths however, a diluted version for casual wear, as well as a full-strength version which lasts a day or more. The shop makes after-shave lotions and things for men as well: perhaps some day you will go there yourself."

"Sounds like fun, but I'd have to start from scratch since I don't have a father or mother to emulate."

"If you are really interested, you might read THE EMPEROR OF SCENT, by Chandler Burr. He describes many great perfumes but most of the book is about biology and how our noses can discriminate among scents. There are at least 4000 different molecules that we can distinguish with our sense of smell. Perfumes are combinations of different molecules and each is like a painting, an arrangement of ingredients that is an aesthetically pleasing whole. To me, the strangest thing about perfume is that it often contains things that do not smell particularly nice, like ambergris or civet glands, yet the final result is wonderful. Maybe you could try "Happy for Men" or "The Dreamer": they are two of his favorites."

"I had no idea that you were so interested in perfume, and that book sounds great. But now, perhaps you would tell me a bit more about Marti, and why it is so important that I come to her funeral. I thought from your phone call that she was still alive, but now you talk as though she has passed away."

"She is dying, and will be gone soon. She must talk to you before she dies. Since I was in Chicago doing research in the Cribb Collection at the University of Chicago Library, she asked me to fetch you to her." Azur changed the subject before Matthew had a chance to ask more about Marti. "By the way, I noticed an Eton school tie in your closet. Where did you find it?"

"Oh, it was nothing. I won it from a snotty exchange student at a party in prep school."

"It is an odd prize for a contest."

"He was such a jerk. He bet me that because of my bad foot, I couldn't turn a cartwheel on the lawn, so I told him that I

11

would do it in exchange for his school tie. He always wore the thing, just to show that he was superior to us. My school mates thought it a great contest and were delighted when I won."

"Where was this, I mean, where were you in school with an Eton exchange student?"

"At Exeter, or The Phillips Exeter Academy, to be more proper. Of course, the guy had a dozen Eton ties, but I wore that one for fun now and then."

"Did you like the school? Did you do well?"

"The math and science were great and I was able to take some university-level classes from MIT via the net, so I loved it. I suppose that I was the best science student in my class, but a couple of girls had better grades.

Azur opened a large old book and started to read signaling the end of the conversation. Matthew persisted. The plane was airborne, and Matthew had not learned anything significant about the trip. His frustration at her evasiveness was mounting. Overcoming his awe at her self-assured composure, he took the offensive. "Azur, we're in the air, I'm coming with you to England, but I do have many questions, and unless you can supply some answers, I'm getting on the next plane back as soon as we land."

Azur began to worry that his queries might be difficult to answer, "What exactly would you like to know?"

"What's so important? Why couldn't Marti just call me if she wants to talk?"

"You have to meet her in person, and study the property for yourself: this isn't the kind of thing you can comprehend on the phone."

"What property?"

Azur was quite surprised at his lack of knowledge. "Surely you know, I mean how could you not know, what I am trying to say is, well, let us start from the beginning. What do you know about your grandparents and their home?"

"Almost nothing except that Floris was in the theater, a magician I think, and my mother was an actress, at least for a little while. My family never talked about them, and I don't even know the names of any of mom's relatives."

"You really don't know who or what they were or any of the stories?"

Matthew shook his head slowly in answer, quite mystified at the turn of events.

"Marti's home is called Redcliffs Hall. It's a large country house on beautiful land by the sea that your grandparents bought sixty-five years ago. Floris was not just a magician, but an extremely famous performer who died shortly after your mother was born. She chose Marti Sedgeford, her best friend, to be your mother's guardian, so Marti has been living on the estate since Floris's death in 1945. Your mother would have inherited the property, but since she is no longer with us, on Marti's death you will inherit. Marti is tired and old and there are many details to cover before she dies."

Matthew was astonished. "I don't know where to begin, but I knew nothing of this property until you mentioned it just now. There are so many questions."

Azur opened her book again, "If you don't mind, I would rather that Marti explain everything as it is quite involved, and she can tell you all about it in person. I have to finish this book for a paper I am writing. Do you mind?"

Azur was very surprised at his limited knowledge of the situation. Instinctively she decided to stop talking before she let him know more. Introducing him to her world was going to be more complex than she had thought, but she also realized that she was in control of the information flow for at least a little while.

Matthew began to understand the reason for Azur's haste and determination to bring him over as quickly as possible. "How sick is Marti? Will she live long?"

Azur startled him again, as she glanced at her watch, "She is perfectly well, but she only has about thirty hours to live."

"How can you know the time of her death so precisely? What happens to her then? Is someone going to kill her?"

"Don't be ridiculous, Marti is an outstanding medium and she has foretold exactly when and where she will die. For your sake, I wish that she had learned sooner, so that we would not have to rush things as we are doing now. It would have been so much better if you had had more time to visit with her. Now, I really would like to finish

13

my book, and you have your school books in your bag, so why don't we study while we have time?"

After a few hours, Matthew tried again to learn a little about Azur and her life. "What book are you reading?" He saw it wasn't in English.

"It's a pioneering study of parapsychology written in France two hundred years ago."

"You mean like E.S.P. and ghosts and bending spoons?"

"You would be very surprised to know that some aspects of parapsychology are subject to verifiable, repeatable, scientific experiment. More is being learned every day. It is probably the fastest-growing branch of science, at least in terms of percentage growth, and is an extremely exciting field in which to work. For example, teams at MIT, Cal Tech, and the University of Washington are doing formal double-blind experiments on long distance telepathy right now."

"Maybe so, but the basics, like how it relates to electromagnetic radiation and time travel don't make any sense to me. For instance, how could a person see the future?"

"You know so little about the field that it is not worth discussing the subject further."

"Are you some kind of expert?"

"I am studying toward a doctorate in parapsychology at Oxford, but I would hardly classify myself as an expert."

Matthew was startled. What baloney! No decent university in America would allow such a bogus course of study. He started to express his feelings, but stopped just in time. She had anticipated his views and gave him a cold look that would have frozen the balls off a brass monkey.

Azur continued, "I have considerable psychic talent. Not only can I do ordinary things like dowse water, but I can also feel the spirit lines and energy flows running through the earth."

"You must have been studying this for a long time."

"Yes. When I was ten, I discovered that my father's second cousin, once removed, Marti Sedgeford, was a famous professional medium. She was in her seventies, living alone in a huge ancient hall, five miles down the road from my parents. As soon as I was old enough to cycle over, I began to visit Marti and learn from her about the spirits."

Beyond this, he didn't find out much. Whenever he asked a question, Azur would answer that he would learn everything he needed to know after they arrived at Redcliffs Hall. Matthew had the strong impression that many things were not being said: an impression that something strange was about to happen, and that Azur was being careful not to tell him any details in advance.

She buried her face in the old French book and read it avidly. Matt suspected that this was a ploy to discourage his questions. Finally, she closed the book and slept. Matthew glanced at her reclining body and fantasized about doing to her what he had just done with Sally. What a different trip this would be if Azur had been a bit warmer and more friendly! With her blazer lying open, he noticed that he could almost see right through the thin silk blouse. Such soft and inviting curves just waiting to be caressed, but definitely off-limits.

The combination of the eight-hour time difference and the eight-hour flight landed them at Gatwick in the middle of the night, at eleven PM. A beautiful old silver gray Bentley and its chauffeur met them.

"Is this Marti's car and driver?" Matthew asked in surprise.

"No, Marti can't afford such things. She has only a daily and a handyman. This is my father's car: it originally belonged to mother's father."

"It's a beautiful car. Do you know what model it is?"

"No, but I can ask. Andrew, what sort of car is this?"

"It's a 1961 Bentley S2 Continental Flying Spur, with Mulliner coachwork, miss Azur."

They rode steadily west in the dark, along the A303, then south through Yeovil, then on increasingly smaller and smaller deserted 'B' roads toward the Dorset coast, between Weymouth and Lyme Regis.

Given the first class travel arrangements and Azur's expensive clothes, Matthew was expecting to arrive at a very fancy house. He was quite surprised when they left the road and drove past a crumbling vine-covered gatehouse, then down a long, twisting overgrown narrow driveway, detouring around trees that had grown too close for the big car to pass. They arrived well past midnight at a large dark structure in pouring rain and stopped at one side, where a few dim lights indicated Marti's presence. As they approached a small door, Matthew noticed a little Honda two-kilowatt generator purring in the rain and wondered what it was doing here. As they entered, Azur commanded, "Pay very close attention to every word she says. You will not have a second chance to ask questions."

To Matt, Marti appeared to be a peaceful and very smart old lady who looked a bit like the Miss Marple character he had seen on TV. She invited Matthew and Azur to sit by a coal-burning fireplace in a small, dimly-lit room in the old stone house. Although there were electric light fixtures, none were in use. Rain was spattering against the leaded diamond-shaped windows, accompanied by a fresh breeze, and waves could be heard crashing on the rocks nearby. Oil lamps cast flickering shadows as their flames wavered in the drafts. Despite the fire's warmth, Matthew was cold, and pooped from lack of sleep. Marti noticed this and handed him a thick woolen sweater, "Sorry about the lack of heat. Here, wear this and you'll feel better."

Matthew put on the sweater, "Thanks, I didn't realize that it would be so cold indoors."

"After Marti passes, we will visit the shops so that you can buy warmer clothes and black things for the funeral," Azur said as they sat down.

"You have much to learn in a very short time. You are about to inherit this place from me, and you will need to learn a great deal in order to manage here, since this is a very old house," Marti continued.

"Why is there a generator outside?" Matthew asked.

"You're quite observant. The electricity was disconnected last week, and that generator is just powering the water pump and the fridge. The rest has been cut off."

"What happened? The unions aren't on strike again, are they?"

"No my dear, perhaps this should wait for morning and daylight, but you see, this house is sliding into the sea, and the electricity board decided that it was unsafe to leave it connected."

Matthew was startled, "Slide into the sea: what's wrong with the house?"

Azur answered, "The rocks below have eroded, and the heavy structure is slowly collapsing: experts studied it, but the situation is hopeless."

"Surely not with proper structural reinforcement: anything can be stabilized with modern materials and engineering."

Azur replied with some stiffness, "Not according to our experts."

"That's ridiculous: if you can afford fancy cars and plane tickets, surely you could afford to have some decent Engineers analyze the problem."

Marti looked curiously at Matthew. He could tell she was interested. "Are you an expert?"

"No, of course not, I'm just a student, but I wrote a paper last year analyzing the failure of Dortington Castle, and showed how easily it could have been saved from collapse by installing a modern supporting structure. I found tons of analytical information on old stone buildings while I was doing the research. This stuff isn't rocket science, after all."

"After breakfast, I will call father and ask him to send over the experts' report on the foundations. You may find the report quite interesting and he will be delighted to receive something useful in return for the money he spent on it, trying to help Marti."

Marti smiled, "See Matthew, fate has sent you here at just the right time, and with the right skills. You'll never leave. The house will draw you to it."

Azur also seemed pleased at the turn of events, "Better write that girl of yours and tell her to find another partner for the dance next week."

"Only if you'll take me to a dance over here instead," he replied with sarcasm.

"Don't let my funeral get in the way. I would love to die knowing that you two were going to dance on my grave."

"Marti, what an improper idea: I could never do that," Azur stated, somewhat annoyed at the suggestion.

"I would have done it in my youth, especially with a handsome young man like Matthew. Of course, I enjoyed doing lots of improper things. About the only fun I had sometimes. Now, you've both had a long trip, and we have much to do in the morning, so let's get a few hours of sleep."

Matthew walked up a narrow staircase to the bedrooms above. He realized that this part of the house might have been servants' quarters originally. The wooden stairs were not carpeted: they creaked with age and were deeply worn in the middle of each tread. His room was small, with a steeply sloping ceiling and a dormer window looking out toward the sea.   The window leaked as rain trickled around the lower edge making rust stains on the wall. A bathroom with ancient plumbing was down the hall. It had a cold water tap and an old coal stove attached to some copper pipes: apparently you had to fire up the stove if you wanted hot water. Matthew had stayed in European youth hostels with better facilities. Azur was in the next room, then Marti in another. As they had come up the stairs, Matthew had inadvertently brushed against Azur's soft body. This touch reminded him that she was, after all, a very good-looking girl about his age, in spite of her serious and intense manner. As Matthew sank into the down pillows in his tiny room it was not Sally he dreamed up but the beautiful Azur.

Chapter 2
Exploring Redcliffs Hall

Morning came early in summer at this latitude, and the sun was over the horizon just before five. Matthew was awakened from a brief sleep by light streaming through his window and the aroma of coffee and bacon cooking. The beautiful view of the sea from his window, clean, blue, freshly-washed sky, and puffy fair-weather clouds, transformed his mood. He knew that this would be an unusual day, and that it was time to learn all he could. It was also time to smile and enjoy this strange experience. He shaved quickly amidst the ancient plumbing and noticed that it really was cold: he could see his breath while in the bathroom even though it was early August. Following his nose he found the kitchen, where Marti and Azur were eating at an old table while the daily helper worked nearby.

Marti greeted him before he entered the room, "Good morning Matthew, ready for breakfast?"

"Sounds wonderful: what a beautiful day. The view from my room is gorgeous."

Azur added as he sat down, "Wait until you see the rest of the property: you're going to love living here."

"I don't know about living here. So far I'm just a visitor, but a very curious one. What should we do first?"

Marti answered, "We'll start with the most important parts, then if there's time we'll wander through the rest."

"Sounds good to me." Matthew looked around the room and in particular at the windows, which were in a style he hadn't noticed before. They went from floor to ceiling and each pair opened outwards. However the unusual feature was that each window had wooden shutters on the inside, with a substantial iron cross bar to close the shutters tight. Virtually every shuttered window he had seen in America had its shutters on the outside, for storm protection or decoration. These indoor shutters looked solid enough to provide protection from burglars, and perhaps to add an insulating air layer when closed: how clever.

Marti explained as they ate fried eggs, fried tomatoes, greasy fried bangers, and fried toast, "Parts of the main building, at least the foundations, go back to Norman times. There have been many changes through the ages as the sea slowly reclaimed the land, and as owners' fortunes waxed and waned. Some of the rooms haven't been used since your grandmother Floris died in forty-four."

"And she and your grandfather never entertained, so much of this estate is just the way it was left when the house was abandoned in 1885 by the Victorian owners," Azur added.

"The plumbing must be amazing," he said.

"That's a polite word for what little there is. I think they all used chamber pots in those days, or peed out the window," Marti said.

"Really Marti, it couldn't have been that bad," Azur reprimanded.

"I saw a castle in Heidelberg where the bedroom toilet was a hole maybe thirty feet above the ground: you could have looked right up into someone's bum if you were standing there at the wrong time," he laughed.

Marti continued to describe the house. "This kitchen and the rooms above and below are a wing that was refurbished around 1850: I'm sure you noticed the old plumbing but it's still working. This wing is where the housekeeper and some of the more important servants lived in the old days. The main house is a mess, and hasn't been lived in for a long time, at least a century. I raised Georgiana in this wing, and this wing is where Floris and Rick lived when they weren't doing shows in London or on the Continent. They had planned to refurbish the whole place eventually, but that never happened. Now let's get on with the important part of the tour."

They went through a squeaky door into the main part of the house, then down a narrow staircase into the servants' offices and kitchens under the main house, then down another stairway and entered an old library lined with books from floor to ceiling. Dark faded drapes covered the windows, which were on the ocean side. The only artificial light was from a kerosene lamp which Marti carried. Much of the stale-smelling room was in dark shadows, with books and papers everywhere. Moldy carpets were underfoot, adding to the musty aroma. There appeared to be other book-filled rooms as well at this level.

Marti became serious, "This is the most important room in the house and I want you to pay attention to what I tell you. The desk over there contains useful records. You'll want to read them as they preserve information that you will need. There are keys in the top drawer: I don't know where all of them go, but with your engineering expertise, you'll figure it out. And all these old books—I've never read them but I knew enough to keep them. They may help you as you live here."

"Funny, I don't think I've ever been in this room before: I didn't know there was a library so low down in the house. We must be in a basement, under the kitchens," Azur said.

"It's odd, but as you say, not many people would expect to find all this down here: quite a secret and private location, not known to the public, perhaps very much on purpose. At any rate, that's not the critical part. The important bit is over here, by the fireplace. These books right here aren't real. See, they're just bindings glued to wooden blocks. This is a door, and you open it by pushing here and here at the same time: you have to push pretty hard," Marti said.

The book-door opened slightly, and Matthew helped her open it all the way, revealing dark dust-covered steps leading both down and up, and many cobwebs.

"Marti, this is amazing: what is in here?" asked Azur.

"Thought you both would be impressed. If you go down, you will find Matthew's grandfather's workshops and all sorts of sub-basements, and the passages upward wander around the house. You can explore with torches later. Matthew, the important part for you, is that if you go down to the bottom, you will be able to see the old foundations and the problems and maybe do something to fix them. And, while you're down there, you will find the entrance to a tunnel that goes down to a cave on the beach. Your grandfather took me down ages ago. I don't know how to find the entrance, but I remember that it was on the wall away from the sea: back deep inside the cliff."

Matthew was excited, "Can we go down now?"

"Later: you'll have time to see it all after I'm gone."

Azur wondered, "This looks like it hasn't been disturbed in ages: did the experts come down here to inspect the foundations?"

"Oh no, they were experts, so they didn't need to get dirty wandering around old passageways. They flew around in a helicopter making pictures and writing reports, then they pronounced the situation hopeless."

At these words Matthew knew almost exactly what the report would contain: a ton of boilerplate and zero practical analysis.

They closed the door, retraced their steps, and came out of the musty basements into the damp but carefully-tended walled gardens. Marti led them to white wrought iron chairs, around an old table, in a brick-walled formal rose garden. She spread old scrapbooks on the table. Unlike the house, the garden was in good shape, with many ancient flowers and herbs. As they had walked around, Marti had sniped a weed here and there: it was clear that this was her domain and that she took good care of it.

Marti picked up one of the scrapbooks and opened it toward Matthew, "This little book is from your grandmother's early career when there wasn't much to tell: she wasn't famous and they rarely advertised her name. Oh, here's a picture of Floris and me in the late twenties: weren't we lovely!"

Azur asked, "Where is the clipping about the night she met Matthew's grandfather?"

"Here, just at the end, on the last page. I put it here to mark the before and after parts of her career. A newspaper man was in the audience that night and he reported on the first time that she did her amazing escape trick. That really marks the beginning of her fame, in October 1935."

"The next day a much fancier theater asked her to perform," Azur added.

"At first she was coy and didn't accept, but then your grandfather, Rick, agreed to be her partner on stage: he wanted to do it just to be with her, and so she agreed, but of course, she didn't need to almost drown each night, but it looked like that was what was happening."

Matthew stared at a particular page: "So this is what my grandfather looked like: he seems a bit weather-beaten."

Marti replied, "That's because he is over a thousand years old. Don't ask me how I know, and for proof and all that. For now, just accept what I tell you."

Matthew thought she was making a joke and laughed, but then he noticed that neither Azur or Marti thought it funny: they were serious. Something odd was going on, and it had nothing to do with the house's structural problems.

Marti turned to Matthew, "Getting back to a question you asked me earlier about your mother, it seemed to me, when I talked with Rick about it, that he and Floris weren't too keen on her. She did something that bothered them, but I never quite knew what it was. Maybe it was the war and being raised by me or something, but there was tension or friction. Your mother always thought that Floris had a secret lover who was her biological father, and that I made up some stuff about Rick being a ghost to cover it up. Your mother left here and married an American stockbroker, then just goofed-off most of her life. Never went to university or took advantage of her brains or psychic abilities."

Matthew was startled, "Wait a minute, you just implied that my grandfather Rick was a ghost, and what was that about mother's psychic abilities?"

"Marti will come to that, but for now, please let her continue in her own way," Azur interjected.

Mathew began to sense something almost unreal about Azur and Marti and their version of past events. He was certain that ghosts and spirits didn't exist, and he recalled Azur's comments about her studies of parapsychology. Perhaps both of them were delusional, imagining tons of far-fetched baloney in Floris' and Rick's history. He tried to interject reality into the conversation. "My uncle and the rest of my father's family tell Georgiana's story with quite a different slant, and they never mentioned Rick or Redcliffs Hall or you to me,"

"I wish I had more time to tell you about all of this and your mother, but after I'm gone, you can talk about her childhood with Julian, Azur's father. In the late fifties, he, your mother Georgiana, and a few other children played here almost every holiday. There used to be a good path down to the beach, and they would go out in a little boat to the island, where there's an old ruined castle. You can imagine how children raised on Enid Blyton's books[1] loved the setting. They kept looking for buried treasure and hoping to have adventures like the characters in the books."

Matt decided to go with the flow and avoid asking pointed questions about the spirit world: probably Azur and Marti were so far out that they couldn't answer factually even if they tried. "Thanks, I'll talk with him and ask about mom and what she was like. What happened to the other children?"

"They grew up and parted company, going in different directions. Azur's father became a sharp businessman and married a very rich French woman. Their daughter here, Azur, is a whiz, getting firsts in everything. You know the story of your parents to some extent. One of the others went to Africa to save endangered animals and do good deeds. And the last one disappeared completely. He left for Australia before finishing school, and fell off the end of the world as far as I can tell."

After they had looked through the picture books, Marti led Matthew and Azur on a tour of the main house. They started outside, in the remains of the original driveway near the front steps. As they walked she explained. "I've been told that the main house is neo-Palladian[2], but with a smaller wing at each side, maybe from

---

1   Enid Blyton wrote books for children. One series of 25 books concerned "The Famous Five", two boys, two girls, and a dog. They often spent time on a little island with a ruined castle, near an Uncle's house.

2   Palladian. "A structure with symmetrical rectangular features, strongly-marked horizontal skyline produced by a crowning balustrade that shuts off the roof from view, rusticated ground floor which gives the impression of solidity and strength, regularly spaced Ionic columns." P62, DISCOVERING ENGLISH ARCHITECTURE, T.W. West, Shire

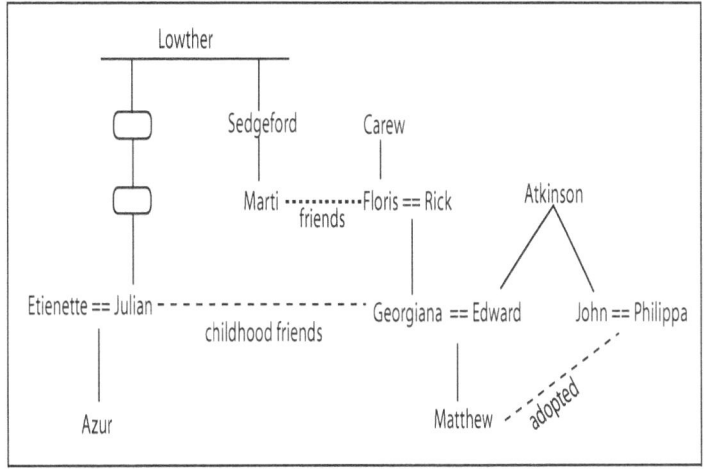

Relationships among the families

1700 or so. The four columns in the middle are solid stone, but it's too bad that one has collapsed. The lowest windows, behind the railing, illuminated the kitchens and the servants' offices. The next row of windows, the big ones, gave light to the public rooms. The smaller windows above illuminated the principal bedrooms. The dormer windows at the top are for servants and children's rooms."

Matthew asked, "Why are some of the windows boarded up?"

"You see, I have only a handyman to help. On this side of the house he tries to either replace the glass as it breaks, or as a temporary fix, nail a few boards over broken windows. He works on the windows he can reach, but it's a loosing battle. On the other side, the side facing the ocean, it's a mess, a big mess. There's no way to access the outside of those windows, and the storms can be fierce. So

---

Publications, 2000. Neo-Palladian buildings, fifty years later, added the suggestion of a temple roof at the center, and grouped the columns under it.

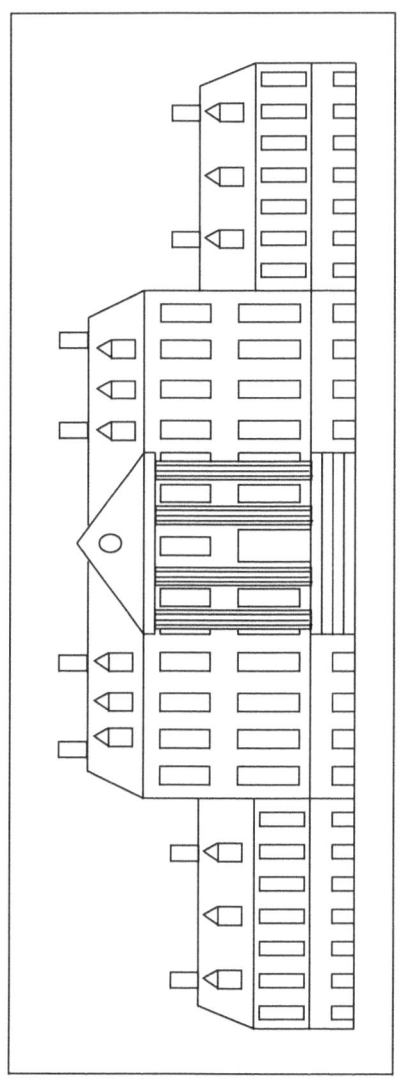

Redcliffs Hall, front view

he's nailed the shutters closed on many of the ocean-side windows from inside: not very pretty, but it keeps the seagulls, or most of them anyhow, outside."

The went inside and wandered through the old rooms as she continued, "The front door, and the servants' door under it are nailed shut to keep vagrants out. My door is the only way in. This must have been a beautiful place when it was fully staffed and freshly painted, and some of the rooms are still very nice."

They went in through the Victorian wing, then through a passageway into the main house and into the formal dining room, an oval-shaped room painted light blue with white plaster trim on the ceiling and the walls. The original dining table was still in the room, scratched and dust-covered: perhaps it was to big to remove. Matthew noticed that although the room was beautiful, dust from the fireplace had covered everything. He asked, "The floor here, it must have been covered with something, I mean these rough boards don't match such a beautiful room."

Marti replied, "Look carefully: I think there was another floor, probably a fancy inlaid design, on top of these boards. A lot of things have either disappeared or been sold over the years, as you will see as we wander around."

Matt examined the floor as they walked and discovered nail holes that showed traces of former layers. Then he noticed that the molding around the walls ended over an inch above the rough planks on which they walked: the finish floor and its substrate must have been substantial, and he wondered what it looked like when new and polished. For a moment, he was almost overcome with remorse: he had inherited the remains of a once lovely mansion, but so much was gone. In some ways it was like walking though an echo of former glory, and his engineering mind told him that the echo was fading quickly, and would soon be lost in the sea if he didn't do something clever.

They entered the main entrance hall, in the center of the house behind the front door. The floor was a black and white stone diamond pattern running diagonally to the walls. The ceiling was at least two stories above. Double marble staircases led up to a balcony and the bedrooms: part of an old chain indicated where a beautiful central chandelier would have hung.

Marti smiled and led them into the other main room on the landward side of the house. "This is my favorite room in the house and we try to keep it functional. I don't know if it was called a parlor or library or what, but it's so comfortable, and the furniture is intact."

Matthew looked around at the orderly bookshelves, comfortable couches and chairs, clean fireplace, and beautiful walnut paneling. This would be a comfortable place to study, and so different from the old dark library under the kitchens.

"Now I'll show you the biggest room in the house, that is if you both will help me open the door. I haven't been in there in years. It runs the whole width of the house on the ocean side. Watch out for seagulls and poop."

They finally managed to move one side of the ornate and warped double doors enough so that they could squeeze into the long gallery. It was dark, musty, and damp but huge. All of the large floor-to-ceiling windows on the ocean side were shuttered. Some shutters had broken and were covered with rough boards and water stains. Light leaked through cracks here and there. The ornate ceiling was perhaps fifteen feet above the warped uneven floor. The chandeliers were gone and one fireplace was missing its mantle and surround. Stains on the walls showed where paintings had once hung.

Azur was amazed. "I had no idea this was here, what a wonderful room this must have been long ago. People could have had huge parties here, and played games when the weather was bad: the view of the ocean must have been spectacular when the windows were open."

Matthew made a different observation, noticing the shapes of cracks on the ocean-side wall, "I think the middle of the floor on the ocean side has sunk: I need to measure, but it looks like maybe it's a bit below the sides. What a sad thing to happen to such a beautiful room."

They walked over to the windows which were shuttered closed on the inside. Matt went to one that wasn't nailed shut, "May I open this?"

"You can try, but watch for broken glass."

Matt undid the crossbar and pulled hard to open one side part way. He jumped clear as glass fell to the floor when the shutter creaked open, revealing salt-encrusted glass and a hole where the broken pane had been.

"What a view of the sea: look, you can see the island," exclaimed Azur as she looked through the hole.

A laughing seagull sailed past the window as Marti said, "After I'm gone you could restore these windows and make this into a lovely room."

"First I need to fix the structure, but then this could be spectacular. You could play badminton in here it's so big!"

They closed the shutter then went up the marble stairs in the main hall. As they walked through some of the bedrooms above, Matthew thought that it was like walking through a museum, except that nothing was clean or orderly, and there were no labels identifying strange objects. Dust was everywhere: they startled the birds who lived in at least one of the bedrooms on the ocean side.

Later they had drinks on the old terrace, facing the sea, watching Marti's last sunset and listening to the seagulls and the crashing surf. Beyond the stone railing on the seaward edge of the terrace was the start of a ruined staircase down to the beach below. When Matthew looked down, Marti told him to be very careful: part of the path had fallen away over the years and the remaining portion could fail any day.

Matthew looked down the stairs. The old stone path ran parallel to the cliff face, slowly working its way down to the beach. At the top of the path, the steps were cut into solid rock, and were sound, even though the iron railing had rusted away in the marine air. However, even from the top, he could see that the middle part of the staircase was missing.   As the path passed the bottom of the house's foundation, there was a large wash-out, where a chunk of foundation, as well as cliff and stairs, had fallen to the sea below. Just repairing this path would be an interesting engineering problem, probably involving building a sloping bridge across the washed-out section. Of course, if more of the foundation fell away, there would be no point in fixing the path, for the whole house would fall into the sea.

When Matthew returned to the table, Marti took both of his hands in hers. "There's something that I had better tell you. It's something that you won't believe now, so don't worry too much about it. As you learn more about the spirit world, and particularly the history of your grandparents, you will come to understand."

"What, what are you getting at," Matthew asked with apprehension.

"It's really nice actually, and not at all scary. The ghosts of your grandparents live here, but they are asleep. You may never see them, but one never knows. They may wake up and then you could have wonderful conversations with them."

Matt could sense that Marti was sincere, that she really believed every word that she was saying, but it was so hard to reconcile her words with his scientific training and experiences. He had never seen a ghost or any manifestation of the spirit world, and he didn't think he knew anyone who believed in spirits. Yet here were two apparently intelligent and well-meaning people talking as though spirits were an everyday occurrence. Half of his brain, the emotional side, wanted to believe Marti and Azur, who were endeavoring to explain a difficult subject, but his rational brain was fighting back.

"You're right about my disbelief: your ideas are so new to me, that, I don't quite know how to put it, but I'm finding it hard to believe that what you are saying is true. But if it were, it would be fun indeed to talk with them." Matthew turned to Azur, "Is there a book about ghosts that I could read to get up to speed? I mean, I don't know where to begin, and the things that you and Marti are telling me are so far beyond my experience."

"There are a few, and if you become serious and want to really learn, then you must enroll in the parapsychology section at Wadham College: it's one of the best places in the world for serious psychic study. You could take beginning courses then work up to more difficult subjects. And you would be quite surprised at the thoroughness and care that we put into our research: we do carefully-controlled repeatable experiments, not spoon-bending as you mentioned sarcastically on the airplane."

"Azur was their top student last year. They want her to become a Lecturer and teach. She'd be the youngest Lecturer at

Oxford if she takes them up."

"I had no idea. Could I learn about Rick and Floris?"

"Not in school. Actually, you will find it best not to mention them in public. Some people think that Floris, and perhaps even Marti, were or are witches, or at least something from the dark side of the spirit world. And we never talk with others about Rick. He's our secret, and now yours as well. Most people are really stupid about such things," Azur said.

"You'll see it at my funeral. There will be almost no one there. People don't want to know the truth."

"And the book learning, what there is of it, mostly covers experiences that normal people have had when they encountered aspects of the spirit world. There is precious little material describing the subject from the other side. Rick may be the only one who has ever talked much about it, but he didn't write anything down," Azur said.

"I don't think he knows how to read and write, and Floris was so busy having fun with him that she didn't bother to leave much, except a few letters to me. I'm sure you can read them," Marti added.

"There's so much that I don't know, and frankly, my scientific background makes it hard for me to even contemplate the idea of ghosts wandering around," he said.

Marti smiled and took his hands in hers, "You're a good student, and I can feel that you have some interesting abilities which could be developed given a strong effort. Azur could teach you many things if she wanted, and perhaps you could teach her some things in return."

Azur was startled at the suggestion, "What subjects might those be?"

Marti smiled but didn't answer. It was almost as if she had said, "You'll be surprised, but I'm not going to tell." There were no words, but Azur looked worried.

After supper they were seated by the only working fireplace talking quietly. Matthew turned to Marti, "Can I ask you something important, but personal?"

"Of course, ask anything."

31

"It will take a lot of money to fix this place. Do I inherit anything besides the house?"

"There's some money and shares here and there, but not much. The papers are in the lower library. You'll have to be resourceful about finances. Rick collected a lot of things, so maybe there is something valuable in his labs that you could sell."

Azur was quite curious, "What did he do down in his laboratories?"

"Rick loved inanimate things so he became interested in machinery. He could somehow feel the way machines worked, how their innards moved, and loved playing with engines and motors and mechanical things. He built a sort of inclined railway that ran down to the beach, but it has since washed away. He made a little steam-powered boat that he kept in the cave down by the beach: it may still be there for all I know."

Azur checked her watch again, "It's close to time isn't it?"

"Just a few more hours. I'll go up to bed now, then you two can come and sit with me at the end."

Marti left Matthew and Azur by the fireplace. Matthew mused to Azur, "What an amazing woman: I wish I had met her years ago. She has so much warmth and knowledge."

"Exactly. I'll miss her very much. She is my only solid contact with the spirit world."

Matthew didn't know what to say in reply. He sensed that Azur was very sad about Marti's condition and instinctively wanted to help her. "Azur, I know this is a difficult time for you, and that bringing me into the picture at the last minute can't be easy. There's so much that I don't know, and as an Engineer, I tend to see the difficulties and problems more than the happy outcomes, so I'm pretty hesitant about all this. What I'm trying to say is that I'm sorry if somehow I have offended you, and that I'll try to be receptive to your world, if you'll let me in."

After a long pause, she replied softly, "Thank you, thank you very much for understanding. Let's go up to Marti's room."

Marti was in bed, reading old letters as they entered.

"Come in children. I was just re-reading letters from Floris and remembering our happy times together. Sorry, but it makes me a bit teary thinking about them. Do you like my funeral outfit? My fancy dress for the occasion?"

Matthew replied, "You'll be surprised when you wake up in the morning and discover that you didn't die after all."

Azur was crying softly, but trying hard not to.

"If that happens, then you can be the medium and I'll be the engineer. That would be a funny switch wouldn't it? Can you see me with a slide rule or computer or whatever they use nowadays? And can you see yourself dowsing and communing with the spirits in the moonlight? We'd certainly be the odd couple, rattling around this old house."

"Please don't go. I'd give anything to save your life," begged Azur.

"Give it to Matthew, he will need all the help he can gather. Good bye children."

Marti closed her eyes and with a long breath died peacefully. A strange wind rattled through the house, swinging the windows open, and blowing-out the lights. It didn't startle Azur, but Matthew felt a cold chill run down his back. The full moon shone through the open window onto her bed, its light centered on Marti's silent face. The wind very slowly subsided as Matthew and Azur sat silently beside Marti's cold and still form.

Matthew couldn't sleep, so he wandered back into the main house, carrying a kerosene lamp, aimlessly looking at things, wondering what to do next. In the parlor he stopped at the piano which he had noticed earlier. He removed the dust cover and opened the keyboard, then played a few notes. How amazing, to find a nine-foot long Boesendorfer 275 concert grand in this old house. Not only was it in tune, but it had an exceptionally warm sound. He tried the four extra bass notes below the lowest 'A' and marveled at the reverberation as their notes echoed off the walls and the marble floor in the entrance hall. Matthew opened the piano wide and began to look through the pile of sheet music on a nearby table. These were old songs from perhaps Jane Austin's[3] days 200 years ago. Music that

3   Jane Austin, 1775-1817, wrote romantic stories many of which happened in old country houses. Her stories describe details of daily life in

people would have played for each other's amusement long before recordings and radio. He wasn't certain but he had the impression that the piano could easily date from the nineteen-twenties or thirties, so his grandparents as well as his mother could have played these very same keys, perhaps even this sheet music. He picked up tunes that looked interesting and started to play by lamp light. Songs[4] such as "The Lamplighter", "Corn Riggs", and "For Tenderness Formed In Life's Early Years". He played a few over and over, and then played other songs from memory, enjoying the beautiful piano. He loved old music, especially old songs.

In Marti's bedroom, Azur was thinking about her PhD dissertation, which focused on Matthew's ghostly grandfather Rick. From what she had been told by Marti, Rick was an incredibly powerful and ancient spirit, nothing like popular conceptions of vague wisps of floating spirit, but a solid and powerful creature. Now that Marti had abruptly passed away, Azur's main source of information was gone, and she was left with fifty pages of useless material. The only consolation was that his grandson might have inherited some of Rick's abilities, which could be documented and folded into the text. Already, Azur knew that Matthew was smart, and perhaps he had latent psychic skills that she could explore, develop, and document.

Azur began to look for Matthew. She heard the music softly echoing through the house and was curious at the source and at the choice of songs. She entered the main house and saw Matthew in the distance, playing by the light of a single flickering lamp which cast long dark shadows in the cold rooms. The music echoed off the hard surfaces. It was a scene from another era: it could have been a few centuries ago with almost no change. She walked over to the piano and sat nearby on an old embroidered chair.

Marti's large white cat, Phil, had followed Azur into the room. It jumped onto the piano bench and curled up against

---

rural England 200 years ago.

4   There is a CD entitled "Music From Jane Austin's Time" which includes these and a dozen other songs, played by small groups of musicians and singers, in the style that would have been used by amateur performers in a remote country house.

Matthew's side. Azur was surprised since the cat was usually not friendly toward strangers. Perhaps it was forming a new allegiance, as it washed itself, then went to sleep against Matthew's side. Matthew glanced at the cat and at Azur , then changed songs. He softly began to play 'Old Deuteronomy' from the musical, CATS[5]. A very slow and sad song which Matthew sang to the cat which he could feel purring against his side.

> *"Old Deuteronomy's lived a long time*
> *He's a cat who has lived many lives in succession*
> *He was famous in proverb, and famous in rhyme*
> *A long while before Queen Victoria's accession*
> *Old Deuteronomy's buried nine wives*
> *And more, I am tempted to say, 99*
> *And his numerous progeny*
> *Prospers and cries*
> *And the village is proud of him, in his decline*
> *At the sight of that placid and grand physiognomy*
> *When he sits in the sun on the vicarage wall*
> *The oldest inhabitant roasts"*

Azur looked on in wonder as she realized that Matthew was crying as he sang to Phil. His voice wasn't perfect, but it was genuine, and he played with such emotion. Matthew repeated the song, then shifted to 'Memories', an even sadder song from CATS. His eyes were closed as the tears poured down his cheeks.

Azur had seen the musical, CATS, ages ago, but had no idea that an engineering student from far away would take the time and trouble to memorize the songs then beautifully play them to a peaceful cat. And she didn't think that she had ever seen any boys her age cry. Maybe a tear or two during a film, but nothing open and flowing, so strong emotionally. Clearly, Matthew was a very sensitive person, one who could be hurt deeply, but also one who could love as well. Perhaps he felt Marti's death much more than she

---

5   CATS, by Andrew Lloyd Webber, based on 'Old Possum's Book of Practical Cats', 1939, by T.S. Eliot.

had realized. Perhaps he really was singing to Marti's cat, to comfort it now that Marti was gone. Azur began to realize that there was far more to Matthew than she had thought. He was turning out to be an interesting and perhaps very useful young man, someone she would like to know much better. She walked to the piano and sat beside Matthew, singing along with him. Matthew smiled. Azur had a good voice and knew all the verses. They sang together for hours into the dawn.

Chapter 3
Visiting A Chateau

The first thing Matthew did later in the morning was to find his way to the lower library and start looking through the old desks. Every drawer was packed with papers and odd things, like ancient letter openers and pens, stubs of pencils. He couldn't begin to make sense of it all. Here and there were locked drawers, which eventually yielded to the keys that he found. Looking at the dates on papers, he realized that at least part of the collection was remnants from the people who had owned the house in Victorian times. So much extraneous junk, like old checkbooks, and things that were valuable once, but which had long since become worthless.

Azur entered the library, dressed completely in black, from her shoes up through a soft black cashmere sweater that showed her figure well. "You really should have a black suit to wear to the funeral."

"You said that there is a town where I can buy clothes?"

"I'll take you shopping on the way home this afternoon. We will have dinner with my parents. You can change over there and stay the night."

"Let's swing-by a place that sells flashlights and batteries. I've got to start exploring the foundations before this place collapses."

Azur looked at some of the papers on the desk. "This is all yours now: what are you going to do with it?"

"All this, all the things you and Marti told me, are just beginning to sink in. Azur, I think that you've always had much of what you wanted, but I haven't. I'm a scholarship student raised by a music professor. I have almost no conception of the wealth that I have just inherited. That magnificent old piano upstairs, it's worth more than a new Porsche. I've only played an instrument like that once or twice. I cannot believe that I now own such a wonderful thing. You ask, what am I going to do, and I can tell you honestly, that I am going to do my very best to save this house and repay Floris and Rick for my good fortune. . . . Please help me, there's so much that I don't know."

"We both have (she paused, looking for the correct word to express her feelings) adjustments to make, and new things to learn. I will miss Marti greatly." A car honked in the distance. "The van is here to take Marti to the mortuary so we had better greet the men."

After the van left with Marti's body and Azur, Matthew refilled a kerosene lamp, entered the secret passage, and slowly began to venture down the dusty dark staircase. As soon as he had opened the door, he had felt and smelled an ocean breeze coming up from below. It almost extinguished his lamp as he looked down the old steps. Many cobwebs and much dust. For an able person this would have been tricky, and his bad foot almost caused a fall on the first step. These steps were steep, perhaps designed for someone with longer legs, and in better physical condition. The flickering kerosene was a poor substitute for bright electric light.

Matthew reached the level just below the library after only falling once, but luckily the light was OK. This floor seemed to contain several storerooms, and many wooden and metal boxes were scattered randomly. Matthew opened an old leather box that had once been quite fancy. Inside he found camera equipment, and realized that it was 35mm gear, perhaps from the thirties. He closed the box and looked around the huge room, then stared at the ocean-side wall. The windows were boarded over from the inside. Cracks in the wood admitted a little light as well as moist sea air.

As he walked over to the wall, he could feel the floor sloping down: the structural collapse was evident and serious. There were large cracks in the floor and in the wall. Only rough boards kept the wind and rain outside. After a quick tour he realized that this couldn't be the bottom level. Marti had mentioned a machine shop where Rick built things, but he didn't see anything like it. He walked around then felt a light breeze coming from a corner. Soon he found an old trap door in the floor and began to lift it by means of an old rope handle. Just before the rotted handle broke, a seagull fluttered through the opening startling Matthew so badly that he dropped the light causing it to go out. In the brief moment that the door had been open, foul-smelling salty air had come up from below, along with the sound of wind, waves, and startled birds. Cautiously he felt his way back up the steps to the Library and closed the secret door: enough adventure for today.

In the early afternoon, a new BMW X5 arrived at the door, driven by a handsome young man, Dexter Arbuthnot, a rich friend of Azur's whom she had telephoned. Dexter had several days of beard growth and was dressed in what Matthew supposed was fashionable clothing, though he didn't care for the gold chain around Dexter's neck and his earrings. Matthew found the two of them wandering around his house, giving themselves a tour, and took an instant dislike to Dexter's accent, manner, and pseudo-rugged appearance.

"Hello, welcome to Redcliffs Hall," Matthew began.

"Matthew Atkinson, this is Dexter Arbuthnot, who has dropped by to give us a lift," Azur said.

"Hello, Azur tells me you're going to save this moldering old pile, and put it back together," Dexter said.

"I'm going to try very hard, but I need to do some research first to analyze the extent of the problems," Matthew replied.

"The first thing you should do is hire a firm of experts and tell them to get busy before it deteriorates further," Dexter stated.

"The first thing that I am going to do, is to investigate the situation *myself*. Your experts have already come and gone, doing nothing more than to waste Azur's father's money," Matthew stated testily.

"Dexter, how old is this place, do you know anything of its history," Azur asked.

"It looks first-generation neo-Palladian, from the early seventeen hundreds, like something Colin Campbell or his imitators might have built using the local limestone. The columns are a bit thin for my taste, but they look original. It must have been quite grand when fully staffed and polished-up, even though it's off the beaten path," Dexter stated with authority.

"Would the floor plans and construction information be preserved anywhere," Matthew asked, his curiosity overcoming his annoyance.

"Contact RIBA, the Royal Institute of British Architects, in London. They have a library of old drawings, and John Harris[1] has done a wonderful job of organizing and publicizing them. Perhaps he can be of help," Dexter said.

"Thank you very much for the information," Matthew said, as he wrote in a small pocket notebook.

"Here, take my copy of "NO VOICE FROM THE HALL", which John Harris wrote, and read about some of the other old houses that used to be grand. You're very lucky that at least Redcliffs is still standing, albeit precariously: most houses like this were torn down ages ago."

"Thank you for the book: I'll start reading it tonight."

"Dexter, if it isn't too much trouble, would you run us by the shops on the way to The Chateau. Matthew needs to buy some decent clothes and portable lights," Azur asked.

As they drove, Matthew felt ill at ease, an outsider who had landed into a world where he didn't belong. Azur and Dexter talked about their friends, about parties that they had both attended, and aspects of a world that was foreign to him. They made little attempt to enfold him into their conversation. Matthew thought of Sally, his school studies and campus friends and missed them very much.

When they stopped outside the shops, Azur explained to Matthew, "You will find lights here, then we will purchase a few clothes over there."

"I don't have any British money: do they take credit cards," he asked with embarrassment.

"Let me pay, we can work out the details later," Azur replied.

In the hardware store Matthew saw tools, rope and ladders.

---

1   John Harris has written many books on old English Country Houses. THE DESIGN OF THE ENGLISH COUNTRY HOUSE, 1620-1920, shows houses much like Redcliffs Hall.

"Do you think we could get these ladders and tie them to the roof of the car. They'd probably be useful for getting down to the bottom level."

"Please let me have them delivered instead." Azur spoke to the clerk, who was quite solicitous. "Take these ladders and all this rope to Redcliffs Hall this afternoon. Just leave them by the side door."

Matthew added, "And this box of batteries, these flashlights, and that big pry bar hanging on the wall."

"And inform your staff that Matthew, here, may charge whatever else he needs to my account. I am sure he will need many unusual things in the coming days."

"Of course Miss Azur, and please accept my condolences on your cousin's death: she was such a wonderful person."

After they walked outside, Matthew asked, "How did they already know about Marti's death?"

"Word travels fast in a small village, and for all I know, she might have told everyone in advance. I am sure that her daily knew it was coming. They probably have some interesting gossip and theories about you, even though you have only been here a few days and have not been to town."

"I'll try to be extra nice to the maid, so that she gives people the right impressions."

"A very good idea: mother says to always treat servants like TV cameras that might broadcast your most embarrassing activities to the world at the worst possible moment."

Buying clothes, with Dexter and Azur proffering advice, was not a pleasant experience for Matthew, and he found himself agreeing too easily, and buying things that were far too expensive in his opinion. The black suit was nice, the seventy-five-pound silk tie was gorgeous, and the sweaters and warm jacket would be useful, but he wished that he had been given time to search for them on his own. Less than ten minutes later, the car softly rode up a long white gravel drive, past perfectly-manicured gardens and lawns, then stopped in front of a French Chateau: a piece of France transplanted into rural England. Matthew stared in wonder as he and Azur walked to the front door, where a formal Butler greeted them. Azur instructed the

Butler, "Please show Matthew to the blue guest room and arrange for his needs." Then she turned to Matthew, "I will come for you in two hours: take advantage of the hot water and modern plumbing if you want." Azur and Dexter walked away as the Butler led him inside.

In the evening, cocktails were served in a beautiful library, with books on shelves painted light blue-gray above a matching light blue oriental carpet. A bright and cheery room, almost the exact opposite of Matthew's gloomy dark old library deep under the house. Julian, Azur's father, told Matthew about his mother and their childhood fun at Redcliffs Hall and showed him books from their youth. Julian was perhaps sixty years old, quite athletic in appearance, though graying slightly.

Julian explained to Matthew, "These twenty-five little red books are a complete set of Enid Blyton's "FAMOUS FIVE"[2] children's adventure series. In many of the stories, the children and their dog spend their holidays at a house in a setting very much like a small version of Redcliffs Hall."

"Marti mentioned that as children you and your friends tried to have adventures just like the kids in the stories."

"Well, the setting was perfect, especially the little island with the ruined castle. Several of the stories take place on a similar island. In the stories, the children find secret dungeons, buried treasure, and a tunnel to the mainland. We looked all over and couldn't find anything. Once we spent the night on the island, and it was a bit scary."

"May I read one of the books: I think I'd rather be a child than a grownup right now."

"Yes, you're taking on an awful lot at a young age."

"A few days ago I was just a student: doing well in class seemed to be my only responsibility."

Julian put an arm around Matthew's shoulders. "Don't be afraid to ask me for help. Azur and her spirit world can be a lot of trouble, and I find that most of it doesn't make sense. You might like to chat with someone from the normal, logical, world on occasion

---

2   For example, FIVE GO DOWN TO THE SEA, Enid Blyton, Hodder & Stoughton, London, 1953.

and I'll be here."

"May I borrow a few stamps. I've written a letter to my step-parents, and would like to mail it," Matthew asked.

"Of course, give it to me in the morning, and I'll send it with our mail," Julian replied.

Azur's mother, Etienette, entered the library. Matthew was struck by her beauty. She wore a thin black dress that shimmered over a very nice figure as she led them into the dining room, which was decorated with sparkling crystal, silver, candles and fresh flowers. A beautiful room, painted mustard yellow with medium blue trim. Julian and Etienette were at the ends of the table. Azur and Matthew were at either side. Matthew could easily smell the bouquet of freshly-cut roses at the center of the table, and he remembered to help Azur with her chair as he saw Julian behind Etienette's.

"What did you make of the expert's report on the foundations," Julian asked.

Matthew began to reply, "If you want my honest opinion."

"Treat us like your own family and say whatever you like. We thrive on frankness and clear thinking," interrupted Etienette.

"Well, if you're sure you want to hear . . . . I thought the report remarkably superficial, even though you probably paid well for it. I was especially surprised that there was no geological study. The properties of the underlying rock should have been the very first area to investigate."

"Yes, you must start at the bottom and work up, just like when building anything of importance," Etienette said.

"I couldn't have said it better: that's exactly what we should do," Matthew said.

"Just investigating the possibilities will take some effort. I've been thinking how we could help and would like to propose to loan you some money and set up a bank account here so that you can get moving quickly. Perhaps ten thousand would be a good amount with which to start," Julian said.

Before Matthew could answer, Etienette interrupted, "No, Matthew we will give you the money, and more if you need it. Heavens, you don't need debts added to your other worries."

If we could have looked inside Julian's mind we would have seen how annoyed he was at his wife's action, but he covered his expression well and perhaps no one saw his suppressed anger. But a glance at Azur would have indicated that she felt that something odd had just transpired between her parents.

"I don't know how to thank you, all of you, for being so understanding," Matthew said.

"The best way you can thank us is by fixing the old house and making it a credit to the county. And if you want to be really nice to me, personally, you could invite me down into the dusty old cellars and rooms. I love poking among old things, the older the better," Etienette said.

"You should see the cellars here. Mother brought all sorts of old stuff over from France," Azur said.

"I don't think it'll be safe for awhile, and it's awfully dirty and dusty."

"That might stop some people, but wait until you see me in Leviis, boots, and sweatshirt. I'll come over in my pickup truck, and we'll get down and dirty together," Etienette said.

Azur's eyebrows rose as she realized that her mother may not have understood the full implications of some American slang expressions. Matthew hid his surprise at the phraseology, "I could certainly use the help and companionship, and your truck is bound to come in handy. If you're serious, you could make a great start by going through the old papers in the desks and there are maybe hundreds of boxes in the rooms below the old library. We've got to see if there is anything valuable in there before the house settles any further."

"I will start soon, and make 'un inventaire complet' of anything of value. I will bring Jeane, my secretary, and she will put it all in the computer," Etienette said.

"There is almost no electricity on the property: does she have a battery-powered laptop," asked Matthew.

"I will bring a generator in my truck: you will see French organization at work. Before you realize, we will have lights, computer, and café au lait."

During all this, Julian was looking a bit worried, while Azur was somewhat bewildered, but not too surprised, by her mother's proposals.

Later that night Matthew and Azur were together, walking in the late summer twilight through the gardens. Although it was after nine, there was enough light to see the gravel paths and the colors of the flowers. "Your mother is amazing. I thought she looked so formal, delicate and proper, then she startled me with talk about her Leviis and pickup truck."

"She really does like investigating and exploring old things. She often goes on archeological digs, or helps in emergency restorations. When she isn't gardening she becomes bored quickly here."

"She's so generous, but I felt that there was some friction with your father about the bank account."

"I felt that too. Often she sponsors activities involving antiquities, so in the larger scheme of things, helping you start work is not a major expense. I don't know why father would care. This project will keep her out of his way for weeks or maybe months, so he should be delighted."

"Her name, Etienette, is strange, to me, I mean I've never met anyone with that name before. Is it a family name or does it mean something?"

"It is quite uncommon, but her great-grandmother had the same name: it means garland or crown in old French. And my name, Azur-Elita, is a combination of old family names too. Azur is a Persian word for blue sky, and Elita means 'little winged one'."

"They're lovely names. Someday I'll research mine, but I don't think it will be as interesting.

Later that night, Matthew was in bed re-reading the report, when there was a soft knock at his door. He went to the door, thankful that he had remembered to buy pajamas, and opened it, expecting Azur. Etienette was there instead, in a soft black silk robe that left little about her figure to the imagination. The robe was thin enough that he had the strong impression that there were no clothes under it.

"May I come in for a few minutes. I was afraid that you might be asleep."

Matthew was embarrassed, confused and excited all at the same time, "No, I mean yes, come in please."

"I didn't want to ask in front of the others, but what's wrong with your foot?"

"It was crushed in a car accident sixteen years ago. My parents were both killed, but I survived."

"Oh, I am so sorry, I had no way of knowing."

"Doctors have examined the foot many times, but the situation is not promising."

"Have you seen the French doctors, at the 'Clinique Podiatric' in Lyons?"

"No, I don't know of them."

"When things calm down here, you and I will make a quiet trip to France. I have seen much worse cases fixed completely. Surely you don't want to spend the rest of your life with one and a half feet."

Matthew was bewildered. He could not take his eyes off Etienette, especially her shapely body, barely covered by the soft robe, and her warm smile and genuine concern for his health. She took both of his hands gently in hers and squeezed them. She was close, and moving closer. Her breasts were almost touching him.

"I know you are confused and overwhelmed by all that has happened in the last few days, but do not despair. Now you have friends and we can be of great help. There is much to do, but it is not impossible, and with a good effort we will see it to completion, together."

With another squeeze of his hands, she smiled and floated away, leaving the scent of her perfume behind as a reminder. A very nice perfume, not too different from Azur's. After she left, Matthew could not stop thinking about the seduction scenes in the film, THE GRADUATE[3]. He had a strong feeling that he had just met

---

3   "The Graduate" is a motion picture about a young man who is seduced by his girl-friend's mother, Mrs. Robinson. He has much trouble when the girl learns about this, and it takes him the rest of the film to win her back. The music, by Simon and Garfunkel, was very popular, especially the song "Here's to you Mrs Robinson", which describes her problems.

a beautiful and active version of "Mrs. Robinson". The Simon and Garfunkel tune stayed in his mind for days afterward. What a body. How to be nice to Etienette, while staying out of her bed, might turn out to be his biggest problem. And what might happen in the dark old cellars below his house, while the secretary typed away in the library? Or on a quiet trip to the French foot doctor?

As Etienette walked back to her bedroom, she passed Azur in the hall and said "Good night" to her daughter. Fortunately Etienette could not read Azur's mind. Azur had taken one look at her mother's skimpy robe, and noted that she was coming from the direction of Matthew's room. Damn, her mother was on the make again, chasing boys half her age. It was so embarrassing to be her daughter. Almost everyone talked about it behind her back. Why couldn't she grow up and behave like a normal forty-five year old mother instead of like a sex-starved teenager.

The next morning, Matthew sought-out Julian. As he had hoped, Julian had an internet connection and was delighted to let Matthew use it to send an email back to school. Matthew just had time to write to Sally. "Sal..you'll never guess what happened. I've inherited a huge old house that is falling into the sea. Fantastic structural engineering problem. I've just started to investigate, but maybe I can fix it somehow. Marti was wonderful, wish I had known her sooner. Don't know how long all this will take to sort. I'll let you know. Sorry, but I won't be back in time for the dance. BTW, there's some funny business about my grandparents' ghosts living here too, but don't know what to believe: need to explore. I'm out in the middle of nowhere, but will write again in a few days. Matt."

As he started to check his own email, Etienette entered and began to rub his shoulders gently. "You can come here whenever you like. Please consider our home as yours." He read a brief message from Sally. "Hey smarty, guess what: I'm in the running for one of the three Amgen bio fellowships: it pays 30K per year PLUS tuition: can you believe it!!! Can't wait for your return. How're you getting along with that smartass brit? Sal"

When Matthew returned to Redcliffs Hall, he found that all the supplies had been delivered, and spent the next hour moving everything down to the box room, piece by piece on the old stone stairs. As he worked by flashlight, he began to look forward to Etienette's generator and more permanent lighting. And the thought of her warm body visiting the old house was something to dream about.

Matt's first task was to use one of the flashlights to explore the box room before working with the trap door. This part, or level, of the house was cut into the cliff and seemed to be solid rock on the three walls away from the ocean. Masonry walls partitioned it into smaller rooms, and the walls gave support to the floor of the library above. The ocean-side wall of the box room was concrete which was cracked in many places: Matt suspected from the wall's probable age that it did not contain steel rebar to strengthen it. The outer wall had five windows which were covered with old boards to keep the moisture and birds out of the rooms. The floor was concrete with many cracks on the ocean side. The ceiling on the ocean side, which was also the Library floor, had dropped perhaps half a foot at the center as the outer wall had begun to fail. A stone staircase led up the back wall to the Library and secret passages above.

Matt could see that the major structural problems weren't at this level: Etienette could investigate the stuff in the boxes and rooms: he needed to get down below and see the real problems immediately. Matt became very excited as he prepared to venture down to the lower area and see the actual structural problems. He had found several old canvas tarps and now used them to fashion a small tent over the trap door. Hopefully this would keep most of the seagulls downstairs. He also closed the door to the Library before beginning to work on the trap door so the birds wouldn't get into the rooms above. He hung an electric light in the tent, closed the cloth behind himself, and began to lift the door with the large pry bar which he had bought. As soon as the door was up a little, he threaded rope around it so that he had a secure handle for opening and closing the door. Once the door was open and tied in place, and the squawking birds had adjusted to his presence and flown away, he shone his flashlight down the ancient stairway. The steps were covered in green slippery moss and bird poop. Daylight in the room below indicated holes in the outer wall, if there was one. He could see outlines of machinery below and realized that this must be Rick's workshop, and also the home of the secret tunnel to the beach. What a find. The fresh smell of salt air and the sound of laughing gulls greeted him as he anxiously looked down the steps.

After his experiences on the box-room staircase, which was dry and in good shape, he didn't dare try to walk down the steps to the machine shop. Instead he laid the new ladders on top of the steps, tied them to the trap door, then gingerly crawled down the ladders feet first into the damp smelly room below.

The machine shop rested directly on the stone. Its floor was brick, overlaying the bare rock. From cracks and fissures in the brick, he could see the approximate geology: a large triangular section of the floor appeared to be failing. The ocean-side wall was a mixture of stones and cement, varying between two and three feet thick, and it had three arched windows. He observed its thickness as he looked out through holes to the ocean below. The glass in the windows had broken ages ago and now salt spray, wind, rain and seagulls entered the room at will. The wall was cracked irregularly and some of its stones had fallen to the sea below, leaving gaping holes. The ceiling was supported by arches with brick barrel vaults running parallel to the outer wall. Matt guessed that the ceiling was over a foot thick, stone, brick and cement, at even the thinnest part, over the high point in the arches. The ceiling on the ocean side sagged in the middle with many uneven cracks. Bricks had fallen from the barrel vault on the ocean side and were lying on the floor. Heavy rusting machinery was scattered around the room. The damaged and slippery stone staircase which he had used climbed against the back wall, on the east side of the room. The back wall, against the cliff, was bare natural stone, as were the side walls. He could see some of the original tool marks made when the room had been cut into the side of the cliff. Bird poop and the remains of nesting material were everywhere.

He realized that the room indeed was an old machine shop, with a lathe, milling machine, various drills and tools and a seeming endless profusion of bits and pieces of ancient machinery in various stages of disassembly, rust, and decay. The room was damp and cold even though this was early August, the warmest part of summer. He wondered what this place was like in the depths of winter. To Matt, the most important thing in the room was a large crack running across the floor, parallel to the cliff face and several feet in from the outer wall. On the ocean side of the crack, the floor and the wall had dropped unevenly, perhaps a foot on average, compared to the cliff side. He wondered how soon the whole wall would give way, allowing the weight of the building above to crush much of the room in which he was standing.

Matt reasoned that when the machine shop had been equipped the geology had appeared sound, or Rick wouldn't have installed valuable things down here. The newest equipment looked to be less than seventy-five years old, since it had individual electric motors, so the collapse of the outer wall was a recent event, probably occurring over the past fifty years. This suggested to him that the rate of change of the rock failure was increasing: time was running out.

He could partially envision the structure above and the various stresses and strains, and had some inkling of the geological formation below, but those dry technical considerations didn't cover the palpable fear he felt standing under so many tons of stone, looking at the very spot where it was falling away.

His thoughts were interrupted by the voice of Azur as she started down the ladder. "Hello down there. What does it look like?"

"Be careful, it's really slippery. I can tell you that I would rather be looking at photos and drawings of this problem than standing here on the edge of disaster."

"It can't be that bad."

"Take a look at this break. The weight of the outer wall has collapsed the floor almost all the way across."

"How much time do you have before it goes into the sea."

"I don't feel very safe standing here is about all I can say at this point. This is a bad problem."

"I see what you mean. Perhaps it is time for some of your modern structural engineering?" Azur said, intending to be sarcastic.

Matt was focused on the engineering challenge and ignored the jibe. "It's so different from working a problem far away, on pencil and paper. Actually standing here is scary."

"Perhaps you are beginning to learn that life is a lot more

complex than you had thought."

"I don't know if we should let your mother into the rooms under the house. This is really dangerous."

"Mother lives on the edge. You should see her on the black ski runs, chasing the young instructors. Father never ventures onto the slopes when she is around."

"Let's go up. I need to think, and in a safe place."

"I looked in some of those boxes upstairs. There's an elaborate Leica IIIA outfit from about 1935, as well as several larger 120 cameras. It looks like Rick had all the fastest lenses that were available in his time. There are two of the Leica Xenon f/1.5 50mm lenses. There's even a Zeiss Ikonta folding camera that looks almost perfect, and it has the rare f/2.8 lens. He must have loved candid photography. I'll bet we could get it all working again if we wanted."

"Do you know much about photography?"

"I've had a few exhibitions, and done some work for charity. If you don't mind I'd like to poke around and see if I can find Rick's negatives. Marti once mentioned that he liked photography, but it is quite something else to actually find and touch his equipment."

"Please do as you wish, and move anything you like up to the more stable parts of the house. I want to take some measurements and if I may borrow your phone, I'd like to call a professor for advice when we're back up in the Library."

"There is something that I feel I ought to say, but maybe not say. I hope you will not take it the wrong way. I feel that I need to warn you about something."

"What, I mean, please go on."

"Did my mother visit you last night, in her rather revealing black robe?"

Matthew was quite surprised at the question. "Er, yes she wanted to ask about my foot."

Azur became embarrassed at what she had been about to say. "Oh, I did not realize, let us skip it, OK?"

"Please, what were you about to warn me about?"

"Well, it is just that she chases all the young men in the area, trying to coax them into her bed. It is a bit difficult being her daughter, especially when a young man turns up."

"I don't know what to say, but that robe doesn't cover very much does it?"

"I see you noticed. Well, let us get back to work."

Chapter 4
A Ghost's Photographs

Marti's funeral was held in the village church, a small gray limestone structure about three hundred years old. The large deep passing bell was rung slowly through the service, once for each year of Marti's ninety-one year life. The service was brief, attended only by a few villagers, the minister, Azur, Etienette, Dexter, Julian and Matthew. Matthew was next to Azur, enjoying her beautiful singing. They sang funeral hymns, then Matthew was surprised as they began to sing his favorite piece of Church music: "Of The Father's Love Begotten" (Divinum Mysterium[1]), an ancient song from the fifth century which is usually sung at Christmas. Marti had requested it specifically for her funeral. Matthew knew the original Latin[2] words and had often sung them in choir, so he instinctively started in Latin. A glance at Azur's surprised face showed that she knew the Latin also, so they sang the slow rhythmic Latin song together. Dexter had no idea what words they were using and seemed to be annoyed that Matthew was capturing some of Azur's attention.

While Matthew was singing he felt something odd, like a person resting a hand on his shoulder, gently squeezing it, but when he looked around, there was no one to be seen. Remembering Marti's comments, he wondered if it had been Rick, or perhaps just the wind.

Matthew, Julian, Dexter, and the Minister were the pall bearers, carrying the casket to the adjacent graveyard under a dark

---

1   Attributed to A.C. Prudentius, 5th Century

2   (first verse) "Corde natus ex parentis ante mundi exordium. A et O cognominatus, ipse fons et clausula. Omnium quae sunt, fuerunt, quaeque post futura sunt. (9th and last verse) Tibi, Christe, sit cum Paatre hagioque Pneumate. Hymnus, decus, laus perennis, gratiarum action, Honor, virtus, Victoria, regnum aeternaliter."

gray sky. It was heavy at about fifty pounds per man, and Matthew wondered if Dexter was having trouble carrying his corner. The casket was slowly lowered into the ground then Azur tossed flowers over the top. After a few words from the Minister Azur carefully placed the first shovelful of dirt back in the ground. She was crying, but Etienette was silent.

As Matthew stood by the grave, watching it slowly fill, a woman's voice, which he did not recognize, whispered clearly in his ear, "Thank you for guarding my home and preserving my spirit". He looked around, but there was no one nearby. He shivered involuntarily as he realized that it could have been his grandmother, and that all that Marti and Azur had told him might actually be true. On the other hand, his logical mind told him that the funeral was an emotional experience and the power of suggestion at such a time was very strong. He could have easily imagined the touch and the whisper.

Later, Matthew took Azur aside and told her what he had experienced. Azur had also been touched, and she thought that she had seen a brief glimpse of Floris at the grave. Matthew asked Azur quietly, "I didn't pay much attention to Marti when she was talking about spirits, but didn't she say something about Floris being weak and needing help, then you added a bit about a really strong spirit well under the house. What gives?"

"The spirit well is supposed to keep her alive, but I don't know any details. From what I have been told, Floris's spirit was quite strong, as strong as Rick's, at least during the fifties when all the children were here playing."

"What's a spirit well? Do they run down, like a battery? Can they be recharged?"

"These wells are at major intersections of Ley lines: lines of primitive force that run through the earth. I'll show you on the map, and we can walk a few. As far as I know they remain strong forever, unless the ground is disturbed. Your house is at one of the strongest confluences in the country. To a sensitive person, it's an incredible presence. I can feel it easily as I walk up the drive toward the house. We'll talk more about this later."

They turned back toward the others. "Your mother, she's

not as sensitive as you, is she?"

"No, neither she nor father can feel anything. Father flatly denies the existence of the whole spirit world. He was furious when I started my concentration in parapsychology. His only kind words were 'at least you are at Oxford'."

"Does your mother believe it, even if she can't feel it?"

"She lives day-to-day, making the most of whatever opportunities arrive. Spirits, God, wars in Africa, anything that isn't right in front of her fades into the background. She can get all dressed up and pray in church with the holiest, but on the way home she'll be swearing and blaspheming as though she had never prayed. She can change emotions in an instant."

"Must be tricky living with her."

Azur nodded in agreement as they joined the group at the car. Dexter and Azur drove Matthew back to his house and dropped him off.

Matthew was all alone: the Daily had left a cold supper of ham, bread, cheese, and pie for him on the kitchen table next to a few kerosene lights. Matthew walked through the house, looking under sheets at the ancient furniture and trying to imagine what it must have been like hundreds of years ago. The white cat, Phil, and the piano were his only friends now. There wasn't even a radio or television, let alone a CD player and some decent disks. He envied Azur and her settled life in a warm beautiful house with her parents and her companions. She was living in the house where she had been born, while he had moved several times, and really had no fixed place, other than this house, to call his own. Azur and Dexter were not especially nice, but Matthew felt he could have interesting conversations with them, and anything would be better than being by himself. After supper, he played the piano with Phil and wondered if he could build a fire in the huge fireplace nearby. Maybe, but the chimney might be blocked, or filled with squirrels' nests or something flammable, so better to wait until it could be inspected.

As twilight faded, he started back to the central hall, then stopped as he heard a strange scratching squeaking noise. The hair on the back of his neck seemed to stand on end, and goose-bumps rippled over his skin. Thoughts of Rick and Floris at the funeral, as well as Marti's and Azur's allusions to his ghostly grandparents living in this house added to his lonely apprehension. However, he noticed that Phil was not in the least disturbed, so it must be a normal noise, or at least normal to a cat. They walked around the small library. The noise seemed to be in the far corner. He examined the wall, and realized that a small doorway was concealed by the moldings. He opened it slowly, revealing an old wooden spiral staircase going both up and down. He wished that he had a flashlight instead of a kerosene lamp, but the good lights were all down in the big library and he didn't want to go there in the dark when there were creepy noises in the house. His flickering kerosene lamp revealed worn wedge-shaped dusty stair treads and many cobwebs: the treads were narrow, perhaps only two feet wide, so the spiral fitted perfectly inside the thick wall. No servants had trod these steps in decades, or perhaps a century.

What a strange construction: the shaft enclosing the staircase was square, rough plaster walls with a round wrought iron post in the center. Each oak tread had been cut to fit exactly, hundreds of years ago. The noise above was louder. Matt stopped and examined the construction details and wondered how to design such an unusual staircase. The rise of each step had to be enough that a tall person could walk up without hitting his head on the steps above. If the rise of each step were around six inches, a typical step height, then the total rise of perhaps eight feet in a complete turn of the spiral determined how many steps were needed, around sixteen. He looked closely at the steps and risers: beautiful inch-thick oak treads and risers held together with rectangular cut nails. Matt started to count the steps but he knew he was stalling, avoiding going up because of the noise above. Finally he shook his body, picked up Phil, and started up the steps toward the bedroom floor. He noticed that the stairs were so well built that they didn't squeak even after all these years. He stopped part way up at a hole in the wall and realized that it was a peep-hole into the long gallery. Someone could have stood here and watched activities unobserved. Matthew wondered how many other secret viewing holes and clever silent staircases were scattered in secret passages around the house. As he reached the height of the ceiling he was surprised to find a landing and a little door, perhaps two feet square, cut into the wall. He had noticed that the main floor's ceiling was at least three feet thick, so it must be hollow and this was an access hatch. Crawling around in the ceiling would have to wait for another day and a good flashlight however.

He reached the bedroom floor and opened a door into a small anti-room outside a bedroom. The noise grew louder, it was in the bedroom. Against his better judgment he pushed open the ancient door, revealing nothing but old furniture in the moonlight. The screechy noise was at the window. "Look Phil, it's just the wind blowing branches across the glass," Matthew told the cat with relief. The moving branches cast dancing shadows on the walls as the moonlight overpowered the faint twilight. Matthew carried Phil back to his bedroom and climbed under the thick blankets. Phil lay by his legs, kneading them with his front paws, licking, washing, and preparing to sleep on the covers, next to the only warm body in the cold ancient house.

With the kerosene lamp on the night table, Matt settled in to read the book that Dexter had loaned him a few days earlier, NO VOICE FROM THE HALL, by John Harris, written years ago. The book concerned old English houses and the beautiful homes that had been destroyed in the 1950's and 60's: they had been ruined beyond repair by wartime occupation with minimal compensation, as well as by a socialist tax system. Harris' descriptions of lovely old houses being destroyed resonated with Matt's feelings about Redcliffs Hall. ". . .[as I] clambered through an open window and walked the deserted rooms I shared the anguish of the house. I caressed the walnut stair balustrade, unable to believe that this precious example of Georgian craftsmanship would be chopped up or burnt." (page 12) "Nothing is more emotive than to visit the site of Wanstead House . . . where a hole in the ground marks the cellars of what was once the noblest Palladian house in England, its great formal gardens still there in ghostly outline." (page 15) ". . . no sound from the chamber no voice from the hall." (page 27)

The next day, Matthew managed to start Marti's small pale green and white 1964 850cc Morris Mini. It had a current registration, and looked functional and quite useable for moving around the countryside. No more rides with Dexter! When Azur arrived they took the car to the village garage for a tune-up, tires, and a new battery. Then they went to the hardware store where Matthew ordered two expensive, but critical items for his investigation. As they entered, he asked Azur, "Were you serious when you said I could charge anything that I need for work on the house?"

"Certainly. I know you will need rulers and things to make your measurements," she replied.

"I would like to charge at least a thousand pounds worth of modern surveying equipment, and there will be more in the days ahead."

Azur was startled at the amount, and realized that Matthew knew what he was doing but that he was moving much faster than she had expected. "Yes, do what you think is right. I see that you are not wasting any time."

His first order was for a Lasermark LMH-600. This is a small box, about eight inches on a side, which contains a rotating laser which paints a horizontal red pencil-point-thin light beam in all directions. There are delicate sensors inside, which create an almost exactly level beam, with an accuracy of better than one sixteenth of an inch, measured one hundred feet away. This would allow exact measurements of the slope and sag in floors, as well as further changes, to be observed.

The other item was a Disto "Classic" Laser Distance Meter, which is like an automatic tape-measure. It can measure distances out to at least three hundred feet (100 meters) with an accuracy of an eighth of an inch. Matthew knew that he must make a detailed drawing of the house, and this would help him do it quickly. He also ordered a standard surveyors transit, tripod, and storey-pole, and bought a short, twenty-five foot, and a long, one-hundred foot, tape measure, a hand level, and several notebooks and pencils. The charge was close to two-thousand pounds, to Azur's surprise, and most of the gear would arrive in a few days.

They returned to the old house, and began to explore the lowest level in detail after crawling down the ladder that covered the slippery staircase. In spite of the summer weather, it was cold, windy, and wet. Matthew began to make sketches and rough measurements of the structural details, while Azur explored the inner wall carefully.

Matthew asked, "Have you found the entrance to the beach

tunnel yet?"

"No, yet it must be over here somewhere."

"Maybe you can find it by dowsing, or by sensing it using parapsychology."

"Actually, that is a very good idea, although I know you're being facetious in suggesting it."

Azur went up the ladder, then returned in a few minutes with a bent 'V-shaped' steel wire. She moved very slowly along the wall, deep in concentration, holding the open end of the wire in her two hands. Matthew watched with much suspicion. He guessed that the tunnel entrance was over in one of the corners, nowhere near Azur. He was just about to tell her where to look, when she stopped in the middle of the wall, near a large old piece of machinery. "The entrance is under this machine: maybe we can move it."

"I doubt it, that's a silly location for a tunnel entrance, and that hydraulic press must weigh at least a ton."

"It is here, and I am certain of it, so please stop whining and help me move this."

"Good grief. I hope it's not as heavy as it looks. (he started to examine the machine carefully). Hey, it's got little wheels hidden underneath: if you push down on this lever (he pushed), the wheels make contact with the ground."

"And then it moves easily," Azur smugly added.

They slid the rusty old machine in the direction which the wheels allowed, revealing a trapdoor, which they lifted together. "I've never seen dowsing in action. I was sure that it wouldn't work. You must be extra sensitive or something."

"You have much to learn, but seeing with your own eyes is a good start. Here, you can have the wire: try dowsing yourself. Walk around and concentrate on what you want to find. I will go down and make a quick look-round: I feel some sort of something down here. Do not ask me to explain, but this tunnel is important, I can feel it."

Matthew looked down after her. He saw stone steps leading down, in the direction of the land, rather than in the direction of the ocean. He looked at the rusty steel wires in his hand. They were ordinary bits of steel. If dowsing worked, and he had just seen an excellent demonstration, it must have something to do with the person, rather than the tool. How could he test this or measure it or figure out how it worked? If he told his professors they would laugh, saying that it must have been a trick, and that Azur had known all along where the trapdoor was located, and just wanted to impress him. After awhile Azur came back up, with cobwebs all over her black Leviis and black Tee shirt.

"I did not go down too far, but it looks very safe. There are no cracks. The tunnel appears to be cut through solid grey rock, and it goes down forever."

"Wonder if it goes to the spirit well?"

"Spirit wells are not physical: you cannot see them or go to them, but we are probably standing as close to the center of this one as a person can get. Did you try dowsing?"

"It must be a trick. Maybe Marti told you more details about where to look."

"I can assure you that I knew no more than you about the tunnel's location. Many people can dowse, and given your genetic background, you can probably learn to do it well, in spite of your scientific education."

"Can you teach me to do it?"

"I can teach you, and I will teach you. I am curious to see how many of your grandfather's genes are expressed in your body."

Matthew thought from the way that she said this that she considered his body to be a specimen which she could examine like a bug under a microscope. "Let's close the tunnel for now. Perhaps we should keep this a secret. No one else needs to know about it just yet."

"We can come back with brooms and clear the cobwebs, then you can survey the stone walls as we go down to the beach cave, and make a map of at least some of the geology under the house."

"Hey, watch out, you're starting to think like an engineer."

At mid-day after serving lunch, the Daily maid and the Handyman approached Matthew and Azur.

"Now that Miss Marti has passed away, we must be leaving too," the Handyman said.

"Yes, we have wanted to get away before, but thought it best to wait until she passed," the Daily continued.

"But, you're wonderful, I mean, you know so much about where everything is and how it all works. I don't know how I'll manage without you," Matthew said.

"Oh now, don't you worry a bit. We're going away for awhile, but then we'll be back in the area and you can call if you have any questions," the Handyman replied.

The Handyman gave Matthew a quick tour of the coal-fired stove in the kitchen, and showed him the electric water pump, then made a vague allusion to problems with the drains whenever it rained. In less than an hour the couple was gone, and Matthew was left in charge of the house.

Later that day, Matthew was working at a big old oak table in the musty library, making drawings on grid paper from a pile of notes, as well as the experts' report. He had pulled back the rotted drapes, but the windows were heavily encrusted with salt and did not admit much light. However, he had two kerosene lamps and several battery-powered lights. He found that the most useful things in the report were the photos of the house made from the helicopter. Matthew was able to measure the photos and compare these dimensions to measurements that he had made on the ground, and so make a crude, but roughly accurate, drawing of the house and its foundations.

Matthew remembered the tidbit of information that the snotty Dexter Arbuthnot had given him, and used Azur's phone to call the RIBA library on Great Portland Street in London. Although the Reference Librarian on the top floor didn't recognize the house by name, she happened to see a retired expert on Dorset architecture nearby and handed the phone to him. The library has perhaps the world's best collection of drawings and books about thousands of old English houses. Matthew described Redcliffs Hall and its dimensions.

"My house is called, at least now it is called, Redcliffs Hall. It's right on the edge of the cliffs above the sea, in Dorset, east of Lyme Regis. I've been told that it's a Palladian design, in the local limestone, from around 1700, with four columns in front. I'm trying to prevent it from falling into the sea, and would love to get an accurate set of drawings of at least the foundations."

"It doesn't sound familiar, but I'll look around here. From your description, it's a wonderful find, and I hope you can save it. If you don't mind, I'll contact a few people who live in your area, and who share our interests in old houses: I'll send them round to visit you, and snap photos for our archives."

"Thank you very much, and send anyone you want. I could use help."

Azur rushed up to him, carrying a large dusty wooden box. "Look at this, it is fantastic. It is full of old negatives that Rick must have made. There are more boxes of negatives downstairs. I cannot believe we have found these and that they are in great shape."

"Are they nitrate[3] or safety film?"

"Probably both: we will have to be very careful or the nitrate will disintegrate into dust."

"Or explode."

"I must scan these into a computer or copy them or something."

"See if you can find pictures that show the house and the cliff as it was then. We might get some idea of the rate of erosion over the past sixty years. And there might be flash pictures of the machine shop, perhaps showing the crack in the floor: maybe the crack has been there for decades."

"First, I will bring all the boxes up here."

As Azur left, Matthew started looking through the negatives, carefully holding some up to the light from his kerosene lamp. He was puzzled by the subjects and didn't recognize what many were. Some photos were of the house, cars, people standing in groups, but others were hard to explain. With a sigh, he went back to his work.

Azur returned with more boxes, of several different sizes. Each was a wooden negative file: a box sized to hold, preserve, and

---

3   'Nitrate' was an early form of plastic, which was used for making photographic film. Eventually it would disintegrate into a very explosive powder. 'safety film', which is acetate-based, eventually replaced nitrate film during the 1930's. This is one reason why many of the oldest movies, from before 1930, have disappeared.

organize camera negatives of a particular size. Unfortunately, none of the labels had been used, though the pictures appeared to be in some sort of unknown order.

"I looked at a few of the negs and some are really odd: you'll have to examine them carefully. Maybe they make sense when printed," he said.

"Let me see what you mean: show me an odd one."

Matthew opened the first box, which held 6x6[4] individual negatives in glassine sleeves. He found one, then another, of the odd shots and handed them to Azur. She looked, then rotated the negatives and looked at them from both sides, puzzled. "Maybe this is a photo of an audience in a theater. It would have been dark, and during the long exposure, some people would have moved, blurring their own images, while other people remained still. The people near the stage would be brighter than those in the back of the theater. When Rick was invisible, he could have stood on the stage and made pictures of the audience without anyone noticing. These pictures could be quite valuable, both artistically, and historically."

Matthew was startled, "Invisible, with a camera, what are you talking about?"

Azur sat on the edge of his table, as she held one of the negatives carefully. "Matthew, in school, and in my research I deal with carefully-controlled psychic experiments. For instance we measure people's ability to correctly guess unseen standardized Zenner cards, or to see faraway objects, which we call remote viewing. The phenomena we study are ones that we can measure, repeat, and analyze. That's what modern parapsychology research is about."

"Well, that makes sense, but what about Rick and these pictures?"

"That is a different world, and one that I believe in, but cannot measure or explain. Like dowsing, I believe in it and can do it, though I cannot measure the effect scientifically, at least not yet. Marti told me that Rick is a powerful spirit, or ghost, something very strange. I have never seen him, but perhaps he squeezed your

---

4   '6x6' is a film size, 2-1/4" square, which is 6 cm square. It is still popular, in cameras such as Hassleblad and Rolleiflex.

shoulder at the funeral. Marti said that he could materialize, marry, and father a child, your mother. You and I have seen pictures of him. According to Marti, Rick can easily shift from visible to invisible and do things that seem impossible, even to me, so it is no wonder that you are surprised at his nature."

"Maybe he could make his body invisible, but how about the camera: he couldn't do that."

"Look at these pictures: most interesting evidence I would say. I am extremely interested in preserving and analyzing them, for they are documents from a strange world, one outside both of our normal areas of expertise."

"Could we sell them and help pay for the restoration here?"

"No, never, these are scientific treasures. I would not part with the negatives for anything: they are a link with the past and another world. However, we might be able to sell a beautiful book of prints and some individual pictures, maybe even a few duplicate negatives. Please do not touch them any more: the oil on your skin may contaminate them. I will go home and get my darkroom gloves and a light box and my laptop and go through these very carefully, listing everything, then we'll scan them into a computer so that we have a duplicate set before anything happens."

"Perhaps the first thing to do is find all of them and move them away from here. This place could collapse any day, and certainly in the next big storm."

Azur nodded, then went back down to the box room to continue her search. Matthew had much to think about. He was quite surprised at Azur's description of her research: he understood what she was doing in school and it appeared to be straight-forward scientific research, not something far-out as he had thought. But the other stuff, the talk about Rick, was bizarre and perhaps frightening. If such a creature actually existed, and lived here, it might be anywhere, and able to cause much trouble.

Matthew realized that he had better concentrate on the house: Rick would appear or not, and worrying about him wouldn't make any difference, so he went back to work on his drawings. By looking at the report's photographs with a magnifying glass he was able to make a guess as to where the beach cave might be in relation to the house, and how long the tunnel must be. He was interrupted by the arrival of Etienette and her secretary, Jeane, an old and very serious woman.

Matthew gave them a quick tour of the main floor of the house. From the Victorian wing, they walked through a service passageway, into a side entrance of the main house. They came into a small hallway, then turned into the dining room. Etienette marveled at the light blue oval room, then opened a small door which Matthew hadn't noticed. "Here's where the servants entered with some of the food. Are there kitchens down below?"

"Yes, I'll show you, but isn't this a bit narrow for big trays and fancy meals?"

Jeanne walked to the east wall and opened a panel, "The main food came up in what you Americans call a dumb waiter, like this one here. There's probably one at the other end of the room for clearing the previous course quietly."

Matthew ventured into the staircase to the kitchen, "These steps go both up and down, why would they do that?"

"The female servants lived on the top floor, under the roof, so they would need hidden stairs to move discretely up and down without bothering the owners and their guests. The male servants probably lived over the stables."

Etienette ran her hands over the ornately detailed white marble mantel, "They lived in another world, with at least three or more servants per person. When this house was built roads were terrible so people didn't travel far. And when they arrived at a house like this, they tended to stay a week or two, before making the return trip. These big country houses were more like hotels than what we would consider homes. Running one was a major undertaking, even if the building wasn't falling into the sea."

They went into the entrance hall, then squeezed through the door into the long gallery, walking past dead plants, old pots and furniture. This was the biggest room in the house, 112 by 37 feet, as he had roughly measured it. Matthew realized that the beams embedded in the ceiling must be massive to cover a 37 foot span with no intervening columns or walls: probably each beam was the heart of a huge ancient oak tree. They continued into the little library where he showed Etienette the piano. She remarked that she played too, but not on such a fine instrument. Etienette asked if Matthew liked to play duets, and he suspected that her version of duets involved sitting very close together on the piano bench.

Matthew had noticed that most of the main walls were at least five feet thick. Their innards might contain two one-foot thick structural walls and a three-foot wide secret passage, in addition to numerous chimney flues. Every room had at least one fire, and the long gallery had two huge fireplaces. He would need to explore each room more carefully, looking for hidden doors and passages.

Matthew then showed the two ladies the lower library, the box room and the desks full of papers. When Matthew offered to help with their long extension cords and generator, they pushed him away, telling him to get back to work saving the house. Soon he heard the generator start and a few work lights came on, as well as two computers and a printer which they had brought. He was working at a large table, so they settled at the desks and began their cataloging work, conversing in French between themselves. True to her word, Etienette was in Leviis, sweatshirt, and work boots, with her long hair tied in a ponytail. Even in this outfit she was stunning, and Matthew thought that she knew it.

Later, as Azur started going through the negatives to catalog them, she began to realize just how unusual some of them were. A few of the photos might be examples of a quite unusual form of Kirlian[5] photography, with Rick and his aura glowing in the picture. She knew that such images are usually fake, made with multiple exposures or retouching, but Rick's pictures appeared quite genuine. Interpreting just a few of these would be a major psychic research project. Perhaps her dissertation was going to be a success after all. Azur had read "The Body Electric" and "The Probability of the Impossible", both of which discussed Kirlian photography and the idea that it might be related to something other than scientifically-explainable electrical discharges. She had been unconvinced and had been unable to

---

5   Kirlian photographs are supposed to show the psychic aura which surrounds living things (see ENDNOTES).

do anything herself along these lines other than duplicate existing techniques, which involve photographing electrically-charged objects pressed against sheets of film in a darkroom: colorful photos perhaps, but nothing psychic. The negatives in Rick's collection were made from a distance, apparently with a normal lens and camera, and clearly showed a glow around his body. He did not appear to be holding anything electric, he was just smiling into the camera while someone clicked the shutter.

As her catalog developed, Azur discovered that perhaps half of the pictures might have been made while Rick was invisible. In addition, many of these might be classified as voyeuristic, scenes that are seldom or never photographed, as least by visible photographers. There were pictures of people on toilets, partially-clothed in bedrooms, eating in restaurants, and to her surprise, inside Parliament. Azur was almost positive that photography had not been allowed inside Parliament until recently, yet here were shots of debates in progress from the thirties and perhaps during the war. By examining old newspapers, she could probably identify some of the people. Many of the photos were excellent artistic compositions in their own right, carefully arranged and snapped at the decisive moment. There were even a few that might have been made inside a royal palace: invisible Rick and his cameras had been very adventuresome indeed. These shots could be worth a fortune, but their publication would raise a hornet's nest of questions. What fun it would be to publish them anonymously and watch the comments fly.

After Etienette left, she showed Matthew pictures of Floris performing at the height of her career. Pictures clearly made by someone standing on the stage beside her. There were also wonderful old pictures of Redcliffs Hall, and of Rick and Floris playing on the beach, boating, and picnicking on the island.

Matthew hadn't quite realized it, but he was beginning to become very interested in Rick and Floris: ever so slowly, they were becoming real to him. He already knew that he would like to meet Rick, preferably when he was visible, and talk with him about his workshop, and about the cars and boats in the photographs, and certainly about ghostly things. Being invisible must be a kick! And Floris looked like lots of fun: knowing a real magician, and talking about how she did tricks, would be fascinating.

After dinner at Azur's home, Julian drew Matthew aside for a serious talk. "Glad to hear that you're making progress in exploring the old place and its contents. But there are some other things to consider."

"I don't know what you mean."

"Do you have any idea how much you owe the government in death duties, what you would call inheritance tax?"

"I hadn't given it much thought: perhaps the place is so dilapidated that it is almost worthless."

"Unfortunately, it's appraised as a grand country estate, with about sixty rooms, over six hundred acres of land, a private island, and who knows what else. You owe at least ten million in round numbers."

"It couldn't be that much, but I see your point: maybe I could sell the land or do something to raise money."

"You've probably got six months or so before you need to do anything, but if you consider selling, let me know. I'm sure you could sell it for at least twice the tax bill, which would leave quite a handsome bit of change for your schooling and your future. Some associates of mine might be interested in forming a syndicate to make an offer should you wish to consider it."

"Thank you for your consideration. At the moment I hope to repair the damage and live in the house, but a lot can happen in the coming months."

As Matthew left to go home alone in his small old car, Etienette gave his hands a squeeze and smiled at him. It was just a moment's fleeting gesture, as she said good night, but her eyes seemed to say much more. It was hard to let go of her hand.

Chapter 5
The Scary Wing

When Azur arrived the next morning, they decided to walk around the grounds and outbuildings since it was a beautiful summer day with a strong onshore sea breeze, blue sky, and few clouds. They passed dry fountains filled with debris and damaged statues, overgrown gardens, and what appeared to be the ruins of a huge maze. It all reminded Matt of the sad damaged homes he had read about in Harris's book.

"Wish we had a giant lawnmower and could clear the pathway into the maze," Matthew said.

"It looks more like you would need a chainsaw. This place is so overgrown, you could employ a small army of gardeners," Azur said.

"I'm afraid that any money I find will go into the foundations, long before we fix the gardens. It must have been something living here in the old days."

"Matthew, look at that side of the house, through those bushes, it seems rather odd."

The house consisted of a large formal central structure, with a wing at each side. Looking at the front of the house, the wing on the left, the east side, had been rebuilt, in Victorian times. This is where Marti had lived and where Matthew was now living. It was the only area with plumbing and a workable kitchen. They walked over to the other, right-hand, wing on the west end of the house.

"I wonder what is inside," Azur said.

"Odd isn't it, the door has been bricked over and these lower windows have been covered with bricks too, then painted to sort of look like normal windows."

"And look at that tree growing through the path in front of the door: it is huge. Judging by the age of the tree, this door hasn't been used in over a hundred years."

"Maybe much longer. This place is really old."

"There must be a way in, let's walk around the end."

They walked all around the wing. It was about fifty feet long, and forty feet deep. On the three sides that weren't attached to the main house, all the lower windows and doors had been sealed. As they walked around the wing, Azur noticed a change in its architecture. "Look, the west end and the ocean-side of this wing are much older, maybe Tudor from the early sixteenth century, judging by the shape of the windows."

"So maybe this was a separate house, before the main house was built, and the builders just redid the front side and tacked it on to the new house as a wing?"

"But why is it all closed up? Someone went to a lot of trouble to brick over the doors and windows and disguise them?"

"There must be a passage from indoors, or some way to get inside, even if it was just used for storage."

They went inside the main house and walked to the west end, but could not find any doors connecting the main house to the sealed wing. However, they noticed one area where the plaster was uneven. It looked like a door had been here a long time ago, but it had been covered over. Matthew had an idea, "Let's go down into the library, then go up through the secret passages. Maybe there's a way to get into this wing through them."

"Bring a broom. Those passages are full of spider webs."

Matthew and Azur entered the passages with flashlights, then started walking slowly, sweeping away cobwebs and sneezing in the dust. They found a long horizontal passageway that seemed to run the width of the house, just below kitchen level. Occasionally there was a narrow staircase going up through walls into darkness above. There were no pipes or electric wires in the passages but they noticed long thin metallic cables that ran from pull-ropes in the various rooms down to an indicator board in the Servants Hall.

Matthew calculated, "We must be about at the end of the main house, near the basement of the old wing. Look there's a door across the passage."

"There does not seem to be a lock or nails or anything. Can you open it?"

Matthew pulled and pushed on the door but nothing happened. By pounding on the door, he realized that it was at least several inches thick, solid old oak.

Azur looked up to her left, "let us try this little staircase, maybe it goes up to the ground floor."

The went up a steep staircase, barely wide enough for Azur's shoulders. He walked slightly sideways, as she went ahead, sweeping away the cobwebs. At the top was an old door. With a shove, Azur opened it and stepped into an ancient room.

"Stop, I can feel something, something very peculiar in the psychic environment. I don't like it."

"May I look, what do you see?"

Azur entered the room, and he followed. Looking back, they could see that they had come through a movable panel into a wood-paneled room. The other panels were fixed, but this one was a secret entrance.

Matthew was amazed at what he saw, "Wow, look at this place. It's so old. It hasn't been touched for centuries."

"We should leave. This does not feel right. There is something wrong with this wing."

"You're not afraid are you, it's just some old rooms. Those sounds are just the wind blowing the trees against the walls."

As their eyes adjusted to the dim light coming through cracks here and there in the covered-over windows, as well as to the light from their flashlights, they discovered a perfectly-preserved scene from another era. The furniture was not covered, plates with the remains of an ancient meal were on the table, a newspaper was on a chair. Matthew looked at the paper: June, 1743.

"This is just like the Dennis Severs House Museum[1]

---

1   The Dennis Severs House Museum, 18 Folgate Street, London, is an old restored row house. Its period is the 1700's and each room looks

in London: a staged scene from hundreds of years back in time. Everything looks like the occupants left only a few minutes ago," she said.

"It's spooky, if you don't mind me saying so."

They walked through dusty rooms, all of which were fully-furnished. It did indeed look like it had been quickly abandoned, then sealed for centuries. Books were open on a table, beds were unmade, clothes lay about. The overall impression was that the people who lived here had run away, taking nothing, and then someone sealed it from the outside. No one had come inside in a very long time.

"Here's a mystery for you: why are there no spider webs in here? There's plenty of dust, and a draft comes down the chimney: see where the ashes have blown out onto the floor, so it's not hermetically sealed," he said.

"That means only one thing: we must get out of here!"

"Why?"

"Nothing can live here, not even spiders."

They turned to go, but they stopped in amazement at a hole in the floor. The edges of the hole were black with charred wood. The hole had the exact size and shape of a person. Even a supporting timber that had crossed the hole was burned completely through. It was as though a red-hot human-shaped poker had been pressed through the floor into the black void below.

"Spontaneous Human Combustion! I've read about it in "Fortean Times"[2], no one believes that it's true, but maybe that's what this is. Damn, wish I had a camera," he said.

---

as though the owners have just departed and walked into the next room. There are hidden loudspeakers making noises from the period. Otherwise the house is silent. Visitors are not allowed to talk. The fireplaces are smoking, the food is half-eaten. The only living thing is a black cat. Each floor shows a different economic class. The parlor and main floor are well-off silk merchants, while the attic is inhabited by a dozen very poor people. The house has an excellent website with more information.

2   FORTEAN TIMES, St Anne's Court, London, Issue 35, page 6, summer 1981, describes a SHC incident from Ipswich, April, 1744.

"Hurry, run, you fool!"

Azur ran through the next room, taking a shortcut back toward the secret entrance to the wing. There was a loud crash and a scream as she fell through the floor. Matthew was limping just a few steps behind, but had enough time to stop before the rotten floor had a chance to give way under his weight. He backed up and shone his flashlight through the hole where the floor had been.

"Are you OK? What's down there? Make some noise if you can hear me."

Only silence and the wind answered his words. He moved gingerly around the rotten area, glancing up to see that the rot had been caused by a hole in the roof, which had allowed water to run down to this area for centuries. The ceiling above this room, as well as the floor below, was riddled with dry rot.

"I'll find the staircase and be down in a minute. Don't worry, I'll be there in a moment."

He scampered about trying doors, thinking of how the house must be arranged. There must be a way down, to get coal for the fires and to retrieve food stored in the cellar. The kitchen area must have a door somewhere, but it was hard to find. Eventually, he found a locked door and bashed his shoulder against it until it gave way, revealing steps down into a cold dark basement.

If he had stopped for a moment to think of where he was going, and of the burned human hole in the floor, he would have frozen with fear. But for some primeval reason he didn't stop, but rushed down the narrow steps to help Azur.

She was lying unconscious on a dirt floor, in a room filled with old boxes. Without even thinking, he lifted her in his arms and started to leave. Looking at the narrow staircase he had just descended, he realized how hard it would be to carry her up. Then he remembered the thick door from this basement into the main house tunnels, and shone his light in that direction.

From this side, the door was easy to see, and it had a large wooden bolt holding it closed. He carried Azur's limp body to the door, removed the bolt, and opened the door. He talked to her unconscious body as much to calm himself as to calm Azur.

"Don't worry, we're almost safe, it's just a little way now, you're going to be all right."

He carried her down the passageway, limping, hurting, and wishing that he had two good feet. Several times they fell to the ground as he bumped into staircases in the dark, then finally up the narrow stairway into the old kitchens and light. He rested for a moment, then carried her limp body out into the sunlight. He was breathing hard and running on adrenaline.

Matthew placed her on a soft, sunlit white garden couch in Marti's rose garden. He held one of her hands tightly in his, wondering what to do. She was breathing quickly, her pulse irregular, her face contorted in pain. He focused his thoughts on her condition, trying to think of how he could help. Matthew realized instinctively that he wanted very much to save her, to bring her back to the living world. She had been a nuisance, cool, bitchy and aloof, but in her own way, a very interesting and attractive person. He wanted to do something, but the only thing he could think of was to stare into her face while gently brushing her forehead with one hand, while the other held one of her hands tightly. He concentrated as hard as he could. Perhaps this was praying, or some form of "healing", or transference of energy from one person to another. If so, it was not a conscious process but somehow he knew that it was the right thing to do. Later, he realized that he had no idea of how long he had crouched over her body. It was quite possible that he had hypnotized himself by staring so long and so hard at her troubled face. Eventually, her expression became calm, and her pulse began to slow. It was hours, rather than minutes, and his knees were stiff from kneeling on the ground at her side.

Azur started to breathe normally, and slowly awoke. "What happened. Where are we. I just had the strangest dream."

"You're so pale. Should I get you a drink or something. Do you feel OK?"

She moved her arms and legs then sat up. "Maybe, yes, I feel all right. Please let go of my hand. Wow, I have never felt such spirit energy, bad spirit energy. We must never open that door again. If you dare to go back, take a hammer and nail the door shut."

Though she dared not say anything about it, Azur was very worried about the dream or experience she had just had. She hoped it had been just a dream but as she moved and explored her body she realized that she seemed to have no cuts or sore spots after falling through the floor. This was not normal, and she began to think over her memory of the dream and her current condition. As she stood, she realized that a trip to the bathroom and some fresh clothes were needed immediately as well. A bad sign.

"We can talk in a few minutes, but first I need to go inside, please excuse me."

They both went up to their rooms in the Victorian wing, then carried on their conversation a bit later.

"There was just a cool breeze in the wing, I didn't feel anything odd." Matthew commented.

"You wouldn't, at least not without much training."

"What's bad spirit energy, or good, for that matter."

"If I go dowsing, for example, looking for water or energy lines in the earth, I can feel positive, negative, water, and other types of energy lines. These are natural things, not good or bad per se. But there are many other kinds of spirit energy that I can feel, sort of like the way that you can see many different colors. Usually the energy is very weak. However, this house, when I walk up to it, feels good, and quite strongly, in a way that I cannot really explain. Especially when we were with Marti. There is some sort of good, or happy or pleasant, energy here, probably related to Rick and Floris, and the confluence of spirit lines. It is sort of a comfortable, warm, feeling. However, there's something really bad in the far wing. If you ever get the foundations stabilized and the house secure, you must tear down that other wing and burn everything. Meanwhile, keep it sealed."

"But it's just an old building, with some wonderful ancient artifacts, and that burned hole in the floor. We've got to go back and photograph it."

"I know you don't believe, but you don't know anything about spirit subjects. For now, you must pay attention to what I say. Leave that wing alone, or I will never set foot on this property again."

"You're really scared of that place aren't you?"

"That is an understatement."

Matthew turned, then winced in pain and clutched his shoulder.

"What's wrong?"

"I must have hurt my shoulder when I used it to bash through the basement door. It was pretty stupid, but I was so anxious to get down to you as quickly as I could. I didn't stop to think. I was so worried about you."

"I am the stupid one. I should never have let either of us into that wing. The spirits warned me and I ignored them. Let's go. I'll drive you to the local doctor for an x-ray."

That night, while eating fried codfish, chips, apples and stilton with a few beers in the local pub, they talked-over what each remembered. The cozy old pub was small, with a bar in the drinking area, and a musty three-table room where food was served. They were the only people eating, although others were drinking and throwing darts in the next room.

Azur told him that "Fortean Times" was usually filled with inaccurate information, but in this case it was right. S.H.C., Spontaneous Human Combustion, was real but very rare, and poorly documented. There was almost no solid evidence that it existed. Azur realized that the fright-filled wing contained a very significant piece of hard data about the spiritual world and S.H.C. It would be quite interesting to photograph and examine the burned hole in the floor, and to do a proper chemical analyses of the surrounding area. And what was on the basement floor directly below the hole? A careful study would make an excellent scientific report, a nice credit on her CV^3, and perhaps a solid addition to her PhD dissertation. For now however, she had no idea how to gather this information. Maybe she could con some students into going into the wing and doing the research, while she wrote the paper from a safe distance.

And what if Matthew had really done something to heal her? She could have just fainted, and then awoken naturally, but it was very odd that she couldn't find any cuts or bruises on her soft body. Azur was surprised to hear about the trip back through the heavy basement door and the distance Matthew had carried her, with his bad foot as well as a sprained shoulder. She had underestimated his kindness and his determination, as well as the amount of concern he could show for another person. "I am sorry that I led you in there.

3   CV, curriculum vitae, the European version of a person's resume.

That was very foolish of me, and you have been hurt, while I, who fell through the floor, have nary a scratch."

"Just hearing your voice again is worth it. While you were unconscious, I hovered over you for hours, wishing, feeling, struggling, crying, willing you to be well again. Somehow it just seemed to be the right thing to do. I suppose that I should have rushed you to a hospital, but I didn't, it didn't even occur to me to take you away. I'm so relieved that you are all right. It was such a strange experience."

"Perhaps you have inherited some of Rick's spiritual powers. Maybe you breathed some of your life into mine and saved me?"

"If so, it was completely unconscious on my part. You just fainted, and eventually woke up."

"Maybe, but maybe not. Tell me about it exactly, what you thought, what you did, everything you can remember. What exactly did you think as you stared at my unconscious body?"

"I don't know, I mean, lots of things, about what we have done, and how pretty you looked, and some things you have said."

"I mean tell me about the healing part, when you really focused on me and tried so hard to heal me, when you cried, when you tried to make me better. Tell me the truth, I know you are embarrassed, but the sexual parts are critical, I want so much to know what you think happened. Please, this is important to me."

"Well, you won't believe what I seem to remember, as it was so strange, and you're right, talking about it is rather embarrassing. I'm sure it was just a dream, but so odd. I felt, that is I think I felt, that I was inside your body, not outside looking at you, but inside literally. I was straining all of your muscles, every fiber of your body trying to be you and to control your movements, to ease your pain and your wounds and bring you back to life: I couldn't tell what was wrong or how to heal it, but I so much wanted to save you, to give you my own life. You were in so much pain."

"What part of my body were you inside? Could you see my naked body and feel its textures?"

"No, it wasn't like that, I didn't see you from the outside, it was such a beautiful experience, I was you, really you, from your toes, through your legs, your pelvis, your body, your breasts, your lungs breathing, I was inside your lungs as they breathed, I saw the air move through your mouth, your face, your hair: I could feel it all, I was a girl and it was so different, I can't explain it. I could wiggle your toes, really, I saw them move through your eyes, and I moved your fingers too. Your lungs were breathing too fast, so I breathed slower to calm them down, to relax your body, then I smiled beautifully and slowed your heart, such a warm feeling flowed completely over me, like warm water. I could feel your belt around my waist, your pants around my legs, your shoes, your bra around my chest, I could feel your soft clothes from the inside. I was all of you for just a moment, looking up at me, and I could see myself from outside, from under my body, and I could feel what it is like to be you, but it was all a dream or auto-suggestion, or something in my head: so lovely, but so unreal."

"While you were straining so hard, inside my body, living your life inside mine, were you sexually excited? Did you feel that you were actually pouring yourself or your energy into me? What did you feel in my pelvis? Was I having an orgasm?" Azur paused for a moment, then added quietly, "I noticed that afterwards, when you went back to your room, you changed your trousers before we went to the hospital."

"You're too observant, I mean, well, you're right, they were a mess. I strained so hard, I gave everything I had without reservation, it just came out. It was so, so complete, to be you and me at the same time. What a dream. I can't tell you, I mean my words don't begin to describe the experience of being inside your body and looking up at me. How could this happen? You understand these things, but I've never had such an experience. Did you feel anything? Did you dream while you were asleep?"

Azur worried to herself, comparing his story to the dream she vividly remembered. In her dream she had felt him moving inside her, not sexually, but perhaps more like a fetus wiggling around. It made no sense and was most troubling. Azur had read of such unusual experiences and had not found them credible. But something had happened to her this afternoon. The scary part, to Azur, was that he might have inadvertently planted something deep in her body, in her spirit, while he was healing her, not in a sexual way, but in some other way. What was it, and what if it expanded and grew? She would need to study this most carefully before saying anything.

"I know something happened, but I do not know what, and wish that I could remember. And, well, don't laugh, but I needed a change of clothes too, so you weren't dreaming alone."

Involuntarily, Azur reached out to Matthew and held his hand tightly, in silence. They stared into each other's eyes and were one together, but just for a few moments. It passed, but they both remembered the closeness of this feeling, always. Azur was torn by worrisome and very serious thoughts. She knew he had mysteriously cured her injuries and was thankful to be healed, but she also knew that something potentially troubling had just happened to her body, and most importantly, she was no longer in control of the spiritual situation: she had intended to study Matthew, but now he was leading her into dubious areas where her logical mind feared to go.

Matthew felt the change in Azur's mood, and decided that it was a good time to ask her about the ghostly side of his grandparents. He had tried a few times before, but Azur seemed hesitant to provide details. "You mentioned my grandfather, Rick's, spirit energy. And the other day we talked about his invisibility and photographs. What other unusual powers does he have? I know so little."

"I do feel that I owe you some explanation of your rather unique family history. I know that you are not going to believe all that I say, but remember that you did not think that I could find that tunnel by dowsing either." Azur was already having thoughts about Rick, and what his grandson might have inherited from him.

"I've been suspecting that there was much more to the old house than just stones, boards, and boxes of stuff."

"Remember that line from the Old Deuteronomy song, the line about 'long before Queen Victoria's Accession'?"

"Yes. . ."

"A very long time ago, Rick was born or created or made: I don't know how he began, but it was centuries ago. Marti was serious when she said he is a thousand years old. That is his estimate, but he is not really sure. He has been a very powerful spirit all those years, and he is just as powerful as he ever was, but he is asleep, and can sleep for dozens or hundreds of years if he wants. I have no idea when he will awaken."

"He was awake for the funeral, and you and I both felt or saw something."

"Correct. I will not pretend to you that I understand Rick and how he functions, or when, or even if, we will ever see him."

"Is he really my grandfather? I mean, is one quarter of my DNA from an ancient spirit?"

"I warned you that this would not be easy for you to believe, but the answer is yes, most definitely."

"How about another beer, or something stronger?"

"They have a serviceable champagne here: let us have a bottle and celebrate your introduction to the world of the spirits."

While Matthew was buying the champagne, Azur spotted a few of his hairs on his chair and quietly slipped them into her purse. She would have a DNA analysis made, and perhaps find something interesting for her paper.

After a toast, Azur began to relate as much of the story that Marti had told her as she could remember. "It was 1937, in London, when Floris, your grandmother, first encountered Rick. Floris was a magician, a normal human being, not a spirit, and a very good magician at that: she was performing on a third-rate stage in a smelly old theater. Floris was handcuffed, under-water in a big glass tank. Marti was in the audience and could feel that something was very wrong. Usually Floris escaped quickly, it was just a magic trick after all. But tonight, she was struggling too hard, splashing about and staying under much too long. The audience was deathly silent: fear gripped everyone as people began to realize that she might not be faking. Her struggle became very real. Her body, wrapped in the locked and weighted straight-jacket squirmed, twisting and turning, but to no avail. She was drowning right before their eyes: Marti could feel her pain as she sat helpless."

"Then, just as Marti was about to rush the stage to try to pull her from the tank, a strange unearthly, sort of shimmering, bluish, glow came over the water. They could not see what was happening inside. Then Floris rocketed out of the water and landed on the stage. She seemed to fly out of the tank and then land softly on her feet. She was shaking and weak. Everyone stood and applauded wildly. No one had ever seen such a magic trick. Marti was simply amazed.

She had seen Floris do this trick dozens of times and it never ended like this."

"Floris limped off the stage, bowing and trailing water. What a climactic way to end a performance. Of course, no one had any inkling as to what had really happened."

"The next day Marti and Floris had lunch at the Odeon Café and Floris told her the most incredible tale. Floris had struggled underwater with the handcuffs but they refused to spring open: there is a sort of secret latch that is supposed to work, but it was jammed. She almost passed-out. The pain in her lungs grew worse and in desperation she was so tempted to take a breath, but it would have been a breath of water. I can not begin to describe how it must have felt, but it must have been much worse than when you hold your breath too long while swimming under water."

"Floris was certain that she was about to die, when suddenly she felt someone's hands working on the cuffs: someone very strong, who just ripped them apart. The next thing she knew, she was standing on the stage, gasping for breath, while someone held her upright and helped her take bows. She was too confused to understand and staggered to her dressing room."

"She was sitting on a little bench, panting from exertion, when she noticed someone beside her. He was there, but he was not. He did not look right, and his clothes were all wet. The strangest thing was that she could almost see through him, like through glass. He was just looking at her, and his face showed such concern. It was almost as if he had been crying."

"Floris reached over and touched him: she was a very touchy person as Marti recalls. She did not know what to say, and he felt strange, not solid and not airy, but something in-between. Then he sort of shook himself and became solid, no different from the two of us here tonight."

Matthew was so surprised, he didn't even know where to begin to question. "You're not making this up are you. This is so strange, I mean, I don't even know what to ask. Floris must have been such an exciting person to know. I wish I could have talked with her, with my grandmother." Azur had a drink of champagne and continued.

"In those days Floris was struggling to make ends meet. She played in dreadful theaters, exploited by an endless string of sleazy Managers and Agents. Men who wanted her body and her money and could care less about her career. The Depression was still on here and not many people were paying to see magic acts, but it was the only craft that she knew. No one should have to endure the things she did, just to stay alive."

"As Floris and Rick came closer together emotionally, he started helping with her magic act, and her shows became extraordinary. Floris The Magnificent, as she then styled herself, commanded top prices at the best theaters: even did Buckingham Palace one night. She and Rick had a wonderful time traveling and performing. Rick loves practical jokes, so their stage shows had most unusual audience involvement, but everyone had fun. She did not tell anyone but Marti about Rick's true nature, so by using an invisible helper it appeared that Floris had very strong and strange powers herself."

"Floris made a ton of money and bought the old house. It was an ancient abandoned wreck, falling down, and overgrown. Rick had been living on the property for a long time, so it had always been a sort of haunted and spiritual place. Once they bought it, they could own it legally and fix it up a little. Eventually Floris and Rick became lovers and were married: your mother was the result."

"Things were fine until the late in the War, when a bomb landed near the house and killed Floris. If you and I have trouble thinking that a spirit could materialize, and father a child, then we should really have a problem with the next bit. In some way, and I have no idea how, Rick managed to salvage Floris's spiritual energy and convert her into a ghost. Most people just die, but a very few bodies, perhaps a couple of dozen in all of England, have been converted into ghosts. Marti said that the process takes a ton of spirit energy and skill, and it has to be done at just the right place and time."

"Now, you are the only living descendent of Floris and in many ways, you owe your existence and your good fortune to her. Perhaps your engineering work will succeed and you will repay her by saving her house and preserving the place where she lives."

Not for the first time in Azur's company, Matthew was

speechless as he considered what he had just heard. Some of it was probably true, but which parts? How could he make sense of such an improbable story.

Azur continued, "I hope we meet Floris, as her spirit is supposed to be sleeping in your house, but Marti said she is very weak. Marti, being a psychic, was very interested in Rick and had some wonderful times with him. She said that his world is not at all like we might imagine: he has a few unusual powers, but many problems and difficulties. You can imagine how excited Marti was to be able to talk with a ghost and to learn from him. In your engineering world, imagine how you would feel if you ran into Einstein, and could ask all the questions you wanted and spend days talking about engineering problems while playing in his lab and walking on the beach. Marti learned a great deal from Rick and tried to pass it on to me, and now I am passing it to you."

"If Rick were here, and materialized, could I tell that he's a ghost, or would he just look like a person," Matthew asked.

"Marti said that he would fool you, or almost anyone else, unless they were very sensitive psychically. Marti mentioned that they were married at the village church, just like any other couple. He did not have a surname, so they made up the name Hauntington as a lark. Supposedly, the church records show your grandparents as mister and missus Hauntington."

Chapter 6, Eviction

On a bright sunny day, Matthew and Azur drove down deserted narrow country roads in her 1970 Morgan Plus-eight roadster. The car looked older than it was, at least partly because of its maroon fenders and light vanilla-yellow body. This was not a modern color scheme and it immediately gave the car an old appearance. In addition, the body design was not too different from the MG and Morgan cars of the 1950's. The car had its original wooden, ash, frame, and old-fashioned wire wheels. However, it also had its original V-8 engine. This engine's 200+ horsepower provided wonderful acceleration because the car was small and light. In reality, Azur could keep up with most modern Porsche and BMW cars when she chose, as long as the roads were fairly straight. They were driving with the top down, the wind blowing their hair in the sunshine, as they sailed down narrow roads between deep green fields. When they came to the top of a hill, Azur pulled over and parked on the grass at the side of the road.

She pointed out distant sights. "Look over there. See that little notch cut into the top of the hill. Then, from the notch to here, you can see bits of straight fences, field boundaries, bits of road, and that church steeple down there. All in a long perfectly straight line, thousands of years old. These lines predate the Romans: they may have been here even before Stonehenge was built."

"So that's a Ley line, like in Watkins[1]' old books."

"Exactly. Take a compass bearing and you can check it on the map."

While he did this, and compared it to a map spread on the hood of the car, Azur worked with her digital Nikon camera to make

---

1   THE OLD STRAIGHT TRACK, Alfred Watkins, describes these straight lines which criss-cross England. He realized their existence around 1900.

a telephoto shot straight down the line. "I wonder if Rick knew about Ley lines. Maybe he made photos from this very spot."

"Too bad he did not read as he would have loved Watkins' books. He would have been an exciting member of Watkins' "Old Straight Track Club" if he had joined it," she said.

"If Redcliffs Hall is a major intersection of Ley Lines, then we should be able to see them all radiating outward from the observation platform on the roof."

"What platform?"

"It shows in one of the helicopter photos in the expert's report. I don't know how to get up there, but near the middle of the main roof, there is a flat place with a railing and some sort of stairway. The view must be gorgeous from up there."

"Let us go up after lunch. Now, look behind you. You can see this line running all the way, perfectly straight, to your house."

After admiring the picture-postcard views over the gently rolling green hills, and the perfectly straight Ley Lines, they drove to the village. The laser measuring equipment had arrived, and Matthew was very excited about the measurements he would make with it. They had a quick lunch at the pub, then drove to the house.

They scampered up the huge main marble staircase to the bedroom floor, then up smaller staircase to the top floor. This floor had guest and children's bedrooms around the perimeter, each with at least one dormer window, then smaller non-windowed rooms in the center. Each of the guest bedrooms contained a primitive bathroom area behind a screen, with chamber pot and wash basin. Matthew did not see any evidence of plumbing or electricity on the entire floor. Most of the smaller rooms were the female house servants' quarters, usually with two beds each. Matthew and Azur walked carefully around the fully-furnished rooms which looked untouched since at least Victorian times: what a museum of ancient life. "There must be a closet or something with a small staircase to the roof, but I don't see anything," he said.

"I believe that houses this old didn't have closets: that's why there are so many wardrobes. I wonder if we need to go back down and enter the secret passages in the library then climb in the old passages to reach the roof."

"I would think that there must be an access hatch or something for workmen to get onto the roof for repairs. We must be almost under the platform right here," said Matthew as they entered one of the non-window bedrooms near the center of the front of the house.

"The wallpaper over there is different from the paper on this side. That is a bit odd," Azur stated as she started to examine the wallpaper carefully.

They felt the wall and eventually found a door, its edges cleverly concealed by innocuous moldings. It opened with a squeak, revealing a dark dusty room behind the wall.

"Hey, judging by where we are, I'll bet this is the way out to the big clock over the front door: I've been wondering how to get up there and see if I can fix it."

They entered the room and discovered that they were inside the triangular pediment over the front entrance. Overhead were the huge ancient rough-cut wood beams that supported the slate roof. Underfoot were dusty boards. On the landward side was the clock mechanism, but before Matt could investigate its workings, Azur cried out, "Look there's a short staircase and a door that must lead onto the roof."

"Children would have a field day playing in this house. Can you imagine 'hide and seek' in here?"

They ran up the stairs quickly and came out through a heavy door onto the roof platform.

"Look at these lines cut into the platform: it is a perfect description of the Ley lines that meet here, right at this spot," she said.

"What a grand view. You could get a great series of pictures, down each of the lines from here. I'm sure that Rick must have known about this."

"Maybe Floris was converted right here, right where we are standing today, and these lines commemorate the event."

"They may be much older than that: look at the wear over there. Are some lines stronger than others, or do they have more spirit energy or power or anything?"

"Of course, just like electric power. There are major lines

and minor ones. The main line is the one going that way, all the way straight to Stonehenge. Then that one goes straight all the way to Glastonbury. This platform is a wonderful find."

Later, that night, Azur was going through a box of 4x5[2] negatives carefully looking at each, when she realized what she had just found. "Matthew, look at these. They must have been made from the roof platform where we were this afternoon."

"Can you scan them, and make positives in your laptop? Then tomorrow we could take it up to the roof and compare the old photos to the view?"

"Yes, if we go up first thing, while the sun is low with long shadows across the countryside, the light will be about the same as these old shots. I will bring binoculars, and be back before six."

"It'll be fun to see if modern civilization has changed the area around here and your Ley Lines."

Azur took the relevant negatives home to her scanner, and Matthew went to bed, his head buzzing with unanswered questions.

Just after sunrise Matthew, Azur, and her laptop, as well as compass, notebooks, camera gear and maps were all on the roof platform. As they compared today's views with the old photos, they were surprised at the lack of change in many directions. Although new roads had been made, and some buildings were different, much of the countryside in this remote part of England was not very different sixty years ago. Most, but not all of it.

"What's that big ugly building right across the Stonehenge line," he asked Azur.

"It is not in the old photograph."

"Maybe it has blocked the power coming down that line, so that's why Floris is weak?"

"I do not think energy lines work that way, but if it goes deeply enough into the ground, and perhaps if it is made of the wrong materials, it could diminish the spirit power."

Matthew looked through binoculars: "It looks like a giant

2   '4x5' these negatives are 4" by 5", and are still used in view cameras, which are large cameras on tripods, with bellows that expand and contract as the lens is moved.

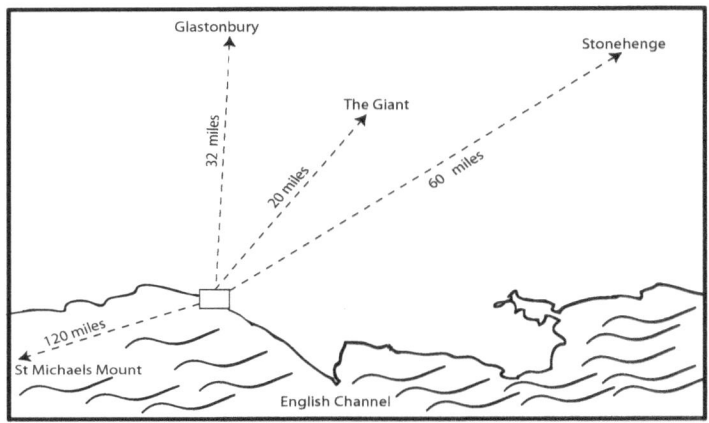

Map of the Major Ley Lines at Redcliffs Hall

run-down warehouse or something dreadful."

"That is odd. All the other lines seem about as they were in the old days, but as you say, the Stonehenge line is blocked."

"Let's drive over there. Certainly you can dowse the line or feel it or something and see if it's stronger on the far side than on the near side?"

"It is your turn to watch out: you might be becoming psychic!"

They drove in the Morgan through a dis-used industrial park from the fifties, and eventually found the building, an abandoned warehouse whose purpose had been outlived years ago. Most of the construction was rotting wood, though parts were cement. Windows were broken and the doors were boarded over. Grass was growing through cracks in the cement. Paint was peeling off the old buildings. The rusty remains of railroad tracks and burned-out railcars were everywhere. Perhaps squatters were living inside, judging by the scattered trash.

They determined, with the compass, the general direction of the Stonehenge line and Azur tried to feel its strength on both sides of the building, but without luck. "Maybe this thing is an energy sink, the opposite of a spirit well, so you can't feel anything here. Let's check it further away, maybe a mile on each side. We can find good spots on the map. Let's go to that churchyard with the markstone up the road as a start. If we're right, the signal there should be very strong as it has a straight shot to Stonehenge," he said.

"I have never heard of anyone making such a test, but you are right. The energy in that churchyard should be fine."

They went to the churchyard, where Azur left the car, then quietly concentrated near a small crooked old stone for a long time. She moved to one side then to the other, then to all four points of the compass. After awhile she commented, "Seems like a normal Ley line here, but a bit weaker on the side away from Stonehenge."

"That's because the ugly warehouse is sucking up all the energy," Matthew exclaimed.

They drove down little roads until they came to a markstone at the intersection of two small one-car-wide hedge-enclosed-lanes. They were on the exact opposite side of the warehouse, between the warehouse and Redcliffs Hall. As much as Azur tried, she could not feel anything psychic in the vicinity.

"So to recharge Floris, all we need to do is remove that warehouse and restore the ground around here. Seems simple enough, if we had tons of money and time," he said.

"And planning permission: it is almost impossible to obtain government permission to do anything. And just think what would happen if you told them why we wanted to do it!"

"I'd be laughed all the way back to school."

When they returned to Redcliffs Hall, there was a government car in the driveway, as well as Etienette's truck. They found Etienette and her secretary, Jeane, in the library. The door to the secret passageway was closed. Etienette and Jeane were conversing quietly in French while two stuffy bureaucrats were sitting primly on dusty chairs. They looked very uncomfortable and were being completely ignored by the two women.

Matthew greeted the visitors, "Hello, welcome to Redcliffs Hall. How may we help you?"

"We would like to see the new owner of this property," the first visitor said.

"That's me: how can I help you?"

The second visitor removed a thick document and handed it to Matthew: "Under section 502.3.8.1 of the Utilities Act, this area has been selected as the site for a wonderful new power plant. The drawings of the plant are in this document, and this site is a perfect location. You will be compensated fairly for the value, and you have sixty days to vacate the house and the property."

The first visitor continued, "Yes, it's especially fortunate that this house is slipping away into the sea, so there won't be any problem with the Antiquities Board about the demolition."

Etienette leapt from her chair, "Leave this house immediately you scoundrels." As she said this, she tried to hit one of them with a poker from the fireplace but Matthew grabbed her arm. "Go, and never set foot on this land again."

The Bureaucrats jumped back and started to retreat.

Azur growled at the visitors as they turned to leave, "You will hear from our solicitors before your feeble bodies reach London: get out!"

Matthew added, "And take the abandoned Telford Goods warehouse with you."

The Bureaucrats were mystified by this last comment, but left in a hurry mumbling to each other. Etienette chased them up the stairs, waving her poker and swearing in French.

Even before Etienette returned, Azur was on her phone to the family solicitor, explaining the problem to him and promising to bring the documents immediately.

"You stay here and comfort mother. I will run this pile of 'merde' over to the solicitor's office in Lyme Regis. The sooner we start moving legally the better."

Matthew was in shock, "I think I'll find Marti's brandy bottle. Sixty days, that's the middle of October."

"I hope it is a big bottle of brandy. Madame is going to be mad for days," Jeane added.

"She would have really hit those guys with the poker, wouldn't she," he asked.

"Oh yes, her temper is legendary, and this house, is how you say, a special cause for her: she will not let those fools rest until the plans are changed," Jeane said.

"But can she really do anything?"

"Maybe yes, maybe no, but she can make life very miserable for them. She is probably pounding on their car as they drive away."

Several minutes later Etienette ran into the room and wrapped her arms around Matthew, hugging him tightly. She was shaking with rage. He'd never seen someone so worked up, so agitated. He didn't know what to do, but almost naturally wrapped his arms around her, patting and rubbing her back. Although she was very disturbed, her body was so soft and warm, and so tightly pressed against his, literally touching every inch from head to foot. He couldn't help but feel sexually excited. If Jeane hadn't entered with the brandy and glasses, he didn't know what would have happened.

They separated and sat down on a couch. Etienette was close beside him tightly holding his hand while talking vigorously with Jeane in French.

He wasn't sure what the two women had discussed in French, but eventually Jeane left in the truck on an errand. Matthew and Etienette were alone. She wanted to see the rest of the house, so they walked through the public rooms then up into the old dusty bedrooms.

Etienette had been casually holding his hand all the time that they had been walking. She expressed much interest in the old bedrooms and at the furniture under the sheets which covered everything. There were beautiful old chairs, tables, beds, couches. Etienette more than once said that a particular piece was quite valuable and that it would bring a good price if extra money were needed.

They were walking through a pleasant bedroom, with light blue wallpaper and a view over the ocean, when Etienette stopped, her body very close to his. Something in her eyes told him that she wanted him, his lips, his arms, his body. Matthew could only think of "Mrs. Robinson" and what happened in the movie, but Etienette was so soft, so warm, and so near. She moved slightly closer, and her hand tightened on his. They embraced and her wet lips moved over his mouth in ways he had never imagined, as her hands explored his excited body.

Something told Matthew that it was time to stop, this was not the time nor the place to go further. He hugged Etienette tightly, but stopped kissing. His fingers ran tenderly through her hair, as he pressed her face onto his shoulder. "Please, please stop. I want to be your friend, more than your friend. You've been so kind to me, you're such a wonderful person. . . I don't know what to say. You're so beautiful."

They slowly and gently separated, while holding hands and smiling at each other, looking into each other's eyes. Then they heard a car honk in the driveway and the tender mood shattered, as they straightened their clothes and hurried down to the door. Julian had just arrived and Matthew wondered if he could tell what he had just interrupted, if perhaps somehow he could smell Etienette's perfume on Matthew or had some sixth sense that would alert him. If so, there was no outward indication. He and Etienette drove off, waving casually, as Azur returned from the lawyers' offices.

Matthew sought relief from the confused emotions engendered by Etienette's approach. He forced himself to become an Engineer and focus on the house's problems. As a start, he unpacked the laser surveying equipment and read the directions. Although it was simple to operate, he wanted to be sure that he knew how to set it up for maximum accuracy. It would be a shame to use such delicate equipment improperly. He decided that a good test would be to check the Long Gallery floor, to see if it really was sagging over the weakest part of the foundations.

He placed the spinning laser on a stone pedestal right in the doorway between the entrance hall and the long gallery. It would be easy to repeat this measurement, as the pedestal, about four feet high, was solid and hard to move. Perhaps it had once held a statue or a potted plant. The machine leveled itself for a few minutes, then emitted a red beam, which painted a bright thin red line on the walls, all around the room as well as in the front hall. With much excitement, Matthew opened his notebook, and wrote "Data: August-9". He then used his tape measure to check the distance from the beam to the floor at the front door. The front door was on solid ground, away from the ocean, and was probably at the height where it had originally been constructed. The beam cast a thin red line across

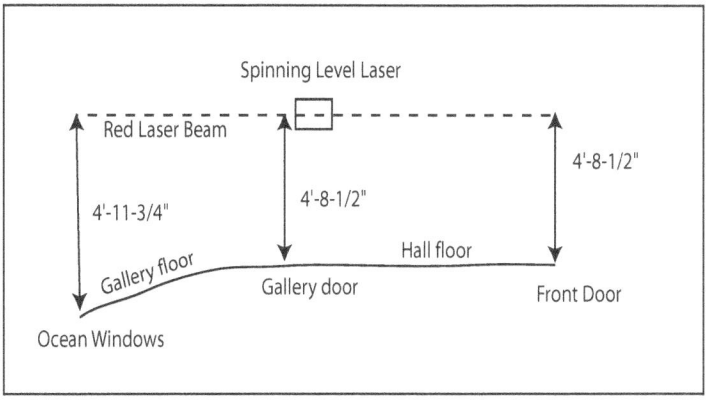

Measurements in the long gallery

his vertical tape measure, giving a quick and precise measurement of four feet, eight and one half inches. He repeated the measurement at the pedestal, and it was the same, so the entrance hall floor was level. Then he walked quickly to the ocean-side wall of the Long Gallery and measured from the beam to the floor, and read four feet, eleven and three quarters inches. Therefore, this part of the floor was more than three inches below the floor by the front door and the pedestal. He moved along the wall, taking measurements. At the ends of the Gallery, the floor was even with the floor at the front door, but as he walked along the ocean-side wall, he could easily measure the sag and find the lowest place on the floor. He took a pencil and marked the position of the red beam at several places on the dusty closed shutters, and the date. Matthew then moved the laser to the front entrance hall and verified that the floors of the small library, front hall, and formal dining room were all at the same level.

The whole process had not taken long, and he now had an exact way to determine if the ocean-side floor dropped any more. He would repeat this exercise once a week, and record any changes. The most important thing that he had just learned was that the sides of the house, as well as the front half, were on solid rock; they had not moved at all in three hundred years. Now, if he could find a way to brace the center of the house to the rock under the sides, there was hope.

He found Azur, told her of his preliminary measurements, then asked if she would take him to a computer store, so that he could buy a strong laptop and order engineering software. He assumed that for practical purposes, her credit card was infinite, so he asked without hesitation for the best equipment that would let him get results quickly.

Chapter 7, Wake Up!

First thing the next morning, Azur, helped by Julian, moved a carload of her clothes and equipment into two of the servant's bedrooms in the area where she and Matthew had first stayed. Julian explained that it was his idea to move Azur over, so that she could continue her psychic research without having to run back and forth between their houses.

Matthew thought that it was nice of Julian to be so helpful, but he couldn't stop thinking about Etienette.   Perhaps Julian already knew, or suspected, a sexual interest in Etienette toward his body. Perhaps Julian was pushing Azur toward him to deflect his interest from her mother? The girl side of his life was becoming too complicated: he needed to focus on repairing the house, then get back to school. He spent the day measuring the house and transferring the data to his new computer. He began to realize that the house was much bigger, and much heavier, than he had originally thought.

That night, while they were both working in the library, Matthew asked Azur how to contact Rick. "Couldn't we hold a séance or something: we could hire a medium or super-sensitive, or something. There are so many questions I'd like to ask."

"Impossible. His spirit is probably sound asleep, and it would be very annoyed if we did manage to make contact. He has to contact us, not the other way around."

"But he could help us save Floris. There must be tons of things he could do to help us, if he were active."

"Maybe, but it is not a real option, so do not waste your time dreaming about it."

"I feel so frustrated. I half wish that I had accepted your father's offer to buy the place, before those utility jerks arrived."

"What offer? You did not say anything about that."

"Oh, we talked about death duties and the tons of money I owe, and he thought that he could organize some business people to buy this if I ever wanted to sell."

"That is a bit odd: maybe he was just being polite."

"He seemed very serious to me: what's so odd?"

"Normally he hates real estate investments, especially in England, due to the planning difficulties."

"Hey, does Rick sleep somewhere special, like Dracula in an old coffin, or something: I mean is there a particular area where he would be most likely to be found?"

"No, it is not like that. His spirit is just sort of here, spread throughout the house. Perhaps it is more concentrated in some areas than others."

"Most of his favorite stuff is down in the storerooms and in his workshop: I haven't seen anything that reminds me of him anywhere else in the house."

"That is true, what are you implying?"

"He's got to be right around here, maybe down below us. Can't you feel his presence, or dowse for him or something. His spirit must be strongest right around here."

"I never looked at it that way."

"Let's go downstairs and look for him!"

"You are crazy, we will not find anything."

"It's worth a try, I'm going to have a look."

Matthew grabbed a flashlight and went down the passageway into the box room below. He stumbled around, shaking boxes and looking into corners, making as much noise as he could, looking everywhere. Azur came down the steps: "What are you doing? You will not find him that way."

"I know it's not the official approach, but I've got to do something; this is too complex for us to handle on our own. I'm going further downstairs."

He went down into the cold wet shop and started crashing around, looking all over. Azur followed, bewildered as much by Matthew's illogical actions as anything else. Matthew started shouting in all directions: "Come out, come out, wherever you are dammit, we need your help Rick. And we need it right now."

He yelled in all directions, and then moved the old machine and yelled down into the beach tunnel as Azur stood with her arms folded across her chest in disbelief. After thirty minutes of yelling to no avail, they returned to the library. As they entered the room, Matt was startled to see a vague blue glow in the chair by his work table.

A voice emanated from the glow, "Fine mess you're making, isn't it?"

Neither recognized the voice, or had any idea how it could be coming from the glow. Matt instinctively assumed that the voice must be Rick and continued, "Yes, and if you want us to preserve this place and keep Floris ticking, you're going to have to help instead of sleeping all the time."

"Matthew! That is no way to talk to spirits: for heaven's sake, show some respect," Azur said as the reality of Rick's presence began to sink in. Her studies of Rick had consisted of listening to Marty's recollections, looking at pictures in old scrap books, and reading obscure reference material: this was her first direct contact and she was wary. She knew that he was a powerful and perhaps unique creature and her curiosity was mixed with fear of what he could do if angered.

"Take it easy Azur, Matthew does have a good point and I have had a nice nap," Rick said.

"How do you know our names? Do you also know what's been happening here and that your house is falling into the ocean, and your spirit line to Stonehenge is shorted out and that the government is going to start building a power plant right over your cave in less than two months?" Matthew asked.

"What a mouthful," Rick said.

Azur mumbled to herself in astonishment, "I can not believe this."

"Tell you what. You're both startled at seeing me, and it takes me a bit of time to wake up, so why don't you two go up to bed, and tomorrow after breakfast, we'll make some plans and see what we can do together. But please be a bit quieter, or you'll disturb Floris," Rick said.

"Great. Lots has happened while you've been asleep, but together maybe we can solve some of the problems," Matthew said.

"Don't look so frightened, Azur. I'm real and I'll teach you a bit about life on the other side. Matthew's rather direct approach is no problem for me. I like action and having fun, and we're going to do lots of unusual things. Now run along, I need time to compose myself."

Matthew and Azur climbed the steps, put out the lights, and walked to their rooms. Outside Azur's door, they stopped, and Azur turned to Matthew, taking his hands in hers. "I do not know what to say. I am so excited and confused that I cannot even imagine sleeping. You were super. Somehow you did just the right thing to awaken Rick. There is so much to do now."

They were both radiating energy and excitement. Matthew could hardly believe that he had just met his ghostly grandfather and that perhaps much of what Azur had told him was actually true. Azur was just as excited, but it related to her PhD dissertation, which was going to be spectacular with Rick's help. Before either realized what was happening, Azur wrapped her arms around Matthew and kissed him passionately, then pulled back with a laugh. "It is so exciting. What do you think we will learn from Rick," Azur asked.

"Maybe we can learn more about kissing," Matthew laughed, but only half in jest.

"Perhaps someday, but not tonight."

Azur kissed him lightly on the lips then they went their separate ways for the night.

In the early-morning light, Matthew, Azur, and her laptop were on the roof platform. They conferred with Rick, who was invisible. Rick had never seen a computer, let alone one with scans of his own photographs inside, and watched in delight as Azur brought his old negatives to the screen, then enlarged details of them.

"So the signal is dead on this side of the warehouse, but strong on the other side," Matthew said.

"We'll just have the warehouse removed," Rick said.

"But how could we do that," Azur asked.

"I've got tons of money, so we'll just buy it and tear it down: piece of cake. Floris is very weak. She needs all the energy she can get, so that warehouse has to go," Rick said.

"What do you mean, tons of money," Matthew asked.

"Lots of gold coins, precious stones, stuff like that. I've been collecting for a long time," Rick replied.

"Where do you keep it," Azur asked.

"Down there, in my park, er, oops, what's that playground doing on my land? When was it built?" Rick asked.

Matthew and Azur looked down on the nearby village, outside the gates to Redcliffs Hall, at the local school and its nearby playground.

"Perhaps twenty years ago, judging by the vegetation," Matthew answered.

"That's not fair, my treasure box is buried there, probably about where that playground is, right where those children are playing," Rick said.

"Do you think it's still there?" Matthew asked.

"Let's find out," Rick said.

"We cannot start digging right in the middle of the school playground," Azur said.

"Let's see if we can feel its presence below, then work out a digging plan if it's there. We need to get rid of that warehouse right now," Rick said.

Azur and Matthew, talking quietly with invisible Rick, wandered around the village school's playground trying to look innocent. Rick was quite excited as he moved about, then stopped and scratched the ground with a stick. "It's here, about eight feet down. We can dig it up tonight when no one is looking," Rick said.

"How big is the box? Is it heavy?" Matthew asked.

"Oh yes, hundreds of pounds, and about a yard on each side," Rick replied.

"That may be a bit difficult to lift by ourselves," Azur said.

"It's my treasure: there must be a way to get our hands on it. Then we can buy the warehouse and tear it down, and Floris will feel much better. We must restore her spirit line," Rick said.

"Well, if we had a back-hoe, we could dig down pretty fast, maybe in a hour or so, and then use the backhoe's bucket to raise the box. I don't see how we could do that and not get caught however," Matthew said.

"The school is deserted at night, and if we worked in the rain, no one might come near," Azur said.

"And if they did, I'd scare the dickens out of them. Now tell me about back-hoe: I've never seen one. Is it fun to drive? How fast can it dig? Where do we get it? Can I try digging," Rick asked.

"Yes, yes, yes, but first, let's call Azur's family solicitor and ask him to put someone onto researching the deeds to this house: perhaps he can show that the school has encroached onto our property. Having a legal claim to the surrounding land might prove useful for future adventures, as well as for the treasure," Matthew said.

"I can show you old maps in the library: they might help whoever's trying to prove our claim," Rick said.

Matthew was fascinated and couldn't wait to see the maps: perhaps they showed geological features, and maybe even the shape of the maze.

"Rick, this may seem an odd request, but can you keep your presence a secret from my family? They do not believe and would not understand. Life will be a bit easier if we do not need to explain you to them just yet," Azur said.

"Of course, I'm much more effective when people don't know I exist. My powers are not so great, but secrecy and invisibility go a long way. Marti and Floris understood that well. I'm not much stronger than Matthew, and although I have excellent psychic powers, I still need to ride in a car or train when I want to go somewhere," Rick said.

"And you need to walk through doors, just like us, do you not?" Azur asked.

"Oh yes, I'm really just like you, except my atoms are all lined up so that you can see straight through me, like a piece of glass," Rick said.

"And you live forever, and have a few other features that we do not possess," Azur said.

"Sure, but in basic terms, I can't do much more than you can, but I can do it secretly, so we can have lots of fun together," Rick said.

Chapter 8
Old Coins, New Money

Even with Azur's family connections, several days were needed to have a Caterpillar 420D Backhoe-Loader discretely delivered to Redcliffs Hall from a far-away rental shop. It was bigger, and certainly more expensive, than Matthew had wanted, but with a reach of over fourteen feet, it would easily dig down to the buried treasure. When the backhoe arrived there was much excitement. Matthew had used a backhoe, but not one this big, during a summer construction job last year, never dreaming that he would be on one again so soon.

His story to the rental house was simple. Matthew told them that he wanted to excavate to investigate the foundations around his home. As soon as the machine arrived, he drove it to an obscure corner of the property and practiced digging and refilling holes like the one he imagined would be needed. He hoped that no one in the village could see or hear his practice runs. They had been as careful as possible about the delivery of the machine and hoped no one in the village had noticed its arrival. Fortunately Etienette and Jeane were in France on business, so the backhoe activity at Redcliffs Hall went off without a need for explanations.

Initially Matt had been awed by the arrival of Rick and all that his presence implied, but Matt had quickly realized that Rick and his treasure could perhaps provide a feasible solution to preserving the house. Money from Rick's treasure could pay for construction materials and perhaps his invisibility and psychic powers might be used somehow to foil the power plant people if they worked quickly. But first they had to get the treasure box.

While learning to use the machine, he put it to good use, burying a decade's worth of junk and garbage in a corner of the property, and digging a new hole for fresh detritus.

Rick was excited about the backhoe, a wonderful new toy with which to play. Rick's innate sense of how machines worked allowed him to master the controls quickly. They delighted in the simplified joystick control for the loader and the automatic transmission which made the huge machine relatively easy to operate. This machine was powerful and fast, and in Rick's hands it might do almost anything. By nightfall Rick was far more proficient than Matthew and Rick had the added advantage that he would be able to feel the treasure box's shape and location psychically. Matthew commented more than once that Rick would be a great construction worker.

That night, in pouring rain, Rick slowly drove the Cat to the school playground, making some unfortunately large tracks on the wet ground. Rick had the brilliant idea of driving around the village, on pavement, then approaching the school from the opposite direction, in case anyone should follow the tracks. Rick started digging in the rain at two in the morning and found the box easily. Azur and Matt were beside the hole. The only problem was getting a chain around the box as the hole filled with muddy water. Rick was able to use the Cat's bucket to gently rock the box back and forth as Matthew, in a very dangerous spot at the bottom of the wet muddy hole, eased heavy chain around the box. No human driver could have been so gentle, or felt so clearly where Matthew's body was with respect to the box. With the chain attached, they raised the huge old box to the ground: it was remarkably heavy, but the big Cat could lift 6000 pounds, so this was nothing for it's engine. Then Rick began to fill the hole.

All of a sudden he stopped and jumped from the machine. "We have visitors, in the car over by that tree."

Azur, who didn't see the car, asked, "How can you tell?"

"I'll be back in a minute."

Rick, invisible, ran to the car and opened a door. In the back seat were a partially-clothed young boy and girl, locked in passionate embrace.

"Sorry kids, time to go home," Rick said.

Before the couple could recover from their amazement, invisible Rick started their engine, put the car in gear, then jumped out the door. The car slowly headed away down the road with the petrified couple in the back seat.

Back at the dig, he refilled the hole as neatly as possible, then motored away with the treasure box in the bucket, leaving a track in the direction opposite from their house. Matthew and Azur quickly walked home, soaking wet and covered with mud. As the backhoe quietly made its way home through the village streets, the town drunk was startled to see it go by, with no driver and no lights, apparently running by itself. Luckily the rain obliterated most of the tracks before morning, leaving a playground mystery for the locals to solve some day.

After they returned to their rooms, Azur undressed and sat at her makeup table combing her soft dark hair. She was wearing little, but who would see: just a very small amount of pink satin and lace from her favorite Parisian lingerie boutique. As she brushed and thought of the day's events, she was briefly startled, thinking that she heard an unusual noise, like a camera shutter clicking. That was impossible. Matthew was down the hall in the bathtub, and he would never take a surreptitious picture of her. Azur's psychic sensitivity indicated that something wasn't quite right. There was an odd feeling to the room. She put on her robe and walked quickly to the bathroom. Matthew was soaking in the tub, reading DOWSING IN DEVON AND CORNWALL, a book she had given him to study.

Azur knocked and then entered without waiting for an answer. "I just had the strangest experience. I thought that I heard a camera shutter click, and I could feel something, but I don't know what it was."

Matthew was embarrassed and tried to cover himself with the book, almost soaking it before he thought of grabbing a towel to cover his nakedness as he splashed about in confusion. "Funny that you should mention that, as I had a similar experience while running the tub. Wonder what it was."

"I do not know, but it startled me."

"First thing tomorrow, let's explore the old passages in the house and see where they go, particularly in this area. Let's make sure that it isn't possible for someone from outside to wander around in them and spy on us."

"If you do not mind, I'm going to stay here with you. I do not feel like going back to my room alone."

Matthew let the water out of the tub and tried to dry himself while covering himself with the same towel. "Would you mind looking the other way, instead of staring at my body."

"You have been inside my body, seeing everything that I have, from the inside, you told me so yourself, so why should I not look at yours," Azur teased, and pulled at his towel.

"Hey, that was just a dream."

She took his hand. "Oh, oh, something under your towel is growing excited when you look at me. Should I untie my robe and let you see my sexy lingerie?"

"Please stop teasing me, or something messy might happen before I can control it."

She ran her fingers through his hair and kissed him. His towel fell to the floor as he reached for her. What an erection!

"What was that? Did you just hear something? Do you feel anything strange," Azur said as she pushed away from Matthew.

"I heard it too. What could it have been?"

"Get dressed quickly. Something is not right. I will sleep on the spare bed in your room; I do not feel like being alone."

First thing the next morning, they went to the big library, then started exploring the dusty abandoned secret passageways with flashlights. The tunnels and steps wandered all over the main house, but there appeared to be no vantage point where someone could have accessed their bathroom or Azur's bedroom. Then Matt had an idea and led Azur to the old Kitchens under the house. He had noticed that the spiral staircase that he and Phil had discovered began in the kitchens and went all the way up to the top floor, to the Servants' bedrooms. As he told Azur about this, they looked for entrances to other spiral staircases, figuring that the walls were thick enough for at least a few more.

Azur spotted the worn entrance to a spiral near the front of the house. It went up in the wall between the dining room and the central hall, and ended next to the front door, providing a convenient way for a doorman or other servant to greet visitors. It had nothing

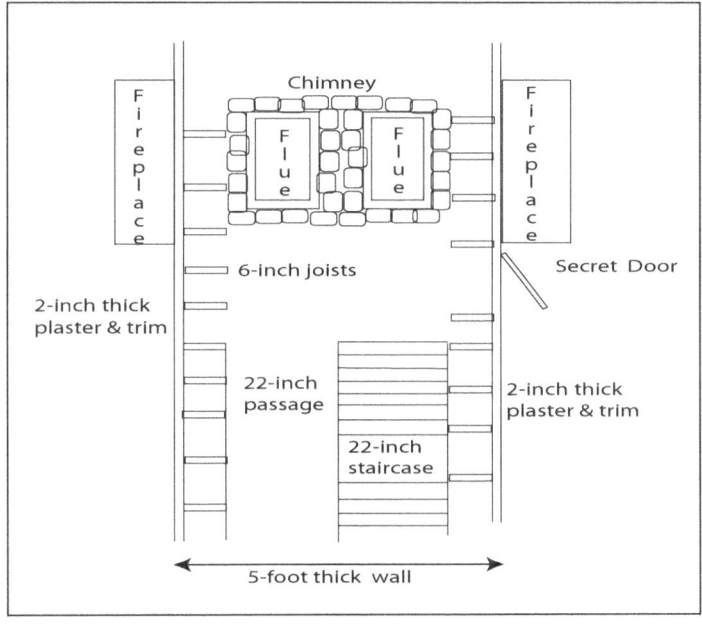

Secret Passages Inside The Walls

to do with the Victorian wing of the house.

As they searched near the eastern end of the kitchens they discovered a third spiral, and it went all the way up to the old Master Bedroom, probably providing discreet access for the personal needs of the owners. They inspected it carefully as it went very close to their bathroom. However the only interesting thing to Matt was Victorian era cold water and drain plumbing that poked through the bathroom wall into the staircase: no secret peep holes or access doors.

Matthew was curious about the passages and could tell that their original purpose was pragmatic. A way for servants to move about the house without bothering the owners, a way to discretely service the fireplaces, chamber pots, and other necessities from a bygone age. There were no footprints in the dust, and cobwebs indicated that the passages hadn't been used in many years. Matthew would love to take the time to make an accurate drawing of the entire house, especially the passageways and old construction artifacts. Azur was still worried about the odd noises.

Rick had used the backhoe to place the heavy treasure box in the back of the stables after washing away the mud and dirt. It was nailed and screwed shut and took two hours to open as he worked carefully, not wanting to damage the old brass and wood. Matthew and Azur were amazed at the collection of jewels, gold coins and other treasures. Azur could have stayed all day examining the treasures, but had to go home and then to town to meet her father.

Rick and Matthew gathered the treasures into small boxes, and moved them down into the basement of the Victorian wing, which they judged to be the safest temporary hiding place. Rick selected a dozen old gold coins and jewels and placed them in a small cloth bag. "Take these to London and sell them so we can buy the warehouse and tear it down. They look valuable, but to me, they're nothing special."

Matthew was attracted to a little ring which he saw, "What is this little ring, in its own golden box?"

"Be careful, that is very special. It's at least fourteen hundred years old, and has a very dramatic history."

"It's so unusual, I mean the heart-shaped diamond is unusual, but the gold band is dented and scratched."

"It has had a turbulent life. . . . Matthew, now that we are alone together, and I have worked a little with you, and begun to know you, and you me, I want to do something special for you. You are my only living descendant, at least as far as I know. I hope that you marry a wonderful woman and have many children. Floris and I would love to watch them playing with you in this house. When you find the right person, an honest and true person, please give her this ring. Even though it is old and worn, it is the most valuable single treasure in this entire chest. Guard it with your life." Rick carefully and solemnly handed the ring and its little box to Matthew.

"Thank you, I don't know what to say, what makes it so special?"

"On your wedding day, I will tell you and your bride the full story."

They buried the treasure boxes, after sealing them in plastic bags, under the basement floor, then arranged old boxes of junk over the area. The ring was in the deepest place.

Then Matthew went to work with his new equipment in the bottom level of the main house. Rick was fascinated as he watched and helped. Matthew wanted to make a detailed study of the elevations of the uneven floor. If anything happened on the rock below the house, it would make a measurable change first in the floor here. He put the rotating laser on a surveyor's tripod, then set it spinning. Back against the cliff, behind the trapdoor, he marked an "X" on the solid stone floor, then measured the vertical distance from it to the red laser line. Then he repeated this exercise all over the floor, making many of the "X" marks, each with a number beside it. Rick was fascinated by the process, and although he didn't know how the rotating laser made its red beam, he could see exactly what Matthew was doing and why. They would come down here every few days and repeat the cycle of

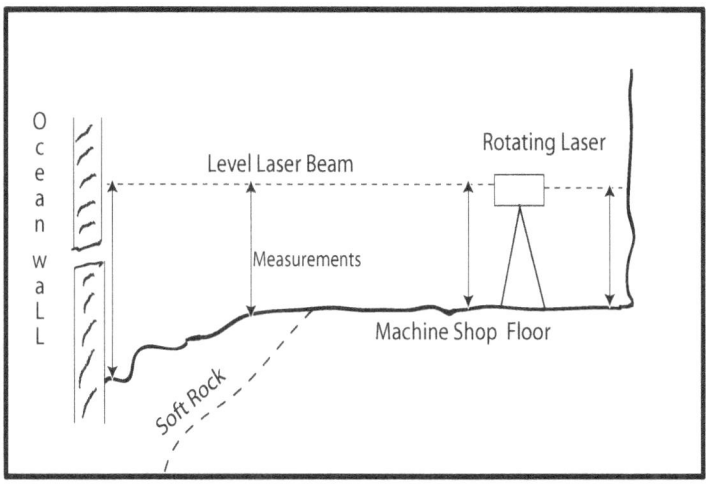

Measuring the collapse of the Machine Shop floor

measurements, noting if any of the floor had fallen further below the beam than it was today. This activity wouldn't repair anything, but it would indicate trouble and how fast it was happening. Matthew also measured the room's dimensions with the laser rangefinder, and showed Rick how closely it matched the numbers measured with a tape measure. Rick loved the new equipment, the backhoe, the laser gizmos, and the computer darkroom. He had awoken at a great time for craftsmen who adore tools.

They went up to the Long Gallery and Matthew repeated the measurements he had made seven days earlier, while explaining them to Rick. The floor had fallen an eighth of an inch further in just a week, as he recorded the data for August-16th.

Rick asked, "Now explain this to me again. What have we just measured?"

"A week ago I set up the rotating laser and measured the distance from the red beam to the ground at several places. Over here, by the windows, is the lowest part of the floor. It is directly over the bad part of the foundation. I compare it to the floor by the front door, which is on solid rock. The difference today is an eighth of an inch more than just a week ago. The floor we are standing on is falling into the sea. At this rate, in less than a month, the floor over here will drop another three inches, probably opening big cracks in this lovely marble."

"So what are you doing about it? I don't see any construction activity."

"That's the problem, I've done some math and know that we should get a big crane in here and lift the ocean side with huge hydraulic cylinders, but those power plant fools would never let such a crew work here."

"Your approach is too complex. We must find a simple way. Let's go down into the basement and talk over the situation together."

Together they wandered over the ruined machine shop looking at the rock and the kinds of masonry in the walls, poking here and there at loose and at solid rock.

Matthew summarized the situation, "First, we need a geological expert, who can tell us how far we need to go into the cliff to hit solid rock. Then we need perhaps a mining engineer to help us drill supporting steel into the good rock, so as to support and stabilize the loose outer rock and the lower foundations."

"Oh, I can tell you all about the rock, exactly, if that is what you need to know first," Rick said.

"Really? How?" Matthew asked.

"I can douse stuff like that within an inch or two. I'll show you where all the rock boundaries fall. Let's start up in the library and work down."

Rick started explaining the limestone walls and underlying geology in the library. The chimney was carved into solid stone, as was the first staircase.

As they progressed, he showed how the inner rock wall changed and detailed the different construction eras represented in the various rooms. Matthew had not noticed before, but there were several building styles in the masonry. Rick was like a docent giving him a tour he had rehearsed hundreds of times, but the difference was that Rick could describe what was beneath the visible surfaces they looked at: it was as though he had x-ray vision that could see into the stone and analyze it approximately. When Matt asked about it, Rick explained that he didn't see into the rock with his eyes, he felt the rock and could sense its inner structure with his hands: more like dowsing than seeing. He had no idea how it worked.

In the lowest level, Rick showed how the hard rock extended out from the cliff about half way toward the sea, but then it quickly became soft shale, which had been eroding for centuries. What was needed was some kind of steel structure to shift the weight of the outer part of the building onto the hard limestone on the inland side. Rick took a piece of white chalk and drew the exact boundaries between hard and soft rock on the brick floor. No living geologist could have made such a map of the subsurface stone without drilling exploratory holes, or by using ground-penetrating radar and shallow seismic techniques.

"We must stop the foundation from falling further, that is the main task. Forget the fancy hydraulics, we just need to wedge some steel in here, so that the weight of the building is carried by the hard rocks, instead of by that soft stone," Rick said.

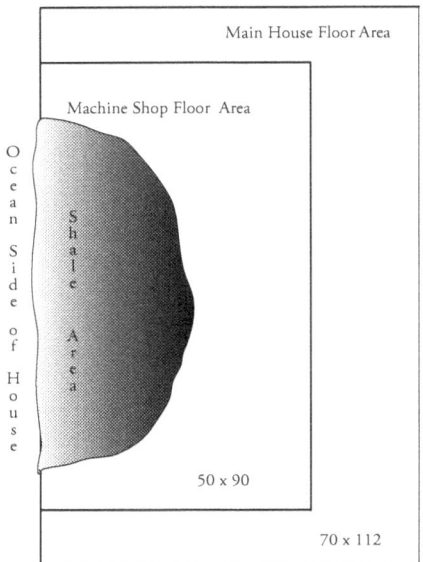

The soft stone area underneath the ocean side of the house

"But, we need to straighten the curved floors and the ocean-side wall," Matthew replied.

"That will come later after we deal with the power plant people. Now time is on their side. Every day the house falls further while they sit and watch. We must reverse the advantage by stopping the collapse. Then we can deal with them and eventually hire big equipment to lift the house back up."

"OK, I'll get busy and calculate how much steel it will take to stabilize the house where it sits now."

"Good, buy lots of little pieces that we can bolt together into big pieces. We can do that without getting permission from anyone."

The next day, Azur and Matthew took the bag of gems and

coins to London, to Christie's, to have them appraised. Azur had dealt with this comfortable old auction house before, and her mother was a well-known customer. However, what started as a simple transaction, soon became complex.

Azur was furious, "What do you mean, you cannot return those stones and coins to me?"

"I'm sorry miss Azur, but the law requires us to hold any suspicious goods until their provenance is determined."

"You mean you question me and my family's integrity!"

"Oh no Miss Azur, it's not that at all."

Matthew tried to explain, "They're mine, from the basement of my old house: they've been there hundreds of years: what could be more simple?"

"Well, how did they come to be in the basement of your house?"

"How should I know: I just inherited it. They're just old family heirlooms and we would like to have them appraised. What could be easier? They've been rotting in an old dusty box for centuries and we need to raise some cash to pay the death duties."

"Well, I understand perfectly, but you see, what you have brought to us is very rare and quite old and valuable. As an outside guess, what you held in your hands is worth perhaps a million pounds, and it is so old that it may well be Crown property, under the Treasure Trove laws. I will need to call Spink[1] and Sons to obtain a more accurate estimate."

"I want those back right now, and I want to see the Managing Director if you ever expect to do business with my family and our friends again," Azur demanded.

After much delay and paperwork, the items were returned, but not until both Matthew and Azur had pledged, with their signatures, to retain them, instead of selling. The materials had been carefully photographed and measured as part of the agreement. An antique coin expert from Spink had walked over to examine the coins

---

1   Spink & Sons is perhaps the most prestigious coin dealer in the world. Christie's used to own Spink, but in 2002, Christie's sold Spink to a foreign corporation.

and was particularly impressed. He asked if there were more coins, perhaps in different denominations, but Matthew and Azur stated that if so, they hadn't turned up yet. It was clear that the business side of Christie's badly wanted to be involved in an auction of the coins and stones, but that they were restrained by the Treasure Act of 1996.

Azur tried to apply her interpretation of the law. In her view, the law said that although old treasure belonged to the Crown, the British Museum was obligated to buy any that appeared at fair market value. They just wanted to determine how much money this handful of treasure represented before selling it to the Museum. They weren't asking Christie's to sell it or engage in anything illegal. The Christie's people explained that although Azur was correct, technically, and that Matt was clearly the "finder" as well as the "landowner" under the law, that the law didn't apply in practice to really old and valuable discoveries. Such things as he and Azur had brought needed research, which implied endless bureaucratic delay.

As soon as they were away, Matthew commented, "Let's take a different bag to New York or Tokyo and sell it there. These guys are impossible. We can keep this handful in an old box in case they ever want to see it again."

"We can sell a little bit in Brussels tomorrow. We will hide it in our clothes," Azur said.

"What do we do when Christie's experts want to see the dusty old box that we found in the basement?"

"Tell them to go away. You would be surprised how often that works, if you yell loudly enough. They really do not want to anger us and they would love to make the sale, then pick through your basements looking for more. They are vultures who have just spotted a fresh corpse."

Without much trouble, they caught the morning train to Brussels, avoiding the ubiquitous metal detectors and x-ray machines found in airports. Azur had a new batch of coins in her purse, mixed in with regular coins. If they hit an x-ray checkpoint, she would seem perfectly normal. They were quite worried as they boarded the train. If Azur lost her purse it would be a disaster. They actually had no trouble, but the fear of having a problem, of being caught smuggling, was constantly in their minds. They appeared to be two conservatively-dressed young people with proper passports and tickets. Completely honest travelers. After minimal customs in Brussels, they went in a taxi from the train station to the jewelry district, which Azur knew from visits with her mother.

The contrast in attitude between the small discreet diamond and gold shops in Brussels and their experience with Christies surprised Matthew. After visiting two shops that Azur knew in Brussels, they found a buyer and walked away with almost a million pounds having been wired to Matthew's new bank account. Matthew wondered about the look on Julian's face if he happened to check the bank balance. At first, Azur had been reluctant to sell even a small part of Rick's ancient treasure, but then, to her surprise, Rick announced that he had more and would busy himself locating it all in preparation for work on the foundations: he wanted to help Floris, and to do it quickly.

Matthew had a feeling that somehow the London people would eventually hear about the mysterious coins appearing on the market and make the connection. But that was far in the future. The Brussels shop which bought the coins, had talked directly with a Japanese coin collector and emailed photos to him during the transaction and having agreed a price, was probably packing and shipping the coins to Japan before Matthew and Azur were even home. It was also clear that the distant collector would take any more of these coins they wished to sell. The coins appeared to be uncommonly valuable and Matt wondered where Rick had found them. Somewhere in the future there would be tax questions, but not for awhile.

Chapter 9
Azur's SHC Paper

Now that he had money, the first thing that Matthew did was to write a check to Azur for his charges at the hardware and computer stores. He wanted to participate in these adventures on an equal basis, not as an inferior. He also bought a cell phone that could attach to his laptop for internet and email access.

The second thing that he did with his new-found wealth was to visit an estate agent and offer to buy the warehouse and its surrounding property. They inspected a map, and related the surrounding area to the ancient Ley line, then marked the desired properties on the real estate map. The estate agent would soon be in touch: she couldn't believe that an American wanted to buy such a mess, but the sales commission would be nice, and his companion, Azur, had parents who were people it would pay to help.

Meanwhile, Azur thought more about the strange things in the far wing of the house. She had read about S.H.C. (spontaneous human combustion) as part of her psychic studies. The stories were always fascinating. Each usually described a case in which a human body suddenly burst into flames and then completely disintegrated. To complicate matters, some of the stories described the combustion as a "cold flame", that didn't even burn the victim's clothes, but only the flesh. But other accounts said the opposite, that as the body burned, the floor on where it was lying burned through. This was just impossible to believe. Perhaps S.H.C. really happened, but the existing accounts were hard to credit.

There were theories about how it might work, on how the human brain somehow directed the protein in all the body's individual cells to change into combustible material. Unfortunately, nothing that she had read had any details that a modern scientist would believe. Everyone knew that a decomposing body could partially turn into methane, and that this gas would burn brightly, but decomposition into methane took years. It was not something that just happened to a living person.

Azur was in an interesting position. She had read much of the available material on the world of the spirits, but she also had studied physics, chemistry, biology, and genetics. She knew, more than most people, where discrepancies lay between the two different views of how the biological world functioned. Azur saw her life's work, academically, as the unification of these views. She very much wanted to scientifically prove the existence of at least some aspects of the spirit world. In line with this goal, she was most excited about her new relationship with Rick, and with his grandson. What a chance to learn what was possible and not possible in a key part of the spirit world.

Now fate had dropped a solid, measurable, photographable, experiment into her lap. The S.H.C. example in the wing was just dying to be analyzed with modern scientific tools, as well as from the psychic perspective. When Azur talked about this with Matthew, they had two thoughts in common. The first was that neither would dare go back to the wing unless they could get Rick to somehow fix the scary aspects of the place. The second was that they should refrain from giving the exact location of the site in any paper or publication. News of something like this would bring a horde of media people as well as too many curious visitors.

Fighting against her scientific curiosity, Azur was very much afraid of actually going into the wing herself. She had survived the first time, though just barely, and she didn't want to do it again. In addition, she wasn't really sure what had happened when Matthew had healed her physically and/or spiritually. The whole experience had been unnerving, and it seemed very strange to her that although she had fallen through a floor, she did not have one scratch or bruise to show for it when she carefully examined her body afterwards.

Matthew and Azur found Rick in the library, looking through his old negatives. "Rick, may I ask your help with a project," said Azur.

"I can sense that this is no ordinary request," he replied.

Azur and Matthew then described their adventures in the far wing, and Azur's desire to study the site and write a scientific paper. "You never should have gone in there. Didn't you see that it was bricked over and sealed," Rick said.

"Of course, and Azur did feel something strange when we entered, but our curiosity got the better of us," Matthew said.

"I sympathize with your interest in applying modern analytic tools to the site, but it's not a good place to be. I wouldn't want to go in there," Rick said.

"You mean that there are places where even you can't go," Matthew said.

"Oh no, I can go in there any time I want, I just don't like it. I like sunshine, and looking at pretty girls, and playing with backhoe. Why go into a creepy place where a bad person died ages ago?"

Rick had seen Azur manipulate negatives with her computer and then print them. He held several of his negatives in his hand and looked longingly at her computer. He could not read or write well, and had never seen a computer, much less one that could make beautiful prints from his negatives. Azur had noticed all of this, and had an idea.

Azur walked to her computer, "How about a deal? I will teach you enough about reading and writing so that you can operate a computer, and then I will teach you how to use Photoshop[1] to process your old negatives."

"And in return for that?"

"You will help Matthew photograph and analyze the material in the far wing of the house."

"I would like to learn about the darkroom inside the computer, and we could confine our activities in the wing to daylight hours, so it wouldn't be too bad. However, you must both agree to do exactly as I say when we're in there. No running off on your own and falling through floors and stuff like that!"

---

1   'Photoshop', by Adobe, is the pre-eminent software for manipulating photographs inside a computer. Any photographic effect that can be done in a traditional darkroom can be done with this program, as well as things that people working in wet darkrooms never imagined.

Azur was startled, "Both? I cannot go back in there. You and Matthew can take the pictures and collect the data, then I will write the report."

"Can the great scientist be afraid to do the experiment herself and collect the data?" Rick mocked.

"You and I could get the data. She doesn't need to go in there again." Matthew said.

"Oh yes she does. Azur, nothing in there is actually going to hurt you, at least not during daylight. You may see things, feel things, and hear things and be afraid, but those spirits are weak. They can't actually do much more than cause you to jump in fright. Now, you are going to learn something from this experiment, and that is to control your body when bad spirits are present. You must not let them scare you and cause you to hurt yourself. Last time you ran away in fear then fell through the floor. From now on, you will walk calmly, slowly, and in complete control of your actions."

Matthew wondered, "Will it help if we whistle a happy tune and pretend that we are not afraid?"

"Yes, and eventually you will actually be calm and not afraid. This project is turning out to be more interesting than I thought it would be," Rick said.

"It is one thing to talk about not being afraid, but it is different when you feel the spirits and your hair starts to stand on end and goose bumps cover your body," Azur said.

"That's when things become interesting. The spirits are more afraid than you are. Give them a good fright. Fire your flash camera. Laugh and ignore them."

"If you are both beside me, I will try it once."

"You won't have any trouble, just stay calm. The next time, and the time after that will be easier. Besides, you will be learning a very important spirit skill, and one that isn't in any books. You will be learning to fight back when faced with a bad spirit."

"Let's order a computer, scanner, printer, and software for Rick," Matthew suggested.

"And some reading and writing instructional software: might as well learn to read and write while learning about computers," Azur added.

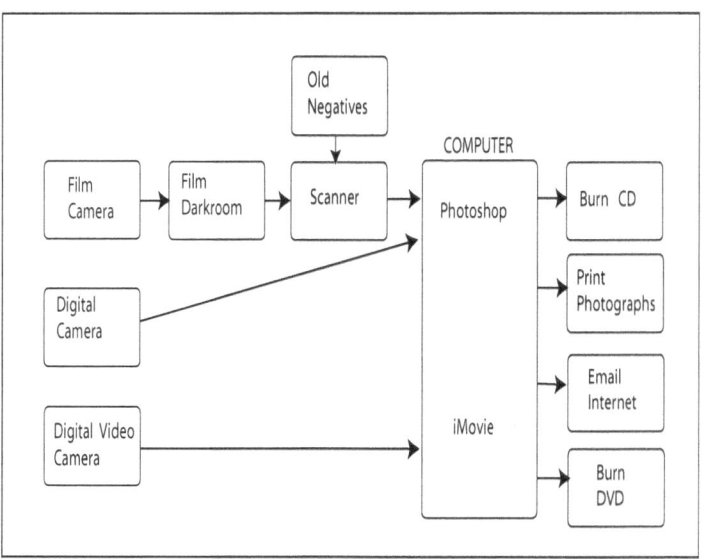

This diagram shows conceptually the major parts of a "computer dark-room". Images come from CAMERAS at the left, then flow through wires into the COMPUTER. Images from FILM CAMERAS need first to be developed in a DARKROOM, then they can go into a SCANNER which converts them into electrical signals that the COMPUTER can process. Old NEGATIVES of any shape and vintage can also be scanned into the computer. Once the images, in electrical form, are inside the computer, they are processed by software such as PHOTOSHOP. Movies from the DIGITAL VIDEO CAMERA are processed by software such as IMOVIE. The processed images can be sent to CDs, DVDs, PRINTERS, EMAIL, or the INTERNET."

      "While we are waiting for all that stuff to arrive, we could do a preliminary investigation in the wing," Matthew suggested.

      "Rick, I have been wondering about something, something that seems a bit strange," Azur said.

      "What might that be," Rick replied.

      "Your speech, your manner of talking, it all seems very

American, yet you have lived in England for maybe a thousand years," Azur said.

"Simple. Floris and I were very annoyed at those Nazis who bombed our country in 1939, so we spent much of the war years helping Yanks who were at a nearby base. Floris and I had a lot of fun with them and we picked up tons of useful words and phrases."

It turned out that Rick knew very little about the contents of the wing. He had been asleep when the SHC occurred, and had no interest in visiting the site when he next awoke. Rick had more interesting things to do when he was awake. His spirit sensitivity indicated that a very bad person had died in a strange way in the wing. Some of the negative energy from the bad person remained, even though he was dead.

Azur called the local Minister who directed her to a pleasant old lady who collected village gossip and historical information. The historian told Azur that a foreigner had killed himself in the house after he had killed the people who had rescued him. The foreigner had been on a ship that wrecked on the coast during a storm. Ever since then, the place where he died had been sealed, but no one seemed to know why. Maybe it was haunted? There had been no village newspaper then so there was little further background research for Azur to do.

The next morning, they made plans for their excursion into the wing. Before Rick would go in, he directed Matthew with a ladder and crowbar, to remove several window bricks so that sunlight could penetrate the space. Rick wanted at least a little natural light to enter, but he didn't want any snoopers or workmen to notice that they were investigating the old structure.

Azur was very curious about Rick's description of the bad energy that had been left by the burning body. She would like to know what it was, how it formed, how strong it was, if it could be measured. Rick however, was not helpful. He lived his life as a ghost, and was not a scientist or student of the supernatural. He knew how to manipulate his body, and what he and Floris required, but as for the details of good or bad energy, he knew as little as Azur. However, Rick could easily detect such things, though he couldn't explain them. He was far more sensitive than Azur.

Now that Rick was participating in the project, he wanted to do it properly, with as few trips to the wing as possible. Therefore on the first visit he and Azur would take cameras, lots of film, tripods, and flash equipment. Rick wanted to make all of the photographs before the dust was disturbed, to the extent practical. He also asked Matthew to make a movie of their activity in case anything strange happened. After a few minutes it became clear that Rick didn't know about small video cameras, and was referring to sixteen millimeter spring-wound movie cameras, like the old Bolex or Eyemo.

Matthew and Azur returned from the shops with a Sony digital video camera which not only was small and efficient, but which also could connect to Azur's computer for digital movie editing. Azur had specifically wanted this particular Sony because it has a sensitive night-vision mode: she suspected it would be quite useful in the dimly-lit rooms. They shot and played back a few scenes for Rick. Almost immediately Rick wanted a video camera and loads of mini-DV tape. He had found a wonderful new toy and was like a child under a Christmas tree. Matthew and Azur wondered to themselves where Rick would take the camera. Judging by what they had seen of his still pictures, the videos would be sensational.

They gathered their equipment as well as two flashlights each and entered through the passageway to the paneled room. Nothing had changed, but the missing bricks provided a little background light. They set up tripods and started photographing everything carefully, especially data items such as the newspaper and the remains of food on the plates. Azur was afraid, but her desire to gather as much data as possible was stronger than her fear. Matthew actually whistled as he paned the video camera over the scene. Rick was visible, so that he would appear in the video. He liked the idea of being in a movie, but kept a careful eye on Azur. He could tell that Matthew wasn't sensitive enough to be afraid, but that Azur was having problems. They covered the ground floor rooms, making many photos and close-ups of the SHC site. Most of the shots of the black hole contained a ruler so that there would be no question about its size.

Rick was using his old Leica 35mm cameras from the mid-thirties and panchromatic film, while Azur used a Nikon-D-200, saving her digital images directly to a miniature computer disk inside the camera. Matthew marveled at the contrast in equipment, and at the fact that both were expert photographers, at least as interested in lighting and composition as in the actual subjects. Matthew saw his role as being strictly documentary, not artistic. He was the neutral observer, covering the unfolding events whatever happened.

They moved upstairs, to rooms which they had not seen before. Azur screamed as she saw a body lying on a bed. Rick calmed her, and they examined the body. It was mummified, and probably much older than the house. In the room with it were old wooden shipping cases and navigational equipment. They tried to touch as little as possible in case the positioning or location of items turned out to be important. Perhaps the mummy, the shipping crates, and the foreigner had all been aboard the same wrecked ship.

"Look at that old compass and quadrant[2]: they're navigational tools from the early 1700's, so they match the date on the newspaper downstairs. We can send our photos of them to the Maritime Museum in Greenwich and have the instruments dated," Matthew said. They wandered the rooms, but none of the others contained much of interest. Each was filled with clothes, furniture, and personal possessions. They were very careful near the hole in the roof, and the rotten floor below it.

Once, as Azur was bending over her camera making a close-up, Rick whispered in her ear, "I love looking down the front of your blouse when you bend over: you have great taste in sexy undergarments." Azur was too startled to reply, but wished that her blouse had one more button. Next time she would wear a sweater. Rick was impossible!

Finally they went down to the basement, through the door that Matthew had bashed open with his shoulder. Looking at it now, they were impressed with its solidity and at the strength of his effort. Then Azur pointed to a key hanging on the wall nearby. It fit the lock

---

2   Quadrants were used before sextants for navigation. Either device measures the angle between heavenly objects (stars, sun, moon, etc) and the horizon. The angular information is used to help locate a ship's position.

on the remains of the door. They had a good laugh, then went down the steps, with Rick leading the way. He stopped halfway down the steps and said, "The spirits are strong down here, so remember what I said and move slowly and deliberately. They can't hurt, but they are good at frightening people." Matthew captured his warning on tape.

The only natural light came from the two holes in the floor, but their six flashlights illuminated everything well. Many old boxes, a pile of coal, indistinct shapes here and there. Flash pictures were made in all directions, including Azur's damage to the floor above. The only footprints on the soft dirt floor were from their last visit.

Azur shivered, "I can feel a cold draft or wind, but the dust is not moving. There is not really any wind is there?"

"No, the cold wind is all in your mind. See, your clothes are not moving, nor the dust by your feet. I feel it much more strongly, and Matthew probably wonders what we are talking about," Rick explained.

"If we measured the temperature, would the cold wind show on a thermometer," Matthew asked.

"I doubt it. These spirits have little control over things, but they can deep-six your brain if you aren't careful."

Matthew was busy capturing all this on tape, hoping that his batteries wouldn't run out. The camera didn't take much power, but now he was using the camera's floodlight, which could run the batteries down quickly. Under the burned human-shaped hole in the floor they saw something that looked like a set of old clothes, roughly matching in shape the hole above. They photographed the clothes, especially the lack of footprints near them.

Suddenly, a shimmering blue glow appeared, and surrounded the clothes on the ground. "Matt, turn off your light and try to capture the movement in the dark. See if your camera's night-vision mode is sensitive enough. Try some different adjustments. Azur, use your most sensitive settings[3] and your f/1.2 lens and try to snap it with a time exposure," Rick commanded. Azur was badly

---

3   Camera settings. The sensitivity of Azur's digital Nikon could be adjusted over a wide range, without the need to change film.

frightened, feeling herself in a cold unnatural wind, with waves of goose bumps rippling over her skin, but she was also very excited. Exploring with Rick was turning out to be fun, and his comments about her underclothes were painless. She would not wear a sweater tomorrow.

The blue glow shimmered and wiggled, expanded and contracted, giving the photographers a good chance to make adjustments, change lenses and film, and try a variety of exposure times[4]. After photographing the glow for twenty minutes, they moved to the basement door, packed their gear after a few final shots, then left the wing. Other than the cold wind, nothing bad had happened and they had seen much.

Matthew rewound his tapes, and they laughed and marveled as they watched the tape play on Azur's computer. This was the best movie any of them had ever seen. The wiggling blue glow was grainy, but they had it on tape, at least when the glow was bright. What a good piece of evidence for Azur's studies.

Azur transferred her images into her computer while Rick watched in fascination. No darkroom work, no smelly chemicals, Azur was already printing a few shots to hang on the wall! Rick went downstairs to develop his negatives in the elaborate darkroom next to the box rooms. They marveled at the quality and detail of the various photos and planned their next move. Azur wanted to do two things. One was to collect samples in sterile containers of many key items around the SHC hole and pile-of-clothes. These would be sent for chemical analysis as well as carbon-dating. The second item was to locate an expert on thermodynamics and combustion, then bring him to the site, blindfolded.

Matthew suggested that the first thing she should do was to have a laboratory make duplicates of all of their images, then store

4   Photography in dim light. Almost anything that human eyes can see can be photographed, if the camera is mounted on a rigid tripod, and if the most sensitive film or electronic chip is used. However, the dim light must last long enough for the sensitive material to absorb sufficient energy to make a recording. These long exposures lead to blurred pictures if either the camera or the subject moves during the exposure.

these far away, perhaps in her college or parent's house. He had experienced enough trouble with computer crashes to have a healthy respect for the fragility of one-of-a-kind data. They decided to make the copies, then collect the samples and see how their analysis went. Rick was reluctant to bring anyone else into the situation unless it became absolutely necessary. He pointed out that with just the photos they had already made, Azur had sufficient material for a spectacular scientific paper as well as a great movie. Rick ended the discussion with the remark that it was one thing to take photos, but another to take actual samples from the site. He suspected that the spirits would not like them removing bits of wood and clothing from the SHC area.

Chapter 10
Collecting Samples

After the estate agent called with information on the warehouse, Matthew and Rick drove to the site. Rick quickly realized that the problem was the foundation. It contained loads of scrap iron and junked cars and went down deep. Perhaps this was a site of severe bomb damage, or a junk yard, but now it was covered with concrete. He also discovered squatters living in the warehouse and gave them a good scare, then made plans to come back late at night to see that they were properly chastened.

"I just tickled them with a feather, then I gave a few "ghostly" laughs and told them to leave my property immediately if they valued their lives. I threw pots and pans around and made lots of noise. That's why you saw those creeps jumping out the window. I'll do it again tonight if any are still inside. This stuff works much better in the dark, and it's harmless. If the owner gives us any trouble, we'll scare him too," Rick laughed.

While the warehouse and scientific paper projects were moving ahead, life in another area became difficult. Etienette received a call from Christie's. The Managing Director was calling to personally apologize for the trouble that Azur and her young man had encountered in London. Etienette was amazed by the description of the jewels and coins which had been shown and wanted to know where they had been found. And she didn't like the idea of Azur and Matthew wandering around together secretly, far from home.

Etienette hadn't seen much of either Matthew or Azur lately, and on a hunch called the family travel agent. She learned that the couple had taken a train to Brussels, then returned quickly. The implication was obvious. That night a difficult situation developed in the library. Matthew and Azur were aware that Rick was also in the room, but couldn't mention him.

"You must tell me immediately about the jewels and coins: they are not in my inventory anywhere," Etienette said.

"I am sorry mother, but it is best for me to refuse to answer questions about them."

"Matthew, what is the meaning of this: where have you been with my daughter?"

"We took a quick trip together. I had business on the continent, and this seemed a good time to do it."

"And did you stay in a hotel together, in the same bed perhaps?"

"Mother!"

"You do not need to answer, it is written all over your faces, the way you two stand close together and keep secrets from me. Your involvement with spirits and this old house was a bad idea from the start."

Matthew started to explain, "Etienette, there is much that we cannot tell you, because it concerns the secret world of the spirits. You have been so helpful up to now."

Etienette tried to interrupt, but Matthew held up his hands to silence her. "Please. I know you do not believe in mediums, ghosts, and that sort of thing, but my grandmother, Floris, as well as her best friend Marti, were very strong spiritually, and they left me this house so that I could carry out their wishes. I did not believe either, but things are happening that I must accept, and these events are forcing us to take actions that will appear strange. However, I am trying to save this property, pay the relevant taxes, and be a credit to the community. As you know, Azur is very wise in spirit subjects and I need her help in order to do this work."

"Azur, you are to come home at once and stay away from this place."

"My work is here. This is my life. You know what I studied, and now I have a chance to apply it and to learn much more. The spirit world is alive and real, and this is a key part of it. And if you say one more bad thing about me, or even imply it, you will see that one of the things I have inherited from you is a terrible temper coupled with a very strong will to have my own way and to follow my own path."

"Etienette, a year from now we'll be looking back on these arguments and laughing, but I know that it is difficult right now. I need Azur's help and if she wants to visit my house, she is most welcome, as are you and Jeane and Julian," Matthew said.

"We shall see, we shall see. I must be going. You cannot take Azur from me so easily."

After she left Rick commented, "Her real problem is that she is extremely jealous: I could see her true feelings. She's furious that her beautiful and young daughter has stolen her boyfriend."

"That is, that is not possible, Rick," Azur said.

"No, it's real. She had hoped to spend much time with Matthew, at least in companionship, and hopefully in bed, and now she thinks that you have come between her and her goal: she's pissed. Part of her problem is that you are young and she is not, but she wants to be young and tries so hard to act half her age. Your actions make her look in the mirror and she does not like what she sees."

The next morning they prepared to collect samples from the scary wing. Azur had purchased a case of small sterile containers that were normally used for tissue samples and drug testing. She hoped to use sterile scalpels and the containers to collect slivers of wood and clothing from the SHC site. Matthew would film the collection activities, while Rick made photographs of each cut. They would be able to show not only the data from the samples, but also exactly how the samples were collected. This was the best that they could manage, as none of them was interested in asking independent investigators to come and verify the site and the collection procedures.

They entered the wing as they had done before, then collected a sample from the old newspaper. Then they collected two samples from the remains of the food on the plates at the table. No trouble at all, though Azur and Rick could feel the bad spirit energy. Even Matthew felt uneasy, though he figured that it related more to Rick's warning than to actual sensations.

Then they moved to the edge of the black hole in the floor. There was a white dusty film just outside the burned area. They had noticed it in blow-ups of their photos and decided that it must be a fire-related stain or maybe powder from the burning body. It evenly surrounded the burned hole. Azur opened a fresh container and a fresh scalpel, then started to scrape part of the film into the container. As her knife went into the film, there was a horrible long scream from the basement. Azur dropped the container and scalpel through the grisly hole and her body nearly fell through, but she caught herself in time.

Rick forcefully commanded, "Move slowly Azur, open another container and knife, and go back to work. Matt, did you get that on tape? We're in for excitement. Both of you, breathe slowly and carefully and focus on your work. We're here and we aren't leaving without our samples."

There were more screams as Azur collected samples of the white powder and the burned wood. The sound of the screams was horrible, but nothing actually happened to the three. Any normal person would have run a long time ago. Matthew was so glad that the spirits hadn't screamed like this the day Azur had fallen through the rotten floor. They collected samples from the mummy and the items upstairs without incident. These things were not related to the screaming spirit in the basement.

Finally it was time to go into the basement and sample the pile of clothing under the hole. They had left this task until last, as it would be in the dark spooky basement, and involved the blue glow that they had already experienced. There were no screams yet, but they knew that they were in for much cold wind and noise. Rick made them bundle their existing samples, film, and tape safely into a case before going down the stairs. Whatever happened, they didn't want to loose what they already had.

Even Matthew could feel a strong cold and eerie wind as they went down the steps one by one. They had examined their photographs of the pile under the S.H.C hole and decided that it consisted of dust-covered clothing, but the clothing was on top of a jumble of old boxes or something uneven in shape. The eerie blue glow seemed stronger than before, and it pulsated, lashing out in their direction as they moved closer.

"Just remember that it can't actually hurt you. Everything is in your mind. Let me have the knife and the container. Azur, try to get pictures if you can hold the camera steady. Matt, brace yourself against that post and shoot away. Don't drop the flashlight or try to help me or become involved," Rick instructed.

Rick carefully opened the largest container and a knife, then walked up to the pile. As he cut a piece of clothing with the sharp knife, the strength of the resulting scream was incredible. Even Rick flinched. He was enveloped in blue sparking flashes and writhing shimmering glows. It was hard to see him in the mass of wiggling blue streaks, but his body appeared to be moving slowly and methodically in spite of the situation. Eventually he managed to get a large piece of clothing into the sterile container. They were out the door less than a minute later.

As Azur organized the samples, she smiled at her prize, a hair from Rick's head that had fallen onto one of the containers during the excitement. Under her portable microscope it looked perfectly normal, though a bit wrinkled. She couldn't wait to get a DNA analysis on it, to see how it compared to Matthew's DNA. As she looked at the hair, something happened and the view faded. What? It couldn't be, but the single hair on her microscope slide had just become invisible.

That night Matthew and Azur went up to the roof platform, to watch the sunset and admire the view as August faded toward September. They were standing close together, as Matthew turned to Azur, wrapped his arms around her and kissed her passionately. Instead of pulling away, Azur responded warmly, encouraging him, pressing her body against his. Their bodies became more active, but then Azur pushed back gently, "Be careful, I am not the right girl for you. I am too self-centered, too wrapped-up in my studies, to ever make a good companion for a wonderful person like you."

"You're so perfect, how can you say such things about yourself."

"We both enjoy kissing now, but I am talking about the future. Email that girl at school and do not let her get away. From the little that you have told me about her, I can see that she will make someone happy for a lifetime. She is rock-stable and normal, while I am neither."

They kissed again, but Matthew was worried and confused. Although Azur's lips were soft and her warm body squirmed against his, something was missing. Nothing was ever simple with Azur.

Matthew repeated the cycle of measurements in the Long Gallery on August 21st and found that it had fallen 3/32", almost as much as it fell in the previous week. Down in the lowest basement, parts of the floor had fallen almost an inch. While Azur worked on her papers, he had made calculations and started to order steel beams, which would be cut and drilled before delivery: preparing the steel and shipping it would take a month or more, dangerously close to the power plant deadline. To guarantee that he could pay for the repairs he air-freighted a small package to the Brussels coin dealer: money was not the problem now, but time was growing short. It was already late August and he had only just ordered supplies that might or might not stabilize the house before it fell into the sea.

Azur had the SHC samples analyzed for carbon-14 dating and chemical composition. All was about as expected. The Mummy was probably Egyptian, given its ancient date and the newspaper and food were as they appeared. However, the white powder that surrounded the hole as well as some of the stains on the clothing were strange. Their chemical composition could be analyzed and discussed, but the reason for its unusual composition was a mystery. Azur decided to put the actual analysis results in her paper and leave speculation to reader. Carbon dating of the powder and stains proved impossible as there was no carbon in the samples, even though they had presumably come from a burning human body which was a carbon-rich structure.

Azur wanted to have her SHC paper printed in 'Nature', "Science', or at least one of the prestigious specialized scientific journals. She knew that before she had a chance of that happening, several professors would need to approve her paper, especially since the subject was so unusual. She sent copies to five professors, as well as a five minute video that she had assembled. The tape showed the highlights of their investigation, from entering the room, to collecting the samples from the screaming spirit.

Matthew explained carbon dating to Rick. "Most living things contain atoms of carbon. Every breath we exhale contains carbon dioxide, and carbon dioxide is what plants live on. We are breathing and eating carbon in many forms all the time, as are almost all the plants and animals on the earth. Our bodies are full of carbon atoms."

"Some of the carbon in the atmosphere gets hit by cosmic rays, and this changes it into a special version of carbon, a version with two extra neutrons, called carbon-14. Normal carbon has twelve neutrons. The carbon-14 tastes the same and works the same so you don't notice that you're eating it. So as long as you, or a tree, or a plant, is alive, carbon-14 is going inside."

"When a plant or a person dies, the intake of carbon-14 stops. Scientists have measured the ratio between normal carbon atoms and these special atoms in living plants and animals. If I kill a plant now, I can look in a book and find out what the ratio between the normal and the special atoms should be."

"The carbon-14 atoms are not stable. Slowly the extra neutrons escape and the special atoms become normal again. After 5730 years, only half of the special atoms are left. After another 5730 years, only one quarter are left. Every 5730 years, half of the atoms remaining fall back to being normal atoms."

"So to do carbon dating, you need a very clean sample from the subject, say an old piece of wood, or a piece of the mummy's skin. Then you use fancy scientific gear to measure the ratio of normal to special atoms and calculate the sample's age with some simple math based on the ratio. This was all invented in 1949."

"There are many ways that this can go wrong since we are dealing with very small numbers of atoms and small samples. Some cigarette smoke or dust or junk could contaminate the subject and confuse the data, but it least the carbon-dating process gives us a good starting point, and if you can get multiple samples from a subject, you can average the data and get more accuracy," Matthew concluded.

"So, even though I may be very old, if you tried to measure my age this way, it wouldn't work, because I'm still breathing," Rick said.

"Exactly, but for that mummy we saw upstairs it all works quite well," Azur said.

In the afternoon, Matthew checked his email, on a laptop connected to his new cell phone. There was a message from a very busy Sally, *"Sorry, but no way I can buzz over to see you and the house, but great progress here. Passed out of dumb stat course thanx to your training, and am working day and nite on my essay for the fellowship. When you coming home red rider? Sal"*

Meanwhile, the combination of Rick's scare tactics and the estate agent's financial approach had led to a quick sale of the warehouse property at a fair price. As part of the deal, Matthew had to accept adjacent land that he didn't want, since the warehouse was part of a large property. Matthew figured, rightly as it turned out, that the low price reflected the difficulty of converting the property into anything of value. Matthew wanted to immediately file for demolition permits for all the structures, claiming that they were not only worthless economically, but also a public eyesore and nuisance. He thought such a permit would be very simple, since it was so logical.

The estate agent told him what would probably happen to his 'logical' application to the planning commission. First, they would state that a full study of his proposal would take months, perhaps a year. Why, he hadn't even considered where he would dump the material from the demolished structures, and both an aesthetic as well as an historic impact report would need to be prepared by licensed experts. And where was his environmental impact report: the work itself might damage the environment. Matthew's argument that he would be making a great improvement in the area seemed so obvious, but the agent showed how hopeless the process might be.

Rick just smiled when he heard all of this. He had expected trouble, and was not about to let bureaucrats block Floris's energy line. "Let's have a little bonfire this weekend, while everyone is asleep. It will be easy to burn down all of those structures with a truckload of borrowed diesel. They're mostly old rotten wood, and I love driving big trucks."

The night of Rick's fire found Matthew and Azur again wrapped in each other's arms, stoked by the excitement of the illegal conflagration and the warmth of their bodies. As they calmed down, Matthew asked, "Do you still feel that you will never make me happy?"

She kissed him gently, "You are happy now and I am not about to push you away. I enjoy your company and you enjoy mine. But there are more important things in my life and in yours. You know I can be cold and calculating so do not give me your heart and expect me to care well for it."

"How can you say such things in one breath, then drive me nuts in the next? I can see the real you, and the real you is much more stuck on me than you dare admit, and you know how much I care for you."

"Your vision is cloudy, but your body is nice and warm, so let us not talk anymore."

On September Third, Matthew repeated all of his measurements and considered the situation. The house was falling slightly every week, and was in a very precarious position. He knew that he needed to focus all his energy on detailed construction planning, instead of on Azur. However, every minute they were apart, he thought of her, and when they were together he couldn't take his eyes off her for long.

One night, Etienette casually invited Matthew over to play duets on her piano and have a peaceful musical evening. She knew that Azur didn't play well, so this was a chance to spend some time with him by herself. They played for each other, and took turns singing old songs in French and English on Etienette's pre-war French Pleyel Grand piano, the piano that she had played all her life. Matthew enjoyed the chance to do something besides work on different aspects of his house and realized that there was much more to Etienette than a soft and rather close body. As the evening ended, he said "Thank you for a wonderful time. I hope that we can do it again, maybe on my piano, though the food and the temperature won't be as pleasant as here."

"I could bring a picnic supper, we could light candles and wear warm clothes. It would be just like hundreds of years ago," Etienette said.

"Well, I had better be going, life is quite busy over at my house."

"Yes it is, and please be careful. You are in danger of risking both your life and your heart."

"I don't quite know what you mean."

"You are sensitive and sincere. You take things at face value, what you see is what you believe. However, sometimes young girls play games to fool men like you. They purr like a kitten when it suits them, and scratch like a tiger when they don't get their way. Unless you are careful, you could give your heart to someone who will not care for it, and who will throw it aside when you least expect it. The lyrics of the old French song "Plaisir D'Amor" (The Joys of Love) are very true, but sadly, it will take years before you understand their meaning."

"Thank you for caring about me and for wishing me well. I have so many things on my mind, but for now, sleep is the thing I need most. Thank you again for a wonderful time."

Matthew's first thought about this conversation was that Etienette was simply jealous of Azur, and was trying to dampen his enthusiasm for her. That was obvious. However, he knew that he didn't know much about girls, and especially grown women, so perhaps there was something to what she said. Perhaps Azur was mainly interested in studying him as a ghostly subject, along with Rick and the house, and not at all keen on him as a long-term romantic partner. What a pain.

He emailed Sally from his laptop, figuring that he had better stay in touch with her in case things here fell apart. *"Sal, amazing adventures here with a real ghost who is my grandfather, a spontaneous human combustion site in my house, and structural engineering. I hardly have time to sleep at night, but wish you could visit and see this stuff. Your genetics prof would go ballistic if he could analyze some of these artifacts. Hope all OK with you. Matt."*

The next day Sally replied, *"Deeper than ever into studies, but your life sounds exciting. Nothing you say makes sense. I hope you're not on dope, and that miss priss hasn't messed with your mind. Why don't you come back here and calm down for awhile? Sal"*

Julian was very surprised to read two newspaper articles when he returned from a fortnight in London.

". . . strange fire last night in the warehouse district. The buildings had just been purchased by a Mr. Matthew Atkinson, a young American Engineer, who recently inherited Redcliffs Hall. The fire brigade responded promptly but was prevented from stopping the conflagration because the buildings had been soaked in oil before being ignited. In addition, several fire fighters, perhaps overcome by the intense

heat, reported seeing valves on their machinery turn by themselves, hoses uncouple themselves, and in one unbelievable instance, a hose lorry drive itself away. . ."

". . . only a few weeks ago the warehouses on this site were burned to the ground in a mysterious fire, leaving a scene of utter desolation such as not seen since the war. The Regional Planning Commission was startled to find yesterday that the entire property had been remodeled by a large construction group over the past weekend. The scale of their effort is hard to imagine. Sufficient labor and equipment was brought onto the site to bury all the fire debris, create several gently sloping mounds, and landscape the entire area with trees and shrubbery. A most peculiar feature of the resulting park is a long straight clear swath cutting diagonally across the entire property from edge to edge. When the Planning Commission contacted Mr. Matthew Atkinson, the owner, about this activity, he begged forgiveness for his hasty work and hoped that people would enjoy this large new park, which is unfenced and open to all. He was apparently unaware of the need for the great number of permits and permissions required for work on this scale. Yesterday, there was criticism of the police constabulary, whose members had watched the furious landscape activity, but who did nothing to stop it. The officers involved stated that their remit did not include checking Permits and Permissions, but only the verification of safe working conditions and the prevention of accidents. . . ."

Julian asked Etienette if she knew why Matthew had just bought an old warehouse property, the scene of a mysterious fire, then remodeled it into a peculiar park. She was amazed. Julian showed the newspaper to Etienette, and there in black and white was Matthew's name. Julian wondered where he had found the money to make such a purchase, and more importantly, why. Etienette provided no information, and suggested that he ask Matthew if he really wanted to know. She, Etienette, was leaving immediately for a French beauty spa, for an extended visit. Julian almost suggested that she make her visit shorter, and thereby less expensive, but he remained silent.

Later, Julian called a friend at the bank and was astonished when he learned the size of the flows into and out of Matthew's bank account, and of the recent large transfer from a numbered account in

Brussels. What could this mean? Azur didn't have access to money like that. He reasoned that Etienette must be up to something with Matthew, and spent the rest of the day analyzing her accounts, trying to discover how she had made the transfer to Matthew without his knowledge. Perhaps she had hidden money that Julian didn't control?

Chapter 11
A Candid Photo

The next day found Matthew and Azur in the little town of Keswick in the Lake Country, at a mountain climbing store: they were buying rope and taking lessons on an artificial wall. The mountaineering skill that they were trying to master was the use of Jumar ascenders. Matthew explained to the staff that they wanted to learn how to go up and down ropes safely. He told them about his house at the edge of the sea, and their interest in scaling the outer walls and the cliff so as to inspect the geology and structural damage. A long day on the artificial wall left them pooped, but sufficiently trained. After a good sleep they drove south, their car loaded with brightly-colored Kemmantle life safety ropes, carabiners, safety harnesses, and other rock climbing equipment.

The ascenders, which allow a climber to easily go straight up a rope, are quite simple in concept. They come in pairs, one for each foot. To climb up a rope, each foot is placed in a nylon loop. The other end of each loop, about four feet higher up the rope, goes to a metal handle (the Jumar device) which alternately slides and locks on the rope. The Jumar, invented by Walter Marti, has a cam which allows it to slide up a rope easily, but to lock tightly against the rope when it is pulled down. To climb, the person takes his weight off one foot, then uses the matching hand to slide the Jumar up the rope a foot or so. Then full weight is put on this foot and the leg is straightened. This takes weight off the other foot, then its Jumar and loop are slid up the rope. By this slow process the climber walks straight up the rope, alternating his feet, almost as though it is a staircase. All the climbing work is done by leg muscles: the hands just slide the Jumars up the rope, one at a time. The process also works in reverse, by unlocking the cams one at a time, for slow descents. Jumars can also be used for attaching safety harnesses to fixed ropes, allowing the climber to solidly and quickly anchor himself.

Back home, they realized that actually using such things outdoors, without an expert nearby, was more challenging and much more scary than climbing an artificial wall in the store.

Rick was fascinated by the equipment and urged them to use it, while he critiqued their developing skill. He made them practice on the landward side of the house, with relatively small danger, while they gained confidence.

Unfortunately, in real situations the rope swings about and the climber is bumped into nearby walls or rocks, and if he or she happens to have any fear of heights, it's time to forget the whole process. For Matthew's purposes, the rope was to be used to slowly go up and down the rugged ocean-side of the house, looking at the foundations and the exterior condition of each floor.

On September 9th, Matthew repeated his laser measurements and observed that the basement floor was falling a bit faster than before, but delivery of the steel was still two weeks away.

On a windless, gray day, they were up early and the three of them went down through the tunnel to the beach, to secure the bottom ends of the ropes, so as to reduce swinging if the wind came up. As Azur had discovered, the rock in the tunnel was solid, with no apparent damage, and very hard.

The base of the tunnel ended in the back of a seaweed-filled cave that hadn't been disturbed in decades. Crabs scurried about the seaweed as they walked in the sand and gravel outside. Rick told them that the tunnel continued further, maybe out to the little island, but that it was full of sand and water. He thought that it would be great fun to clear the rest of the tunnel and look for buried treasure, but Matthew focused his attention on the task at hand. Under the seaweed, they found two of Rick's old boats in fairly good condition. A fun project that would need to wait for more leisurely times.

That night Rick reported that Floris was much stronger and was sleeping peacefully. He was elated at their success with the repair of the Ley line and hoped that soon Floris would be her old self again. Soon in Rick's time frame seemed to be years, not days, however.

"Rick, why don't you materialize more often? I hardly ever get to see you," Matthew asked.

"It takes a lot of energy, and it isn't necessary to be visible to talk with you so why should I bother," Rick replied.

"There is continuum of states between completely invisible, and fully-visible, isn't there," Azur asked.

Rick demonstrated, "Right, without much work, I can become a blue fog, here, now you see it. A thin fog is less work than a thick fog, and then with more work, I can be slightly visible, sort of a ghost as (laughing) some people say. Then with lots of work, I can become completely solid, just like you two. It takes work to sustain the solid self, so if you don't mind, I'll just fade back now."

"You look just like you do in your pictures from the nineteen thirties: do you ever get older or weaker," Matthew wondered.

"I don't know, and we've only had photography for a hundred years or so. At the moment, I am feeling younger each day as I soak up the restored energy field. I'm beginning to feel like my old self, strong and ready for fun."

"How old are you? When did you arrive," Azur asked.

"I don't know, and who cares? I'm here right now but I sleep for long times, dozens of years at a stretch. I've been in this area, more or less, for ages."

"Do you need to eat or sleep or do human things," Matthew asked.

"When I am fully-material, then I can run my body just like yours, and the best part of that is sex! It's worth materializing for, at least with the right girl."

"Like with my grandmother, Floris," Matthew said.

"Right, can't wait for her to recover. It's a great treat that we both materialize for, but she's been too weak for a long time."

"You can't float through walls or go up chimneys or anything like that can you," Matthew said.

"Oh no, I move just like you do, by walking or crawling. Strangely though, I can swim, even when I'm not materialized. I don't know how it works really. When I want to go somewhere, I hitch a ride in a vehicle, or on a wagon, or a horse."

The next day, as the three were preparing ropes for the first descent down the cliff beside the house, Julian paid a surprise visit. From his attitude and approach they could tell that something wasn't quite right. He was wearing a dark business suit and a serious expression.

"Hi kids, what are you up to," Julian said.

"Just about to go down the cliff to inspect the geology at the base of the house," Matthew said.

"What brings you over here, father?"

"Just curiosity. I've been following the news reports about your warehouse property. Quite a project you have there."

"Yes, it's all finished. Just need to install some sprinklers before next summer to make it complete," Matthew said.

"Sounds like it cost a pile of money, to clear it all and make it nice again: did you need to borrow much to do it?"

"No, just a few cash transactions. It's a long term investment. I plan to leave the land in its natural condition for years. Maybe I can get an agricultural or wilderness preservation tax rate eventually."

"Not my kind of investment I'm afraid: er, do you need any more money for your projects or repairs?"

"No, but thanks for asking. Do you have any other questions," Azur said.

"We're hoping to go down the cliff before the wind comes up. This is the first calm day we've had in ages, so that's why we're in a bit of a hurry," Matthew said.

"How is the house doing? Is it still sliding into the sea," Julian asked.

"Very slowly. We found some photos from the thirties and also from the late fifties, and they aren't much different from today, so the rate of slippage is very gradual. Of course, a big storm could take a piece out of the cliff at any time, so it's quite precarious," Matthew said.

Julian looked over the side and saw that the rope was anchored to rocks far below on the beach. "How did you get down there, to tie the other end of the rope?"

"Oh, we have these gizmos that let us walk up and down the rope: want to try going down," Matthew said.

"Oh no, of course not, well I must be going."

After a bit of trial climbing, Azur went down and photographed the base of the foundation extensively, while Matt explored with his sketchpad and laser ruler. Then they moved the ropes and repeated the exercise. By the end of the day they had many photos and measurements of the problem area, and had seen it up close.

It had been a long exciting day and now a thunder storm loomed. They could see rain squalls at sea and hear distant thunder. After dinner, Matthew and Azur went up into the old house's sleeping quarters to be together by themselves. Matt wanted to explore by candle-light, and experience a bit of what it might have been like during a storm in the past. There were so many bedrooms, each in a different style, and all fully furnished with dusty old beds and furniture. They entered the master bedroom, with a corner location and a wonderful view of the gathering storm in two directions over the sea. The lightning and thunder came nearer, as they embraced with excitement and passion. Perhaps it was the lightning, or the booming crackling thunder, or the physical exertion of climbing the dangerous ropes, or the growing awareness of their desire for each other. More and more of their clothes peeled away as they rolled on the ancient squeaky bed. There was no hesitation as the last scrap of cloth between them fell to the floor. They were thoroughly involved in their first deep sexual contact, with absolutely nothing between their bodies.

Just as they reached the peak of enjoyment, their bodies straining rhythmically together, there was a bright flash, and they heard invisible Rick's excited voice, "Wow, what a snap: you two are just like dogs in heat: I can't wait to develop this for my collection: it'll go perfectly with my shots of both of you undressing and my beautiful close-ups of Azur in her knickers getting ready for bed, combing her wonderful hair. I love that lacey French lingerie you wear. You're so sexy! I watch you undress every chance I get. I'd wet my pants if I were materialized. And Matthew, what a shot I got the other night, of your erection practically bursting through your undies. I put the print right next to a blow-up of Azur."

The yelling and screaming, the frustration at not being able to see Rick, and his laughter coming first from one side of the room, then another, as they threw things at him, made a horrendous mess. While they stood naked by the bed yelling and throwing pillows, books, candles and clothes in the direction of Rick's voice, there were more flashes, and more laughter from Rick. Most of the words, in French and English, are unprintable.

In the end, under the dusty old covers, Azur cried herself to sleep, wrapped in the comfort of Matthew's arms. He didn't sleep for a very long time, wondering to himself if maybe it was time to go back to school and sell this whole mess to the first bidder. His comparatively simple student life, and his normal relationship with Sally, looked very attractive in retrospect.

When she awoke, Azur looked around the room. At first she was disoriented by the location and by the mess, then she remembered and realized that Rick's photos were far from a bad dream: it had really happened. Azur was about to leave the bed, when she stopped, realizing that she was completely naked. She shook Matthew and he slowly awoke. "What are we going to do? Do you think he is watching, waiting for me to get out of bed so he can make another picture of my body," Azur said.

"It is a beautiful body, but I don't know what to do."

"I cannot believe this is happening to us."

"Rick if you're here, get your camera ready cause we're going to the bathroom. Want to get a close-up as I take a leak? Maybe I can piss on your camera if you come close enough. (to Azur) Let's go, if he's watching so be it. This is like jumping into a cold swimming pool. You have to do it all at once. Don't stop to think."

Azur threw back the covers, "Check it out Rick: one healthy girl ready for action. Sorry, but I cannot find anything sexy to wear just now."

Both naked, carrying their clothes, they walked down the main stairs, and back to their rooms in the wing, then down the hall to the bathroom, talking on the way.

"Azur, humor is our only defense."

"In a strange way, sex might be more exciting with someone watching, but I would want to control who and when."

"After breakfast, let's find his other darkroom and wreck it."

"Good idea. Rick, if you are watching, why do you not select some sexy clothes for me to wear and lay them out on my bed:

it may be your last chance to get a good crotch shot."

"Remember all those negatives from the thirties that he made in bedrooms and bathrooms? He's been doing this for a long time."

"I wonder if Floris knows about this side of Rick?"

"And if maybe she does it too."

"Looking at this academically, perhaps neither of them can materialize easily, so to compensate they are very active voyeurs, watching and wishing for something they cannot have easily."

When they returned to their bedrooms, Azur's clothes were spread on top of her bed. Rick's selection included a tight black sweater, next to black lingerie.

"I do like that sweater: it shows your figure nicely, but it's awfully distracting while we're working together. I keep wanting to feel those soft breasts under the cashmere."

"Please ask first, and be gentle and considerate. Stay with me while I dress. Tonight I am going home and start sleeping in my own bedroom, with the door locked. I do not want to be here with him ever again."

Matthew realized that his cozy life with Azur had just ended with no more than a few words. He also knew that trying to talk her into staying, while invisible Rick ran around with his camera, was pointless. What a difficult grandfather!

Chapter 12
Work & Dancing

After breakfast, Matthew and Azur were in the library, looking through Rick's old negatives. "If he could make shots like these, then he could have made much more intimate shots if he had wanted," Matthew said.

"Look at this one in the bedroom with the girl in her slip. She must have just put it on, or be about to take it off. If he is so excited by girl's bodies, why did he stop here, why not wait for her to take it off?"

"I'll be that somewhere there are boxes of other shots, shots that are much more provocative. These may be just the rejects, the shots that weren't too exciting."

"Or the shots that he showed Floris, while keeping the others hidden."

"I've been thinking about it all, and I have sort of a plan."

Matthew looked around the room, then shouted in all directions, "Rick, if you're listening, here's the deal. We know that you can wander around making snaps of our bodies whenever you want. We don't like it, but we can't stop you as long as we are living in this house. So, we will go on with our lives just like before: you can watch, but you can't stop us from loving each other. We're not going to tell Floris about your activity, and we're not going to even look for your secret stash of trash, or mess with the darkroom. You can have your private life, even if we can't have ours. We know that you are powerful and that you could kill us in our sleep without a moment's thought, if you wished. Therefore, we need to take preventive measures. In a few minutes, we are leaving for London to visit our lawyers. If we get there alive, then we're going to make wills that state that if anything odd ever happens to us, this place is to be torn down, the ground pushed into the sea, the cave filled with cement and scrap iron, and the power plant constructed. This will kill Floris, and remove your energy center, so watch what you do."

Azur grabbed Matthew's hand "The Morgan has a full tank of gas. You drive and I will call the solicitors on the way and explain everything to them."

They did not hear a reply from Rick, and for that matter, they had no way of knowing if he had even heard Matthew. Perhaps he was busy in his darkroom or sleeping. In the little car, there was just enough room for two people, especially with the top up. If Rick was hitching a ride, he was on the outside in the wind and rain, as the car zoomed down the A31, then the M3 at close to one hundred miles an hour. Azur talked for over an hour with the solicitors arranging uncommon and legally-binding wills for both of them.

They checked into The United Oxford and Cambridge Club at 71 Pall Mall, a large gray Victorian stone building where Azur and Julian were both members. There was no indication that Rick was watching or following. They were assigned two little bedrooms up near the top of the comfortable old club: each room had a small window facing Marlborough House. Azur had lost interest in sharing a bed with Matthew, and was looking forward to a peaceful night alone.

However this was Matthew's first night in London with a bit of free time and he very much wanted to visit a dance club that he had read about on the net. Although Azur was dubious about the idea, she didn't want to reveal that she knew little about night clubs and late-night dancing. After dinner they walked through Leicester Square to the entrance of Snowy-Rockz-All-Night which was in an alley near Seven Dials, in the basement underneath the TinTin bookstore on Floral Street. At first they couldn't find the club, but then Matt remembered that the entrance was an unmarked polished six-panel wooden door beside the shop. Matthew was impressed as it cost $100 a couple just to get through the door. Anticipating great fun, he had worn the thin-soled dancing shoes which he had thrown into his backpack weeks ago, as well as black slacks and a white sweater. Azur looked OK in her black spaghetti-strap dress but she felt uncomfortable and apprehensive and she didn't know what to make of Matt's surprising interest in night clubs. He had neglected to tell her that in compensation for his mangled foot, he had been taking acrobatic dance lessons for years and had won many contests in spite of his handicap.

The dark smoky basement was filled with loud music and dancers. It was only ten and the club was warming-up, waiting for the post-midnight crowd: the music was already full-blast. They could hardly hear each other as they started to dance. Unlike some clubs which alternate slow and fast pieces, this was almost all fast, and mostly classic rock 'n roll from the fifties and sixties (e.g. surfing songs, Buddy Holly, The Coasters, Elvis) Matthew sang along, knowing the words to almost all the songs. Azur was amazed at his skill, range of moves, and arcane musical knowledge. Matthew had often danced with girls of varying experience, so he eased her into faster and more complex steps, showing the way.

When a medley from the original version of the film "Grease" started, Azur showed signs of fading, and with a quick 'excuse me' smile to her, he grabbed the hand of a nearby girl who he had noticed jumping through intricate steps. Azur couldn't believe her eyes as the couple leapt to the center of the floor, doing spins, flips and the tricky up-and-over-the-back roll-turns. Matthew's favorite film was "Grease" and he had carefully studied the choreographed patterns in the dance contest sequence. He was in paradise and the star of the floor. Azur was used to being the sophisticated person in their relationship, the one with clearly superior social skills. Now she had entered a field where he was far in advance of her abilities: catching up was going to be an adventure. None of her fancy friends danced like this.

After the medley of fast songs (Greased Lightning, Rock N Roll Is Here To Stay, You're The One That I Want, Hand Jive), Matthew bowed to his partner and returned to Azur, took her hand, and said, "How about a break?" Azur was relieved as he led her to a glassed-in room with tables and chairs where the music was attenuated so that people could talk quietly. As they drank overpriced champagne, Azur began to relax. This was a new world for her, and it was turning out better and much more differently than she had expected.

"I love dancing with you, We've got years of fun ahead of

us", Matthew began.

"Where did you learn all that? What about your foot?"

"After the accident, a Physical Therapist told me that I could get either a wheel chair or dance lessons: you know which I chose. I love the music, the steps, the movement. I can go all night if you can".

"Do you know slow formal dances like waltzes and foxtrots too?"

"Sure and I love the Latin dances like Tangos and Sambas, but the fast ones are the best foot exercise: let's go salsa dancing next time we're in town: I'll teach you all about it".

They enjoyed a series of dances interspersed with quiet breaks. Azur began to feel comfortable with Matthew in a world where she had rarely ventured before. As the crowd thinned in the early morning, Azur decided to take a chance, to open her heart and expose a little of her inner feelings. She walked to the D.J. and requested her favorite song, by Abba, and a microphone. Something about the way she spoke showed that this would be special.

Azur stood alone in the spotlight, a small five-foot-five vulnerable young woman in a thin black dress: nothing fancy, no cover-up, her heart, mind, and body open to the world. She looked out at Mathew and began to sing as he watched in wonder and surprise.

"I have a dream, a song to sing
To help me cope with anything
If you see the wonder of a fairy tale
You can take the future even if you fail
I believe in angels
Something good in everything I see
I believe in angels
When I know the time is right for me
I'll cross the stream - I have a dream

(Azur asked the audience to join her and others began to sing along)

I have a dream, a fantasy

147

To help me through reality
And my destination makes it worth the while
Pushing through the darkness still another mile
I believe in angels
Something good in everything I see
I believe in angels
When I know the time is right for me
I'll cross the stream - I have a dream
I'll cross the stream - I have a dream

(The rest of the dancers joined her for the final verse)

I have a dream, a song to sing
To help me cope with anything
If you see the wonder of a fairy tale
You can take the future even if you fail
I believe in angels
Something good in everything I see
I believe in angels
When I know the time is right for me
I'll cross the stream - I have a dream
I'll cross the stream - I have a dream[1] "

Azur began to cry as she sang, giving her all to the song: she lived these lyrics, this poetry, these secrets never told. Matt could tell instinctively that the words expressed deep private feelings, but he had no idea what the lyrics meant to her. If he had asked at that moment, she couldn't have told him either, as the message for her was emotional, not literal. Azur was longing to be free from a deep fear, she dreamed of a life unrestrained by her past, to break the chains of her worries, but these words did not begin to show all that she felt deep inside.

As she finished, several dancers rushed to Azur, hugged her and cried. Somehow they understood a bit of what she was feeling, but Matthew was confused: to him, her song was beautiful, but so hard to understand.

---

1   Composed by Andersson and Ulvaeus of ABBA, released 1979.

Matt rose to greet her as she returned to their table: he hugged her tightly, but without words, he didn't know what to say. The DJ played a slow song and they danced close together, silent in their thoughts. Something had changed in their relationship, but neither was sure what had happened: they had each opened a little of their secret lives tonight.

Azur hesitated and in the end did not tell Matthew what her song meant, the meaning that resonated with her emotions. For many years she had been aware of her psychic gifts but had feared that they were from the dark side of the spirit world. On the surface her gifts were nothing unusual among similarly-trained people, but she felt, somehow she knew, that she was special, and that she would become powerful but that she would use her strength for evil. It was hard for her to put in words, and the closest she came was a deep longing to be free, to dream of sunlight and happiness: she longed to become a bright angel, but feared that she was a malevolent spirit.

They left the club hand in hand just after four in the morning and walked in the faint misty pre-dawn light. Down the bricks of Floral Street, past Covent Garden, past sleeping-bagged homeless people in the shadows who had replaced the throngs of tourists found here in daylight, down a strangely deserted Southampton Street, down the steps behind the Savoy, through the Embankment gardens and sleeping statues, to Cleopatra's Needle beside the Thames. The bronze lions were like shadows watching over them as they sat close together on the stone wall. Matt's arm was tightly around Azur as she rested her head on his shoulder, but they said little: just being together sharing the warmth of their bodies was enough. The river below their feet rippled quietly, hidden beneath a thin fog. Sunrise began to peep over the horizon behind Waterloo Bridge marking the start of a new day as tiredness began to overtake them. They smiled to each other and walked hand in hand in the shadows of tree-lined Northumberland Street, onto Pall Mall to the Oxford Club, then slept until noon.

After lunch in the little dining room surrounded by boat race memorabilia, they lingered over coffee and newspapers: at heart they were both academics and took pleasure in the peaceful quiet surroundings, the book-lined walnut-paneled rooms, thick carpets, and comfortable old red leather chairs. An environment for study, reading and thinking: a far cry from chasing a horny old ghost around a cold and dangerous lonely house. In the main Lounge, they passed an internet terminal offering free email, but Matthew walked by without a thought of Sally.

In the early afternoon, they walked the few blocks to the Floris perfume shop on Jermyn Street and Matthew bought a bottle of after-shave with Floris's signature JF fragrance. This was the very shop whose name his grandmother Floris had adopted many years ago. He liked having something to remind him of her.

"When I return to Redcliffs I'll tell Rick about the new wills: wouldn't want him to do something without knowing the consequences," Matthew said as they walked back.

"Did you think that there was something odd about father's visit the other day? I could not put my finger on it, but he seemed so worried, and I do not think it had anything to do with our rope work or the old foundations. Let us have dinner with him tonight and ask him to share his troubles with us."

"Maybe we can help him for a change."

Matthew reluctantly left Azur at The Chateau after an uneventful dinner with Julian, who had been touched that they wanted to help, but who didn't volunteer any information on his own problems. Etienette was still living an extravagant life in France.

Back at Redcliffs Hall, Matthew found quite a surprise. A naked woman was running around the house, lost and afraid. She was trying to find her clothes and the man she had come with.

"What did he look like? Where did you meet him," asked Matthew, suspecting that Rick was involved.

"He's a real handsome bloke, always laughing and making jokes, I met him in the pub and he offered me a hundred to spend a few hours with him. What's a girl to do, with an offer like that staring her in her face," she replied.

"And what happened when you came here?" Matthew asked.

"Well I can tell you he was something else: what a horny bastard. I hardly had time to get my clothes off before he was all over me. But, and when you see him don't tell him I told you, he couldn't get it up! He had plenty of desire, but no matter what I did he was as limp as yesterday's spaghetti. Then he ups and disappears and the next thing I know, while I'm lying there naked on top of the bed, I see these bright flashes and hear him laughing, but can't see him anywhere. Then I looked around and couldn't find my clothes. I was trying to find a robe or something and get the hell out of here when you arrived."

"I hope you at least received your money," Matthew asked.

"Oh, that I did, but I want my clothes too."

He followed her back to the bedroom which they had used and found her clothes neatly folded on the bed. She was out the door a moment later. As she was leaving, invisible Rick made a ghostly laugh. She ran down the steps and into the distance.

"Rick, do you do this sort of thing often," Matthew asked.

"Oh, now and then for amusement. It's more fun than watching and wishing and taking snaps."

"Would you consider telling us when you want to take pictures of us, and leaving us alone otherwise," Matthew wondered.

"Do you really want to know?"

"Yes, that is, I'm not sure. I'd like to believe that it isn't going to happen again. Azur has gone home to her bedroom and locked the door."

He told Rick about their new wills, about their new defense plan, a protection against getting themselves killed, but not against being photographed. Rick's only comment was, "Better go to bed, it's been a long day."

Later as Matthew thought about Rick and his sexual escapades he had two ideas. The first was curiosity about Rick and Viagra: perhaps modern medicine would work on Rick, and it was an experiment Matt might be able to suggest to divert Rick's photographic activity. The other idea was curiosity about Rick's contacts over the centuries. Tonight was just one of many adventures, but relatively fool-proof contraceptives were only a modern invention. Perhaps in the past, when Rick was more functional, some of his adventures had resulted in children, who would be distant relations, at least genetically, to Matthew. He wondered if ghostly DNA had a unique marker that could be readily identified.

Chapter 13
Visiting The Island

Matthew was asleep, having a bad dream about Marti, who was talking very seriously about Floris.

Marti's face was almost touching his, she was holding his hand tightly, painfully, imploring, "You must promise that you will never let this ground be disturbed. The building may rot, but the ground here is what counts. If the spirit well is ever broken, Floris will no longer exist: she will disappear forever. Now swear to devote your life to this goal!"

"What! You're not serious? I just got here! I haven't finished my studies. I already have a job and the start of an engineering career in Palo Alto. We're sitting in an old house out in the middle of nowhere. What would I do here?"

Azur turned quickly to him, "That was yesterday. Now grow up and assume your responsibilities."

Marti continued, her hand squeezing even tighter on his, "You have her genes. You are her flesh and blood. You are her only hope. You must live here and protect this site: there's no other way."

"But, that's not practical," Matthew complained.

"Life is not practical: you owe Floris and the bill has come due," Azur hissed.

"I need time to figure this out," he pleaded.

"Matthew, you have no choice, fate has drawn you here: you can fight, you can run away, but you'll be back, you can never leave," Marti added with finality.

Matthew awoke shivering and drenched in sweat: his left hand hurt, then he saw that his right hand was holding it tightly and slowly let go. He heard a strange gentle female voice. "You were having such a violent dream, I thought it best to wake you and maybe have some fun."

He was totally confused. Daylight streamed through the window: a glorious blue-sky day was beginning, but the dream was still alive in his mind, and this strange voice, was it real or part of the dream. "What? Who are you?"

He made a guess, "Floris?"

"Yes dear, thanks to you I'm on the mend. I just had to get up and have a chat with you first thing."

"Is Rick in the room too," Matthew asked, then he started to look around, but didn't see her. Floris was invisible.

"No, he's down in the darkroom playing with his latest snaps. He's been up to his old tricks again, chasing the girls and taking pictures where he shouldn't. At least he hasn't tried to take girls' clothes off in public, well I hope he hasn't anyway. He's done that a few times and I can tell you that it was not appreciated."

"Can you control him, or divert him?"

"Now that I'm awake, he'll stop chasing skirts and follow me around. We do lots of things together, things that he couldn't do with a live person. I think you'll have more peace and quiet. Rick told me that your name is Matt, but what's your full name?"

"Matthew George Atkinson, but why do your ask?"

"Curiosity and a hunch. Your mother loved mermaids, but I bet she never told you who Matthew George was?"

"I just thought it was an old family name or something."

"It's an old mermaid story. Matthew George Trewhella was lured to death by a mermaid, near Zennor over in Cornwall. They say he was lured to his death in the dark waters near Pendour Cove by the singing of a beautiful mermaid. You can go there and see a carved bench in the Zennor church which depicts the mermaid."

"Holy cow, I had no idea: wish I could have known my mother a lot longer."

"Don't be sad, you've got me instead, so let's have a fun day together. I'm going to borrow a bit of that Floris after-shave lotion I saw in the bathroom: it's my favorite scent. Then we'll go down to the beach, fix the boat, and go over to my island and have a picnic. The weather's perfect. Get dressed, and I'll send Rick down to get the boat ready."

"I'll bring Azur's camera and take pictures of you and Rick and the island, that is, if you can materialize: you can, can't you?"

"I don't know if I have the strength for that, it's been a long time, but I'll try for you."

Slowly a glow, a sort of steamy cloud, appeared near a chair, then it became almost the shape of a person sitting on the chair. Gradually Matt could see that it was a woman, in a striped old-fashioned dress with shoulder pads, like a picture of someone from the early forties.

"I can see you, but I can see through you too, you're not solid like Rick when he materializes."

"Can you see my face at least?"

"Yes, you're smiling and you look just like your photos in Marty's album."

"After awhile I'll be stronger, and don't worry about getting dressed: I don't take pictures of men or spy on them, so you can dress and bathe in peace."

With that she walked out the door, returning to invisibility on the way. Matt didn't know what to make of the dream, which was still firmly planted in his brain, and of his meeting with Floris. So much had changed in the past month and a half. He wondered if somehow Floris had made the dream occur, to remind him of her situation and his responsibility for her future. He thought it strange that she had appeared right after such a strong dream about her welfare.

Rick found his old Seagull outboard motor, an indestructible British product that used such an oily 9::1 fuel mixture and such loose tolerances that it would run forever, but with great clouds of smoke. He and Matthew cleaned the fuel lines and the spark plug, then it started even though it had been idle for perhaps forty years.

The trip to the island was rough as the smoking motor powered the heavy wooden boat against the wind. However, they would be able to sail back unless the wind changed. Rick and Floris acted like young lovers. They walked holding hands, and they were never far apart. Floris became stronger and more solid in appearance as she walked in the brisk wind and salt spray. She had died when she was thirty-five years old, and still had her youth, as well as the same clothes and vintage hairstyle as when she had died.

Matthew made many beautiful photographs as Rick and Floris showed him the ancient ruined castle and the places where Julian and his mother had played as children, and where a generation before, Rick, Floris, and Marti had played and picnicked. The pictures of the island, the ruins, the sea birds flying, the happy people, and the old wooden boat could easily have been from a hundred or more years ago. There was nothing newer in the shots except their clothes.

Floris recalled that on the memorable night of her rescue, after sitting a while in her dressing room with Rick, she had examined her handcuffs and realized that her Assistant had jammed the locks on purpose. She had refused his sexual advances the night before and saw that this was his way of getting even. A few days later, Rick arranged the Assistant's disappearance: perhaps he had died of fright. Rick became the new stage assistant.

She explained that the Depression was particularly hard on performers. One cold gray snowy London evening, just before Christmas, she had happened to be standing on Jermyn Street, shivering in the cold, and wishing that she had a few warm clothes, like the swells in the fancy stores nearby. She was just outside a shop named Floris, catching whiffs of the expensive perfume sold inside, when several fur-clad foreigners stopped their immense limousine and went into the shop. As they passed her shivering body, they bumped into her by mistake and said something that might have meant, "Sorry didn't see you there." They tossed her a foreign gold coin, with a cheery comment about Christmas Spirit. She was so mad: she realized that she was essentially invisible to these fat rich people. Then and there, she vowed to become someone, to do whatever it took to get to the top of her profession. As a start, she changed her stage name to Floris, and vowed that someday she would shop in this very street.

Rick said that when he heard this story he went to the Floris shop and entered with a snooty old lady. He materialized in front of the clerk and asked for their biggest bottle of Number-127[1], the

1   The Floris perfumes were originally numbered, with the number referring to the page of a recipe book where the recipe for making each

fragrance that the lady had just selected. She fainted to the floor. Others in the shop stared. The clerk gingerly handed over a beautiful bottle worth hundreds of pounds. Rick thanked him then faded from sight. As he left he told the speechless clerk, "Don't worry about the money: you're going to have wonderful publicity from a most unusual magician. When you see an advert for Floris The Magnificent, be sure to come to the theater. You won't be disappointed."

Matthew also learned that there are good and bad spirits and many gradations in strength: Rick was one of the most powerful, but he was usually lonely and alone: there were more bad ghosts than good, and more weak than strong. Matthew also learned that even while Rick is invisible he can affect things by acting through people's minds: he can make people do strange things, but he has little strength of his own. To really make something difficult happen, he must materialize, and this requires much energy and effort.

Floris amused Matthew by making cards appear behind his ears, and out of the sky. She was very adept at the I'll-tell-which-card-you-picked tricks, and demonstrated her manual dexterity by rolling a coin, on edge, across the backs of her fingers just by wiggling her finger muscles in some way that he could not understand.

"Do you ever go to magic shows to see what other magicians are doing," Matthew asked.

"Oh yes, we love to go to live performances whenever we're in London, and we often help with the show," Floris replied.

"Do the magicians on stage know that you are helping," Matthew asked warily.

"They know that something interesting is happening. We try to make the shows better so that the audience has a good time and comes back for more," Floris answered.

"We also help children. There's an orphanage about fifteen miles away from here, and we go there and look for the kids who are having the most trouble, then befriend them," Floris said.

"We act like invisible friends, and help them play and not feel so bad. It's easy for us and it makes such a difference for them."

---

customer's favorite scent was kept. Eventually some numbers became so popular that they were kept in stock for anyone to buy.

They raised the old sail, and enjoyed a smoke-free return to shore.

The next morning, Matthew's cell phone rang: it was Azur calling from The Chateau with a problem. "Matthew something has just happened here. I think there is a spirit in our cellars, among antiques that mother just brought from France. She came home yesterday and took her boxes into the basement, then came back screaming".

"What happened: what did she see?"

"She does not know, or will not say: why not come over this evening with Rick and Floris, visible and posing as spirit experts? They will sort it and we will learn something in the process."

"See you at six for cocktails."

Rick promised to be on his best behavior as he, Floris, and Matthew drove over to the Chateau. Floris was fully materialized and all were excited at the prospect of doing a little spirit investigation. Floris said it was just like putting on a costume and preparing to go on stage: there was a mixture of anticipation and fear. A mild case of stage fright. Rick was very excited as he had seen Etienette.

At the Chateau, Rick and Floris were introduced as experts from London who were visiting Redcliffs. Etienette was charmed by the warm attention that Rick paid to her. Floris played-up to Julian in compensation for Rick's closeness to Etienette. Matthew and Azur laughed quietly to themselves as the four adults maneuvered around each other.

All six went down into the basement. Rick was holding Etienette's hand and asking her questions about her encounter. Floris told Julian that he didn't need to worry.   Rick's warm manner was just his way of extracting as many facts as possible from the victim.

They entered a room filled with old boxes piled helter-skelter. As they entered, Matthew felt some sort of cold shiver or vibration: he couldn't pin it down, but it was something that he hadn't felt before. It was clear that Rick felt it too, but the others seemed not to notice. Rick glanced at Matthew, and made an odd expression, like he was passing a "so you felt it too?" query to Matthew. Visually, there was nothing out of the ordinary as they moved around the room, toward the corner where Etienette had seen something glowing and moving about.

Her explanation was cut short by the appearance of a dim glow around one of the boxes: it was shimmering, emitting coldness. The lights in the room went out. Rick held Etienette tightly as she shook with fear. Rick felt that the evening had turned into a very promising situation and told the others, "That's nothing to worry about: it won't hurt you, it's just a poltergeist playing."

"Rick, can't you tell it to go away and play somewhere else," Floris said.

"I'll need to think about how to fix this. May Floris and I stay here tonight," Rick asked.

"Of course, stay as long as you like," Etienette replied, holding Rick's hand.

Floris, Matthew and Azur were surprised at the turn of events, but decided that they couldn't stop Rick from fooling around with Etienette: she was a big girl and they knew he wouldn't hurt her. On the contrary, he would probably provide her with a memorable experience.

Later, Matthew had a private moment with Etienette, and told her, "Rick's not quite what he seems. Please be careful."

"In what way is he unusual: what have I to fear?"

"He loves taking pictures of girls with their clothes off, while they don't even know he is in the room, and he's really hot for your body."

"Matthew! How can you say such things!"

"The good news is that he won't hurt you, he just likes having fun, especially in sexual situations."

"I can take care of myself in that area, thank you very much."

"Just be careful: Azur and I care very much for you."

Matthew decided to stay the night also. He and Azur were having fun watching the four grown-ups and their adventures. He whispered to Azur, "I think Rick and Floris will become frequent visitors here. Julian and Etienette are in for some excitement."

"I bet Rick could chase that Poltergeist away with a few words if he wanted, but it will take him weeks if mother is friendly enough."

Matthew and Azur entered her bedroom suite; a bedroom, a huge clothing closet that was also a dressing room, a bathroom, and a study lined with books on all sides as well as a desk and a comfortable old reading chair. Matthew wandered around looking at and gently touching everything. This was a side of Azur that he hadn't seen before, a window into her mind, showing the things that she had cared about in the past as well as now. So much of Azur was here. As he moved about the rooms, he smelled powder in one area, perfumes in another, and an unusual French milled soap in the bathroom.

"I love these rooms: they're so full of you and your thoughts and ideas. And they're so sensual. I feel you, smell you, touch you, everywhere I turn. I can almost taste your lips and feel your arms about me as I walk around. I could stay here forever."

Azur smiled and explained pictures of parents, cousins, aunts, uncles, grandparents, in a variety of settings in England and in France. Etienette's favorite sister, Marie, lived on a large French estate and many of the pictures of children and adults playing had been taken there. There were pictures of Azur with her favorite cousin and best friend, Claire, Marie's eldest daughter. Both girls were strikingly beautiful, but different. While Azure had dark hair, Claire's was blond. They were the same age and had played together often as children. Matthew was startled to see one of the pictures: "This picture here, is this you with Olivia Neutron Bomb, I mean Olivia Newton John?"

"No, that is Claire in her costume for a stage production of your favorite film, GREASE. She was the star, as she dances and sings quite well."

"She looks perfect for the part, with her blond pony tail, white blouse and yellow skirt. It could almost be a picture from the film."

"Maybe someday you will dance with her. You two would have a wonderful time together."

Matthew was polite enough to end the conversation and not express too much interest in Claire. There was one picture that interested him far more than the others. A shot of Julian as a child, playing with Matthew's mother and other children on the little island.

"Would you like me to make you a copy of this? I think it is the only picture I have of your mother, and she looks so happy playing with father and the others," she asked.

"Yes, and would you make me a copy of this picture of you. It's perfect, you look so beautiful in it."

"Of course, well, I do not think I look all that special, but I am glad that you think otherwise. Tomorrow I am going to make a proper photograph of you, to add to my favorites here."

"When we entered that room in the basement, did you feel the cold, the faint vibrations," Matthew asked.

"No, what do you mean?"

"I've never felt it before, but as we entered I felt this odd set of faint sensations and when I looked at Rick, I could see by his expression that he felt them too: he gave me a strange glance, as if to say that he could see that I could feel it too."

"Maybe you have some of Rick's psychic sensitivity: after all, a quarter of your genes came from him".

"But I'm supposed to be an Engineer, not a mystic."

"Remember that Rick can feel how machines work: maybe your Engineering interests and abilities are also from him."

"I wish that I could give the psychic features to you, and keep the Engineering ones".

"There is an old saying, 'make the most of what you have, and let the rest take care of itself'. You must develop your psychic abilities to the fullest. Think how useful it would be if you could see into the foundations and the insides of the rock walls. Just that one skill would be of immense use to you, and think of the undeveloped skills that we do not even know about"

Azur took Matthew's hands in hers, "It is time to go to sleep, time for you to go to your own room."

"But we could both stay here. I'm sure Rick has other things on his mind besides making pictures of us. This is so perfect, so much of you, I could sleep on the floor, just to be near you, to hear you breathing, to know you are all right."

"Remember what I told you before, I am not the girl for you."

"You said that, but you didn't really mean it, I'm sure of it.

I know you care so much for me, and I'd do anything for you."

Azur kissed him lightly, "I know, but tonight I would like to read for awhile, then go to sleep, alone."

Matthew realized that he was getting nowhere, and slowly walked to his own bedroom. In bed, he tossed and turned, and could not think of anything except Azur's warm body a few doors away. Eventually he slept, but it was restless and unhappy. He wished so much that they were together.

The next morning when he met Azur she had a puzzled look on her face as she approached. "Did you dream about me last night, and wish that we were together?"

"I always dream about you and wish for your happiness and that we would be together. Why do you ask?"

"I had a strange feeling during the night. I could almost hear you calling to me, whenever I closed my eyes, it was so unreal. I was not hearing you with my ears, but with my mind."

"You were just having a dream, and I'm sorry if somehow I disturbed you."

Azur was much more concerned than she appeared. She was worried that perhaps Matthew had inadvertently implanted a little bit of his ghostly energy in her, during either the healing process or during their unprotected sex in the old house. This energy might be growing, making her body a part of his. She needed to start studying immediately to find out how to reverse the process if it had indeed happened, and she knew that she must avoid any further activities along these lines.

"Let us go down to breakfast. We both have busy days ahead."

Chapter 14
A Few problems

Matthew went back to Redcliffs to work on plans of the house and to put finishing touches on his design for the new foundations. Floris asked him for a lift to an orphanage several miles away so she could visit children and see if conditions had changed: she would be back in a few days. As they parted, Floris told him not to worry so much about Azur and to get on with fixing the house.

Matt grabbed his tape measure and notebooks then went to the old kitchens: his immediate goal was finishing the measurements of the secret passages. This wasn't strictly necessary, but he was curious and wanted to make a complete drawing of the house. Today was the sixteenth of September, and the steel wouldn't arrive for five more days. The math was done, plans were made, and all the rental equipment including a generator and air compressor were near the house waiting. He had plenty of tools, a year's worth of diesel, and even a small hydraulic crane that Rick loved to drive around the property.

Around ten o'clock, his cellphone rang. It was an agitated bank manager calling with news regarding the recent activity in his account. The trouble was caused by the government's computers which were programmed to detect drug smugglers and money-laundering activities. Somehow the computers had decided that Matthew's rather large and rapid financial inflows and outflows were suspicious, especially in a new account held by a foreigner. A large block of untraceable money had arrived, then in a few days it was converted into a large piece of real estate, and within weeks much of the money had disappeared into construction projects. The bureaucrats wanted details, and they were pressuring the bank to provide answers.

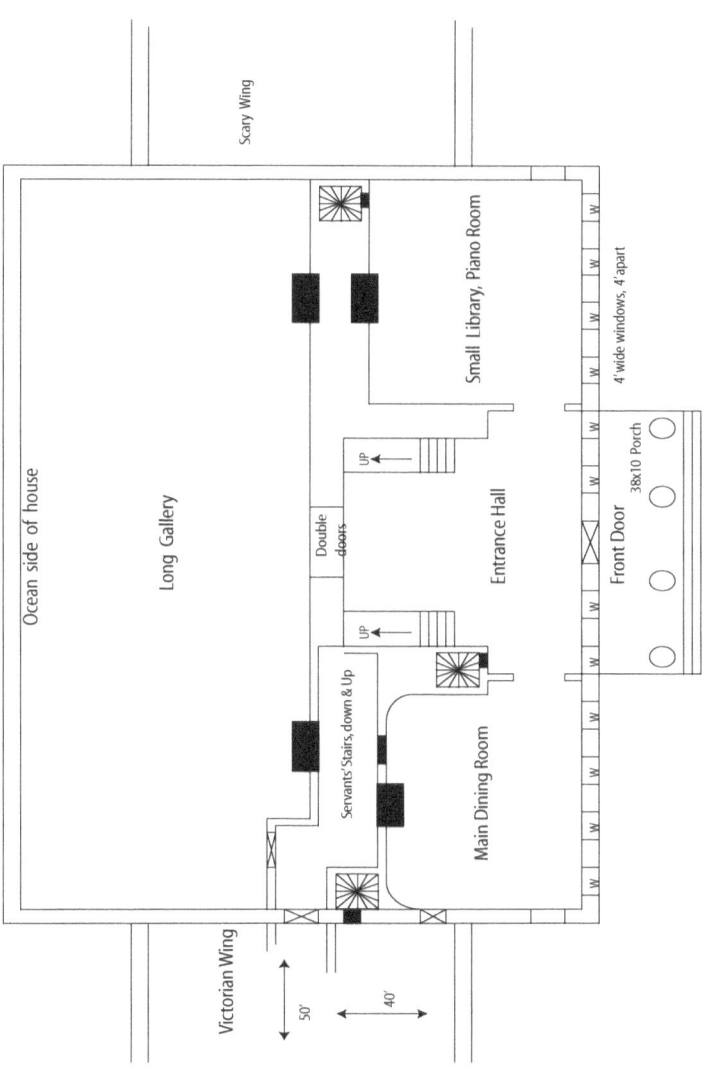

Redcliffs Hall, The Main Public Rooms

Matthew fudged a bit, making up a semi-plausible and partially-true story. He told the bank that he had sold a few pieces of old jewelry which had belonged to Marti to a dealer in Brussels which was the source of the funds. The real estate was a long term investment related to a promise he had made to Marti on her deathbed. She had wanted that particular piece of land cleared and beautified because the ugly buildings on it interfered with the view from her house. Matthew apologized for his rather unorthodox actions, and hoped that his explanation was believed. Unfortunately he had to reveal the name of the Brussels shop to the banker so that the legitimacy of the source of funds could be verified. Although the banker did not ask, Matthew knew that eventually there would be additional questions relating to inheritance tax on the jewels. And if the Christie's people ever made contact with the government people, there would be more trouble, much more trouble.

Today was not starting well.

Then Azur called with news from Oxford. She had been invited to give a guest lecture to an advanced class, even though she had yet to formally accept the College's offer to join the faculty. He asked, "May I come to the lecture: I'd love to hear you speak professionally. There's so much I don't know about the spirit world. Every day brings new questions and surprises from that direction."

"Certainly. The lecture is tomorrow night, so I am going to stay home and start preparing my notes."

"Can't you do it here. I'll promise not to interrupt or bother you while you work?"

"All my books are in my study, and I have to go to a faculty dinner tonight if I am going to play by the rules. Just drive your Mini up to Oxford tomorrow afternoon. I will call your mobile with exact directions. I cannot wait to be the teacher instead of a student."

Matthew had been expecting Azur to visit, but now he was alone in the big old house. Although he knew that there was much to be done, he was seized by melancholy. He missed Azur very much, even though he had just talked with her. And he missed Rick. When Matthew stopped to think about it, he realized that although Rick was a lot of trouble, he was also a wonderful companion, always upbeat and full of new ideas. Now Rick was busy chasing Etienette and her poltergeist, while Azur was showing interest in the academic world. What use was a huge mansion when you had no one to share it with?

Almost without thinking, Matthew went down to the box room where Rick's darkroom was located. Matthew poked around with his flashlight looking for a picture of Azur. That would be something to find, a memory of her to hold in the empty house. Quite by accident, he found a second darkroom, concealed behind the first. He felt guilty entering it, even though his logical brain told him that it was part of his own house.

He didn't need to look far. The walls were covered with candid pictures of people, most of whom he didn't recognize, but almost all in various states of undress. There were many pictures of Azur, and to his surprise, a picture of Etienette working in the library. He selected a beautiful picture of Azur, and moved it to the library. He would have loved to frame it and hang it on the wall, but that wouldn't be possible as long as anyone else was allowed in the room. The picture was the one Rick had mentioned, showing Azur combing her hair. Cleverly, it showed both sides of her face, by using her reflection in the mirror. A very beautiful and artistic black and white photo with soft lighting. Unfortunately the picture also showed her minimal French lingerie since that was all that she was wearing at the time of the exposure.

Matthew decided to work hard to shake off his loneliness. A good time-consuming project might be to clean the library windows, to bring fresh light onto his new picture and his work table.

The only window that showed signs of moving was at the far east end of the room. After an hour with putty knives and a hammer, the old wood moved enough so that he could raise the sash and step out onto the library balcony. What a view! Below him the waves crashed against the shore as seagulls circled and called to each other. The ocean stretched to the horizon in three directions, with happy sunlight dancing on the waves. He could taste the salt air. The balcony where he stood was stone, and seemed to be in excellent condition, except for an ominous bend at the center, directly over the washed-out foundations below. Two floors above his head was the main balcony for the public rooms: it looked perfect, at least from this view.

The library balcony had an unfortunate accumulation of seagull droppings, but that could be washed away. However, the windows were a different story. He worked at the nearest one for a long time, using every substance he could find. The crusty film on the outside would not yield to bleach, acetone (Azur's nail polish remover), alcohol, darkroom chemicals, or kerosene. Finally he attacked it with a wire brush, and although this removed some of the encrustation, it also scratched the glass beneath. The real answer was to replace all the glass, and probably the window frames and all the adjacent wood as well. A major project that it would be unwise to start until the foundations were solid.

He poked at the putty around a window, and noted that it was so weather-worn and hardened that it fell away with little effort. This would make it easy for him to replace the glass, but also it meant that a good storm could wash away a few windows with ease, flooding the library with salt spray.

That afternoon found Matthew on the balcony with cans of putty and white paint. The glass in two of the windows was sparkling new, and the view from inside the library was worth the trouble. Matthew moved his work table, the photo of Azur, and all his notes to this end of the library. A hard day's work, rewarded by a lovely sunset over the water. Time for dinner at the local pub, where he could at least chat with a few people after spending the day alone.

The next evening, Matthew and invisible Rick entered the Oxford lecture hall where Azur would be speaking. Matthew realized that she probably didn't know that he had brought Rick along, and decided that it would be best not to tell her as she was sure to be nervous about her talk. Rick and Matt were impressed by the old paintings of professors on the walls, the lovely cream colored room, and the large number of students who had gathered to hear Azur. The room had a beautiful chandelier, and was ringed with high windows, below a ceiling perhaps thirty feet above their heads. Azur was wearing her academic robes and chatting with Dexter and members of the faculty. This was her world, and she fit perfectly, using technical words and phrases from various languages with ease.

Neither Matt nor Rick felt comfortable, but both were most curious to hear what she would say. Dexter ignored Matt, even though they had been together both at his house and at the funeral and had carried Marti's coffin to its grave.

As the lecture started, a Professor introduced Azur as the newest member of the faculty with a series of glowing remarks including references to her soon-to-be-published SHC paper and academic honors. Matthew and Rick had no idea that she was so highly-regarded, and that she had accomplished so much so quickly. There was a round of polite applause, but Rick's sensitivity revealed that many of the students were put-off by her achievements. They suspected funny business and felt that nobody so young and pretty moved to the top quickly without inside help, probably in bed, as well as in cash. Rick whispered all this to Matthew as the lecture started. His discomfort increased as he realized how little he knew of Azur's school experiences and friends.

Azur's topic was a discussion of Ley Lines. She started with a few comments on Watkins' books, summarizing his description of the things that normal people can see on the surface of the land. She had slides showing lines containing fences, markstones, steeples, hill-top notches, and reflecting pools. The same sort of thing Watkins discovered a hundred years ago. Matthew was pleased to see some pictures of the lines which met at his house. So far nothing controversial. Azur was careful to point out that all the things that she had shown were available for anyone to see. Watkins had not been a psychic.

Then she moved into the psychic world, describing[1] these same lines from the viewpoints of 'sensitives'. To these gifted people, Ley Lines marked the location of earth energies and secret deep water lines. Intersections of Ley Lines marked the locations of spirit wells, and places where cosmic forces entered and left the earth. She stated that probably few in the room had the ability to actually feel, or dowse, the spirit lines beneath the Ley Lines.

One student started to rudely object to this interpretation,

---

1   The website www.geo.org contains information on 'earth energies' and the characteristics of Ley Lines.

but invisible Rick placed his hand over the student's mouth, silencing the objection abruptly, much to the surprise of the others sitting nearby. Rick whispered in his ear, "Shut up you ignorant fool". The student was petrified. Azur continued, probably not even noticing what had happened.

She went on to describe how the energy lines had both positive and negative aspects. People living over positive lines would be hyperactive, while those over negative energy lines would encounter tension, anxiety and perhaps neurosis. The best place to be was at an intersection, for there the energy was strong and yet balanced. This knowledge had been used for thousands of years by the Chinese (the art of Geomancy) for locating favorable positions for houses and sacred buildings. Then she talked about primary water, which flows deep below the surface, only appearing at spirit wells and major psychic centers.

Matthew had thought that the audience would consist of students who shared Azur's views of the spirit world. He did not realize that many of the students in the audience were non-believers, people who had come to question, rather than to sit passively listening. From the far side of the room, a student stood up and demanded proof of her assertions, "How can you be so sure of all this: where's a photograph of cosmic energy, or a well tapping into your spirit water? What's its chemical composition?"

Before he finished another student stood, "We aren't living in the dark ages: this is Oxford in the twenty-first century and we want proof, instead of vague B.S. from kooks and weirdoes."

Another student started to speak, "Where's an independent verification of all this: maybe you're just making it up so you can publish lots of papers."

Matthew whispered to Rick, "There're too many, you can't silence all of them."

Rick replied, "Watch this!"

Rick picked up the nearest speaker and carried him to the front of the room. The student appeared to float through the air, waving his arms and legs. A stunned silence fell over the room. As he walked to the podium, Rick shouted to the startled audience, "You want proof, here it is. Look with your eyes and believe what they tell you. You can't see me, but I'm holding this jerk in the air. I'm a spirit, and I live over a spirit well, drawing energy from it. In fact, Professor Azur and her handsome lover, Matthew, who is in the back of the room, just helped me remove a blockage from one of the Ley Lines that supports my well. Matthew's an engineering student, so you can get the pragmatic side of things from him. By drawing on the well's improved energy, I'm getting stronger every day, even though I'm a thousand years old."

"Now, I'll put this fellow down, and return to my seat to hear the rest of Azur's talk. She's speaking the truth, so be quiet and listen."

There were no more questions as a very rattled and embarrassed Azur finished her talk. Afterwards a professor remarked to her, "I don't know how you did that, but I wish I could get your spirit friend to help with my lectures."

Matthew and Rick made their way to Azur, who was busy conferring with Dexter and the other academics. "Wasn't that great. Afterwards we had many more believers than before," Rick said to Azur.

The other academics jumped back on hearing Rick's voice.

"Do not EVER do that to me again," Azur commanded a very startled Rick. She was absolutely furious at him, and by extension, Matthew.

"But it worked: they wanted proof and I gave it to them."

"That is NOT the point. I am supposed to be the professor, to teach, and to answer their questions. The students need to ask and I must answer them. You have short-circuited the whole process. I am not an accessory on one of your cheap magic shows."

"I'm sure Rick only wanted to help, to get you out of a difficult situation," Matthew pleaded, trying to restore peace.

"I can do that myself, thank you very much. Now, if you will excuse me, I have my professorial duties to attend." Azur turned and started to talk with other professors.

Several students approached Matthew and were directing questions to him, interrupting the conversation.

"Did you help her fake that paper on spontaneous human combustion?"

"I've been to the site, seen it, felt it, and smelled it. It's genuine. It gave me the creeps," Matthew replied.

"Will you come talk with our class: we'd love to get the real story on all this stuff?"

"Only if you invite Azur too," Matthew replied.

"What's she like in bed?"

"You'll never know," he replied with finality.

A very senior Professor walked over to Matthew and Rick, "I don't care what she says, you were excellent, providing believable proof exactly when it was requested. You can both come to my lectures any time you like. Don't let her chase you away. She's just beginning to learn what life is like at the front of the class, while you already know instinctively."

On hearing these comments, Azur stormed from the room, with Dexter trailing behind.

"Let's go. We can get home by midnight if we hurry," a sad Rick said to a bewildered Matthew.

Chapter 15
Violent Separation

Matthew awoke to hear a storm beating against the house. He walked by Azur's room, and cast a forlorn glance at the empty bed, then went down to the old library and looked longingly at her picture then at the rain pouring off his new windows. A sad day. There was an odd noise from somewhere below in the house. Perhaps Rick was working in the machine shop. Matthew started down the stairs, but stopped. To his horror, he saw that a new hole had opened in the wall. More of the rocks had washed away, and the noise was made by the sound of waves crashing below. Spray from the waves was blowing through the hole. He didn't need his laser measuring equipment to see that more of the foundation was gone. He scampered up the stairs quickly, shouting for Rick all the way. Finally he found Rick and told him of the problems. They conferred in Marti's old kitchen while making a simple breakfast of oatmeal. Matthew was startled to hear sounds from upstairs: they went up to investigate.

Azur was in her bedroom packing her books and notes into a suitcase. She was wearing an expensive dark silk travel dress. Dexter was nearby, leaning over a chair, smoking cigarettes, the ash falling to the floor. Matthew rushed into the room. Although they couldn't see him, Rick was right behind.

"Sorry to be so abrupt, but I am moving back to my flat in Oxford immediately," Azur said.

"You can't be serious. You're not leaving today," Matthew begged.

"Oh, but I am, in just a few minutes. I am giving a guest lecture tomorrow evening, by myself, without help from either of you."

"But the guys from Christie's will be here tomorrow to see the rest of the stuff and meet with us," Matthew implored.

"It all belongs to you, it is not my problem."

She closed the heavy suitcase and locked it with finality, then picked it up herself. Dexter made no move to help, but stood up awkwardly.

"I thought you loved me? What about our life together? I love you, I love you with all my heart," Matthew, almost in tears, pleaded desperately, oblivious of Dexter's and Rick's presence in the room.

"Do not be so infantile! You are just infatuated with my body. Rick will get you another one."

This cut Matthew to the bone. His heart shattered. Invisible Rick could feel his grandson's pain deeply. Her words hurt Rick more than they hurt Matthew. Rick was furious. He ripped the silk dress from her body, sending buttons and zippers flying, "Bitch, your problems are just beginning. Get the hell out of my house before I pull your face off and drop kick your fat ass into the ocean. You're going to regret those words for the rest of your very short, and very painful, life!"

What a curse! As he said this, he picked her up and started to give her a violent spanking, as she screamed at the three men. Dexter did nothing to help: he was frozen with fear at the invisible ghost's violent rage. Matthew struggled with Rick, trying to make him let go of Azur , "Please Rick, don't hurt her any more. Please let her live. Please stop. Please."

She escaped as Rick relented, then ran from the room, clutching the remains of her clothes. Dexter grabbed the suitcase and ran after her. Rick and Matthew followed.

As Dexter ran to his fancy car in the pouring rain, Rick shoved him to the ground and stood on top of his wiggling muddy body, "If you ever kiss her, if you ever touch her, if I ever see you two in bed together, I'm going to cut your balls off one by one and stuff them down your throat. Now stop shitting in your pants and get out of here. You smell as bad as you look."

Azur had entered the car and closed her door, but Rick tore it open, "You're doomed, my curse will follow you everywhere, stealing your sleep, and erasing your beauty. Never again will you bed a man who loves you, you self-centered, cold-hearted, scheming whore. Now get out of my sight before I kill both of you."

Rick slammed the door with such force that the car's side window shattered in a thousand pieces, covering Azur's partially-naked body with broken safety glass and rain. The car splashed its way down the driveway as Matthew and Rick stared after it.

"Rick, you came close to killing them," Matthew whispered.

"Yes, it would have been easy, but for your sake I let her live a bit longer. Perhaps she will grow up and learn that she owes much to the world, just for the privilege of being alive. Then she might be worthy of your affection. Let's go for a walk in the wind and rain and make plans. She's got a tough ass, my right hand's going to hurt for a week after that spanking."

Rick and Matthew walked all day through the deserted stormy countryside, splashing through puddles, talking over their problems and plans. Dusk found them at Matthew's car, soaked, cold, and covered with mud.

"Do you really think Julian will want to see us," Matthew asked Rick.

"I'm sure of it. I made a few discoveries while I worked on their poltergeist, and we need to help him out of a jam."

They climbed into the old Mini and drove to the Chateau. The formal butler met Matthew with surprise. He couldn't see Rick. "Mr. Julian isn't expecting anyone that I know of, and Madam has gone to France."

"I must see him, even if he's in the bathtub, and I could use a few towels to protect your beautiful floor from my dripping clothes."

The butler brought the two wet visitors, and a robe and a pile of towels, into the library, where Julian was sitting at his desk with a glass of whiskey and an almost-empty decanter. "What a surprise. What brings you over here?"

"Rick and I thought we might join forces with you. Sort of form a boys' club to help each other."

"Rick, I don't see him. Is he outside?"

"No, I'm right next to you, but I'm invisible."

"Don't worry Julian, it takes getting used to. We have a lot to talk about," Matthew added quickly.

"Why don't you ring for a few bottles of champagne and sandwiches. I'd materialize for that in a heartbeat," Rick said.

"Please don't upset the butler. He has enough problems as it is. Perhaps there are a few bottles left in the cellar and we can share them together." Julian said.

Julian and Matthew made small talk as the butler served champagne and sandwiches, then once the butler had left, they settled into conversation.

Rick began, "Julian, I'll give you the quick tour. See, now I'm partly visible, a cloud. Now I'm more visible, like a ghost. And finally, I'm just like you, fully visible and capable of drinking a lot of champagne."

"Amazing. Does Etienette know about this. We thought you were a, er, normal, person, just flesh and bones."

"She doesn't have a clue about that, or about lots of things for that matter."

"Well, she certainly seemed to like you. I thought you two would be lovers the first night you met."

"I thought so too, but just as it became interesting, you know what she had the nerve to tell me, me of all creatures?"

"What did she say," Matthew asked.

"She said that I was remarkably virile for such an old man, but that she'd rather bed someone younger!"

"She was being polite. What really turns her on are pubescent school kids with their first erections," Julian sadly replied.

"How can you put up with her," Rick asked.

"Sometimes, after she has a bit of champagne, she remembers how I used to look."

"Maybe she should look in the mirror and realize that she's no spring chicken herself," Matthew added.

"Is that why you're almost out of champagne," Rick asked.

"Oh no, can I refuse to answer, or I'd like not to answer, or?"

"I knew there was something seriously wrong here. Out

with it. We're here to help each other. Each of us has big problems, and I have a cellar with lots of very old champagne if you're running dry," Rick said.

"How much do you know? What do you suspect," Julian asked.

"Suspect? What do you mean," Matthew said in astonishment.

"I know there's something very wrong financially, aside from our mutual problems with silly women," Rick said.

"Exactly, I'm broke, in fact, I'm worse than broke. I've just mortgaged this place to the hilt so now we've living off the last of our capital."

"What went wrong," Rick asked.

"Long story, but you could put it all down to a combination of bad luck in business combined with unlimited spending by Etienette. You have any idea how much she can burn in a week?"

"But why don't you stop her. Doesn't she know," Matthew asked.

"Matthew, there are some things that may be practical, but which may not be easy, emotionally, to do. What would Etienette think of Julian if he told her that he had lost her family fortune," Rick replied.

"But it is almost all gone: she's got to focus on saving what's left," Matthew said.

"You're right. I should have told her earlier, but I keep hoping to make it back somehow. Now as we are being frank with each other, I want to know how a million pounds came to be transferred from Brussels into your bank account. Did Etienette give you that money, and where did she get it?"

"No, but she knows what happened. I sold some old coins that belonged to Rick. Azur and I had to smuggle them out of the country in her purse because Christies wouldn't touch them. In fact, Christies almost confiscated the coins when we tried to get an appraisal. I sold them to a Brussels dealer, who passed them to a Japanese collector. He wired the funds here then I spent some of it restoring the Stonehenge spirit line, to save Rick's wife, Floris."

"My word, Floris? Is she a ghost too? And are you talking

about the strange warehouse project, with the fire and clearance and all the planning commission trouble," Julian asked, bewildered.

"Yes, Floris died in the War, and needs energy that comes down a spirit line, which the warehouses blocked. Then I bought a generator and some electric lights and a few other things to start work on the house."

"I've got more coins and we're going to try to sell a few tomorrow, but if that doesn't work, we can all sneak over to Belgium. Both of you could use a bit of serious cash, and we could have fun on the continent," Rick said.

"That's the best news I've had in ages. Now what can I do for you in return. And where's Azur by the way?"

Rick and Matthew explained Azur's disastrous departure to Julian. To Matthew's surprise, Julian said that Dexter was a childhood friend that Azur had played with for years, but that he was usually in London with his gay friends. There was no romantic entanglement at all.

"Now are there any other secrets we need to share," Julian asked.

"Remember when you were five and were sent away to school, and were so sad and lonely," Rick asked Julian.

"Yes, it was a terrible time," Julian cautiously replied.

"And you had a secret, invisible friend, who helped you by pushing a bully over a cliff," Rick continued.

"No! How could you, I thought it was God or some sort of heavenly blessing when that monster went to his grave," Julian exclaimed.

Matt hesitated, then began, "Rick, can I share something embarrassing about you with Julian, and perhaps help you have some fun?"

"Fun? Of course, what do you mean?"

"Remember that girl from the bar, the one you brought into the house, then hid her clothes?"

"Oh yes, that girl," Rick said with hesitation.

"She told me something of your troubles in bed, and if you're willing we could try an experiment. You probably don't know about Viagra and Cialis, but they are medicines that might give you an amazing erection with the next girl you meet."

Rick was too startled to reply.

Julian caught on quickly, "Problems like that happen to lots of older men, and the new medicines are great. I'll get a prescription from my medico and you can give it a go."

"I am embarrassed, but this is so amazing, I had no idea that doctors could fix such things. Just thinking about the possibility is very exciting."

"Well, my secret is that I'm going back to school to finish my studies. This is too much for me. Rick, why don't you give the money to Julian and he can save the house. You don't need me here," Matthew said sadly.

"Don't quit on us Matthew! With your brains, Rick's money, and my help, we can whip your house into shape in no time at all. Bet you don't know that I'm an expert welder, and did a German apprenticeship when I dropped out of college. I can't wait to get my hands on some steel and prop your house into position," Julian exclaimed.

"You can't leave now, your psychic skills are just starting to appear. I'm going to teach you all sorts of useful things if you'll just be patient," Rick implored.

"I don't need psychic skills to be an engineer, Rick."

"Maybe not, but your left foot could use some improvement, and I'm sure that between us we have enough energy to make it grow properly. Bet you can't learn how to do that in school."

Matthew was shocked. Such an idea had not occurred to him, and he wondered if it was idle talk or real. "Are you serious, or just saying that to get me to stay?"

"I won't lie. Your foot has been sick and covered with scar tissue for a long time, so it will be very difficult to re-grow. It will never be perfect, but it can be a lot better than it is. Your foot is an interesting challenge, and developing your abilities will be part of the cure."

"Let me think about it over night. I'm pooped right now."

Matthew was still in a state of shock and didn't realize how badly he felt until he walked away, leaving Julian and Rick with the last of the champagne. He wandered upstairs, through Azur's rooms, wanting to cry as he smelled her perfume, touched her things, and looked at the happy pictures from her childhood. For the first time he knew that heartache was a real phenomenon, a physical pain in his chest that burned as he thought of her, far away. Tears were so close, his eyes hurt, but were dry. He went down to the music room and opened Etienette's French piano, and began to play softly. He knew many sad songs, but now they had the extra bite that came from playing with a freshly broken heart. He had a brief laugh playing Jerry Jeff Walker's "I feel like Hank Williams Tonight[1]", a country and western song which expressed his mood exactly. Matthew guessed that perhaps this was the first C&W song ever played on this old foreign piano. He played quietly, crying by himself until dawn.

Two surprises awaited the three men when they went to Redcliffs Hall in the morning. The first was an expensive black Jaguar parked by the front door, and the second was a freshly-dug hole in the yard, near the rose garden. The hole was empty, so it could wait, but as they drove to the house, two men in proper business suits emerged from the car. Julian recognized one of them immediately.

"That's Sir Edward, he's the Managing Director at Christie's. I'm very glad you told me what happened. I'll talk, while you get the coins and stones that you showed them. Rick, just be quiet for now: let's see what happens," Julian directed.

"Why Edward, what brings you down here, so far from London. Want to buy an old house?"

"Hello again, I remember you from London. Hope you had a pleasant drive down," Matthew said.

"Yes thank you, and you haven't met Richard here, he's an expert from America on the subject of very old and rare coins."

"Great, I'll get the coins so that he can study them. Let's go down to the library, there's some good light and furniture down there, if it hasn't fallen into the sea while we've been at Julian's."

They entered the library, and were examining the coins when Julian saw Matthew's picture of Azur combing her hair. He

---

1   The song tells the story of a sad cowboy who plays different music depending on his mood. Hank Williams' music is reserved for the most painful occasions.

nearly jumped out of his skin, and quickly turned the photo face-down on the desk, hopefully before the London men noticed it. Rick was even more startled, and quickly searched the room for any of his other shots. Fortunately Matthew always closed the secret door to the lower rooms.

Richard explained that the gold coins dated from before Roman times: they were extremely rare, and in outstanding condition. He suspected that no museum in the world held better specimens.

"How can Matthew convert these into money. The foundations below are collapsing and he needs cash right now, to buy more steel and equipment," Julian asked.

"Could I rent them to you or to Christie's until they're sold? They aren't doing me any good and I can see that you'd love to study them and exhibit them to scholars," Matthew said.

"How about a loan, with these as collateral: you say they're worth millions. Just a few hundred thousand would help get the ball rolling here, but it must be done quickly," Julian added.

"Another chunk fell out of the wall during the storm yesterday: I don't dare look at it until I can find more money," Matthew said.

"The problem is that you, Matthew, might not have title to these: they may be crown property," Edward said.

"But if it's just a loan, then Matthew could pay it back eventually, if they do turn out to be crown property. Meanwhile you would hold the collateral," Julian quickly replied.

"Richard, stick these in your pocket and fly back to the States: you can wire the money to Julian and nobody will be the wiser. You can have them for half their real value, and I can see how badly you want them," Matthew said.

"Why that's just not done, that's impossible," Edward said stiffly.

"Are there more of these hidden here perhaps," Richard asked, with undisguised curiosity.

"Maybe, but I don't suspect that I'll find any more until I know how to convert them into cash. And if the house collapses, they might be lost forever," Matthew said with a smile.

"I'm sure that Christie's in New York or Tokyo would love

to auction the others, if they turned up. Perhaps you would like an exclusive on other treasures that may be hidden here, that is if any others are found before it all washes into the sea," Julian added.

"I'll bet you ship rare coins all over the world every day: these would only need a small box, and what's a few hundred thousand among friends," Matthew said.

"You and Julian don't mince words do you? If you can provide a solid provenance, that is, tell me how the coins came to be here, in a way that shows that they are yours and not the Crown's, then you've got a deal, for as many as you can find," Richard said.

"Can we shake hands on that? Half price for the coins to Richard, and an exclusive to Christie's for anything else of value that needs to go on the block," Julian asked.

"You mean you know how they came to be here," Edward said in amazement.

"Yes, but first we all shake hands," Julian smiled.

After many hand shakes, Rick startled the two visitors, "Please be seated, as it's a long story. The coins are really mine, but since I'm a ghost, and my house is falling into the sea, you can have them on the agreed terms. Don't faint, here, I'll materialize for a minute so that you can see that I'm real."

Rick told them a long story about how he had befriended a group of lost people long ago and that they had rewarded him in gold. There was no way to check the story, but it sounded authentic. Richard knew that if this ever went to law, it would be the trial of the century, since Rick agreed to testify in open court.

As Rick talked, Matthew went to the wine cellar and returned with one of Rick's prize bottles of champagne and five glasses. When Edward saw the label he almost fainted. "You're not going to open that right here are you: that bottle's worth a fortune."

"So is our new agreement," Matthew replied.

Rick took the bottle from Matthew, "Please let me do the honors, I haven't opened one of these in at least fifty years and I'm dying to see how it compares with my memories."

Later, as the two men were about to leave for London, Matthew excused himself for a moment, then returned with a dozen coins of other sizes and denominations. He wrapped them in a handkerchief and placed it in Richard's hand.

"Here, this will improve your collection, and substantially boost the amount that you need to wire into Julian's account. Don't peek until you're on the road. These coins are even better than the others," Matthew said.

After the startled men drove off toward London, Matthew, Rick, and Julian walked to the strange new hole in the front yard. It was about three feet deep, and there were fragments of old rusty pipe projecting from the side of the hole.

"Those damn detectorists have been digging in your yard," Julian fumed.

"What? Who are they," Matthew asked.

"Detectorists run around with metal detectors looking for buried treasure. They trespass all over the place, and would you believe it, the law is on their side! If they find anything, they can legally claim it as discoverers, even though it's on your land," Julian fumed.

"Not in my yard, they won't," Rick growled.

"Let me call a proper fencing company to repair your wall. Your first legal defense is to be able to show that they climbed over your wall, past clearly visible 'no trespassing' signs," Julian said.

"Yes, do that quickly, and have them put broken glass along the top of the wall, like they do in Mexico," Rick added.

"Oh no, that's illegal in crook-friendly England: why they might get hurt as they climbed over," Julian replied sarcastically.

"Floris and I will stand watch, in fact, I think we'll have a bit of fun with the locals. In a week or two nobody will dare set foot on our property. This house is about to become extremely haunted and dangerous. Why trespassers might be blown over the cliffs, or die of fright, or be chased by strange apparitions. I don't like people wandering around my property," Rick said with finality.

Floris returned from the orphanage, and was startled to hear all that had happened. "I'm sorry to hear about Azur, for I like her very much. We all know that she is too self-centered, but she can also be quite pleasant, and her spirit knowledge would be useful to us. What she needs is a good ghostly grandmother to shape her up."

"I think you would be wasting your time. Her problems

are deeply-rooted, and something about her spirit feels wrong to me. After we get the house fixed, let's find Matthew a real woman, someone with a warm heart, who will make him happy forever," Rick replied.

During this conversation, Matt looked at the mid-September rain, and at the early autumn leaves that were starting to fall and thought that he had never felt so miserable. He went down to the basement and was startled to see the size of a new hole in the wall where big rocks had fallen away. He didn't need fancy gear to measure the problem and there were only twenty-one days until he was supposed to vacate the property.

Late in the day, Matthew found himself alone in the Long Gallery, a huge room, with a checkerboard black and white stone floor and red marble columns. The beautiful ornate painted and plastered ceiling above was intact in spite of the mess on the floor below. He tried to imagine what this room might have been like originally, when filled with people, candles, and furniture. The large windows on the ocean side would have been clean and clear: perhaps the moon was visible across the sea, reflected on the ripples of the waves. A few windows were open, allowing a gentle breeze to float through the room. He could almost hear music and murmurs of conversation from women in long dresses and men in powdered wigs. Happy people, playing the pianoforte and violins while entertaining each other. An idyllic setting.

Then his imagination moved forward in time, and envisioned the same room in the second war, with lights blacked-out and anxious people looking across the sea for enemy submarines, while Vera Lynn sang "We'll Meet Again" on a glowing vacuum tube radio. This room could have seen so much history. He knew that he must preserve it: the house was far too wonderful to slip into the sea just because the foundations were weak. Structures were a problem that he could solve. He knew it instinctively. If he couldn't fix this, his own house, how could he ever call himself an Engineer. Time to stop dreaming of the past and begin to think victory instead of defeat, solutions instead of problems, action instead of endless calculation.

Matt busied himself, grabbed Rick, and started to clear the box room, making it ready for the steel which would save their home.

That night Floris dressed in a provocative diaphanous stage costume, then materialized in front of a group of local boys who were walking home. She laughed and played with them, encouraging them to chase her toward Redcliffs Hall. There, she floated over the wall, calling to them to hurry after her. After they climbed the wall and dropped to the other side, they found no one.

To their surprise, invisible spirits started removing their clothes and tickling their naked bodies. Whenever one tried to climb back up the wall, he was pulled back down. The boys screamed in fear, which made Rick and Floris emit what they imagined to be creepy laughs. The clothes floated by themselves toward the edge of the cliffs, and the boys followed. Then the clothes went over the side, to the waves below, to the boys' horror. No one was dumb enough to follow the clothes down, and besides, now the boys were being spanked and chased up the drive toward the gate, which mysteriously opened as they arrived. The stories of the ghosts and the haunted house spread rapidly, with magnification at each re-telling.

Rick's best catch was one of the detectorists, who had been busily searching through the old gardens in broad daylight. He was so intent on his work, listening to his headphones and moving his detector about, that he never would have seen Rick, even if Rick had been visible. Rick tore his clothes away and threw them and his gear over the cliff. Then he chased the unfortunate creep to the top of the old beach steps, and halfway down, with pokes and jabs and vigorous spanks with a paddle. The man stopped, as he realized that the steps ended in a great hole, where the foundations had fallen away. Rick gave one of his best scary laughs and told the man to go on, to go on and die, or to sit on the stairs and rot forever. The naked man sat there for hours, shaking in the cold sea breeze, then slowly made his way up to the top of the cliff, where Floris tripped him, then chased him out the driveway. He was still shaking with fear when the TV people interviewed him the next day.

When television news people showed up to investigate, and had the effrontery to drive their van down to the front door of Redcliffs Hall, Rick adjusted their cameras and equipment randomly, turning every knob and pushing every button he could find. Floris tickled the crew people and let the air out of their tires. While the crew tried to control the situation, their van began to drive itself down the road, trailing cables and people. As they left, Rick admonished them, "This time we just played and no one was hurt. But when you come back, stay outside the gate, or we'll play for keeps, and you won't like it. You can make all the pictures you want from the other side of the wall, but don't ever trespass on our land if you value your lives."

Chapter 16
Construction Begins

While all this happened outside, Matthew finished his plan to stabilize the house in its present condition before more washed away. He ordered additional equipment, and bribed the steel fabricators to deliver all of his steel immediately: he had plenty of money, but little time.

For those readers who like to know details, a technical account of the house's problems and the design of its repair is included in the Appendix, at the rear of this book. This is a good time to read it, in terms of story continuity.

In less than a week, the front yard looked like a proper

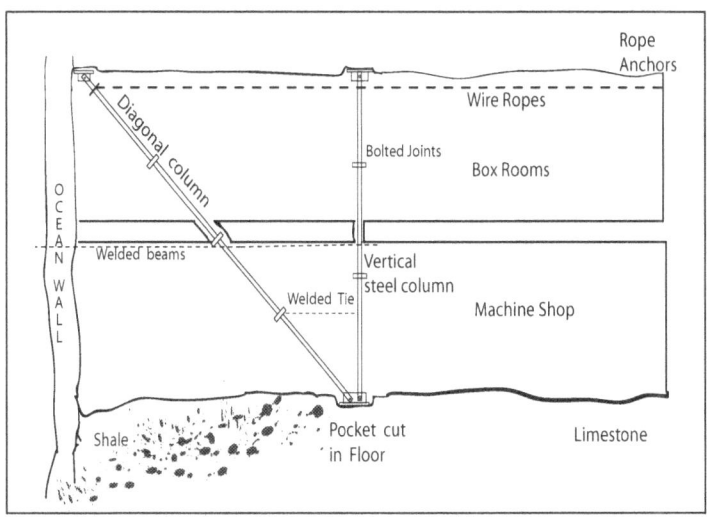

Steel Framework Being Built Under Redcliffs Hall

construction site. A Smith 130 diesel air compressor hummed next to the big electric generator and the industrial welder. Dozens of 55-gallon barrels of diesel fuel stood nearby. An orderly pile of galvanized steel beams and plates was near the service entrance, as well as a six-foot diameter wooden spool of stainless steel wire rope. Boxes of other items were arranged neatly. There were even two construction toilets. A team of laborers was slowly preparing, then moving, the material into the house under Matthew's and Julian's direction.

Rick's favorite toy was a small Japanese crane. It could be driven anywhere, and its hydraulic boom would go in and out, up and down. Rick played with it for hours at a time, carefully lifting, moving, and arranging the various supplies. He was careful to appear visible and non-ghostly to the other workers. Meanwhile, Floris stood invisible guard, watching for trespassers.

True to his word, Rick helped Matthew with his foot several times each day. Short sessions, where Rick encouraged him to focus all his thoughts and energy onto the foot as it is now, and then as it should be, carefully thinking of the differences. Rick told Matthew to feel himself inside his foot, to look around at the damaged structures, and to see the repairs that were needed. The same approach was used whenever they talked about walls and rocks. Rick always wanted Matthew to go inside things, to imagine himself penetrating just a little and looking and feeling, especially feeling the textures of what he found.

Matthew expressed confidence in his plans in a simple and direct way. He hired four construction crews to work on the house and yard while he and the others worked on the steel. The first crew was installing seven-foot high electric replicas of old gas street lamps at his gate and along his almost mile-long driveway. Wiring was buried in a trench along the drive, and while they were trenching, the crew buried conduits for telephone, cable television, fast internet, remote gate control, and electric power in the same trench. For now, he ran the new lights from his generator, in defiance of the electricity board which had cut off his street-power, and as a demonstration of his faith that his house would stand a long time. The second contractor had begun to replace the old windows in the long gallery, starting with those furthest away from the crack over the soft foundations.

The view of the ocean in two directions would be spectacular. The third contractor was engaged in general yard work, removing the overgrowth from a hundred years of minimal maintenance. They would make the driveway passable, clear the maze, and re-activate the fountains. The fourth contractor was a chimney sweep who started on the fireplaces in the public rooms. Winter was coming and the yard work would generate plenty of firewood.

After the first week of intense work, on September 28th, Matthew received a surprise call from an Architect, who had been in touch with RIBA (Royal Institute of British Architects), and who lived in Lyme Regis. He was coming to Redcliffs Hall, carrying a present. When he arrived, Matthew discovered that the RIBA expert, whom he had talked with weeks before, had found some of the plans for his house and gardens, and had made a set of copies. The plans were gorgeous, and Matthew hoped to frame them and hang them in the Library for reference. Matthew showed the Architect over the house, from the roof platform on top to the construction activity at the bottom, as well as the plans that he had drawn for steel reinforcements in the basements. They also talked about the power plant people and the problems that they presented. The Architect loved the house, and urged Matthew to litigate in the court of public opinion, since the government and the laws were biased in favor of the power plant. As a start, the Architect wandered the house making beautiful digital photographs, then called television friends in London.

A few days later, with Rick and Floris on their best behavior, the Architect returned with a small television crew. He filmed the old plans, and showed how they related to the house today, with emphasis on the rarity of some of the house's features. He pointed out that the house was an architectural treasure that should be saved and preserved, rather than being replaced with an ugly pollution-spouting power plant. Then the crew showed the men working to save the house, and introduced Julian, who added an enthusiastic artistic preservation speech.

When it was over, Matthew was careful to invite the television people to come back and do follow-up stories whenever they wanted. When they asked about the haunted nature of the house, Matthew brushed it aside with a comment that only unfriendly people and trespassers ever had trouble with ghosts here.

Matthew missed Azur very much and hoped for a letter or a note, but there was no contact. Etienette wrote to Julian from a French beauty spa, mentioning that she had seen Azur in France, and that she was worried about Azur's health. Azur seemed weak, mean-spirited, and very unhappy. Etienette's letter described an evening that she had spent with her at a fancy-dress party.

"We sat with her flashy cinema friends. They are so stupid. They think that a film must have a sad ending or no one will take it seriously. Of course, they have never made a film that I would go near, and if they didn't have family or government money they would all be in the gutter where they belong. I don't see why Azur tolerates them. They just sit there, smoking too much and talk, talk, talk. The band played some good music, but they sneered because it was too American. To my surprise, Azur stood up, walked to another table, took the hand of a young man and danced for the rest of the evening. It was less than a minute later that I did the same thing. Later, Azur told me about the dance club in London that she and Matthew had visited. They danced until dawn, just like you and I used to do. I don't know why she left Matthew: what a young fool she is."

Julian wrote back to Etienette, and casually mentioned that although their bank account had been having difficulties and was nearly empty, Matthew was now quite solid financially and was helping Julian cover Etienette's extravagant credit card bills. Julian figured that if anything would bring Etienette running home, talk of financial distress, coupled with exciting news about Matthew, would do the trick. He laughed when he imagined Etienette's reaction to this simple letter. Perhaps she would show it to Azur. Julian had decided that when Etienette returned, she would need to know the truth about their finances. Their relationship would re-start with fewer secrets and perhaps more pleasure. For now, he was living with Matthew, Floris, and Rick, as they all worked twelve hours a day, trying to save the old house.

Julian's fence people had done an excellent job rebuilding

the old walls, which were over a mile long, covering open areas with new wire fence and installing government-approved no-trespassing signs. At least now, detectorists would face physical obstacles if they dared to trespass. Into the midst of this activity arrived a truck containing several surveyors. Finding the gate open, they drove to the front door, and started looking for the owner. They found Julian instead.

"Hello, we're here to do a detailed survey of the site," the first surveyor said.

"We didn't ask for one: who sent you?"

"We were hired by the contractors who are building the new power plant here."

"You're mistaken, there will be no power plant here, it will be re-sited to another location. Now please leave, we're very busy as you can see."

"Do you know where the new site is: maybe we have the wrong address?"

Invisible Rick arrived and started messing with their truck. As the mystified surveyors watched, their truck's engine started, then the truck drove itself along the drive and through the gate. The men ran after it. Instead of staying on the road outside the gate, the truck made a sharp turn, then went straight across the adjacent pasture, and over the cliff, crashing onto the rocks far below. The men ran to the edge of the cliff and stared in disbelief at what they had just seen. While they were standing on the edge, invisible Rick (who had jumped out the door just as the truck reached the edge) poked them, "Don't you ever come back here, or you'll be smashed into the sea like that truck. Nothing will ever be built on my land. Now, run as fast as you can." Rick jabbed and poked at the two as they started running toward the village.

Matthew received a phone call from the regional planning commission, asking what was happening. At first he resented the interruption, but then he became polite, carefully explaining that since his foundations were crumbling, he was doing emergency steel work to stabilize the house. Unfortunately he hadn't had time to hire an architect or a licensed structural engineer, so he didn't have approval from the coastal commission or anyone else, but they were welcome to visit and see the actual work if they liked. The planner asked if Matthew had received the eviction notice from the power plant committee. Why was he still living in and working on the house?

Matthew told the caller that he doubted that the plant would be built here, and that the house would be structurally stable by the end of the year. After that, he proposed to do a proper, architecturally-correct, restoration, with all the legal plans and permissions. It would once again be a beautiful house, and he would open it to the public for special occasions and public events. The call ended with a friendly chat about the correct way to do restorations and the difficulties of maintenance near the ocean. Matthew was learning the value of good public relations, even as Rick and Floris worked to expand the house's haunted reputation. At the end of the conversation, he asked if the planners might arrange a visit of the Antiquities Board to examine the house. Matthew mentioned his Architectural friend and the television program that they had done, as well as the old and unusual rooms, which might interest people with historical knowledge.

As Matthew returned the phone to his pocket he reflected on his "new friends" at the planning commission. These were people from his own county, rather than from the national government. They would be interested in improving the local area and its attractions. It might well be possible to enlist them on his side in the coming battle with the power plant people from far-away London.

Down underground Matthew worked hard on the new foundations. Much of the work involved drilling holes in the rock walls and in the masonry floors. Many hours pressing on heavy air-powered drills and jack-hammers, while wearing dust masks, hearing protectors, and safety glasses. As Matthew drilled, Rick was often at his side, whispering instructions to him mentally, rather than through his ears, urging him to feel the rock and stone as he worked.

"Relax your mind. Focus on the tip of the drill. See it moving against the rock. Sense the rock, see how it is now hard, but there is a soft layer just an inch below. Imagine yourself as the drill bit. Look around, see the stone you are passing," Rick said as Matthew drilled.

After days of trying hard to follow Rick's detailed advice, Matthew began to be able to run his hands over bare rock, and somehow feel beneath the surface. He didn't call it dowsing, but he was beginning to develop some of Rick's skill. While Rick could see down hundreds of feet, Matthew could only sense an inch or two into the rock, but he realized that his accuracy was getting better, and that it was pleasant to feel the rock, to feel himself inside it, to live inside the earth just a little bit. As they worked, this daily practice became more and more useful.

The first part of the steel that they installed consisted of thirty-eight vertical columns, running from the base of the machine shop floor up through holes in the ceiling to the box-room ceiling, a total of nineteen feet above. This was the easiest part of the overall project and it immediately added substantial reinforcement to the structure under the house. Matt made a perfectly straight line across the box-room floor with his spinning laser, mounted sideways. The line was twenty-five feet from the ocean-side wall and parallel to it. Then he located the holes, twenty-two inches apart, and marked the location of each with orange surveyor's paint. He and Julian drilled holes through the box-room floor with a big heavy core drill which made six-inch diameter holes. The drill bit was a long hollow cylinder with diamond dust around the bottom edge. Water was forced into the holes during drilling, to keep the cutting edge cool and to clear away chips. The holes were exactly vertical, straight down through the floor. After each hole was drilled its core fell through with a crash into the machine shop below. Then a plumb-bob was lowered through the hole: it marked the spot on the machine shop floor where a sixteen-inch square baseplate would be installed. Each plate was recessed several inches into the floor, which meant a few hours with a small jack-hammer chipping away brick and the rock below it to make a pocket in the floor. Each steel column consisted of three eighty-pound pieces which interlocked with brackets that the steel fabricator had attached. At the top of each column was a two inch diameter screw which allowed Matt to tighten the columns, wedging them solidly in place to support the house. He and Julian used a pair of wrenches with three-foot long handles to tighten the big screws: they could almost feel the house lift slightly as they made their final push. Matt felt a strong sense of accomplishment as he saw the columns march across the floor: although they had been easy to install, they were real, strong, and clear evidence that the house would not fall into the sea.

Installing the diagonal steel, which would actually support the outer wall was not as easy to do. The diagonals went from the baseplates they had installed up through the box-room floor, to the outer edge of the box-room ceiling, just inside the wall. The main difficulty was accurately drilling big holes through the box-room floor at exactly the right angle, fifty-nine degrees. Each hole had to be at the correct angle, and in the correct spot or the steel diagonals would not hit the box-room ceiling at the correct location. Although six-inch holes would work, on paper, Matt realized that they could never cut the holes perfectly. The floor where the diagonals penetrated was uneven, sloping slightly, and cracked: they would never be able to hold the drill at a perfect angle for every hole. To allow for errors, they used an eight-inch core drill, which was slower and heavier, but it gave them room for adjustment when the steel was installed.

Once the diagonal holes were made, each diagonal beam, consisting of four one-hundred-pound pieces of 4x4 wide flange I-beam, was installed, accompanied by much swearing and heavy-lifting. Installing the first diagonal through its hole took more than a day, but they gradually learned tricks to temporarily brace the heavy pieces and make their work easier. Drilling and positioning the diagonal was only part of the task. After each was in place, a six-inch hole had to be drilled through the outer wall right next to the top of the diagonal. This involved mounting the six-inch core drill on a temporary scaffold up against the box-room ceiling, then pushing it hard into the wall as it slowly ground its way to the outside air with cooling water and muck running everywhere. Another hundred-pound I-beam went into each of these wall holes: it was then welded to the top of the diagonal, so as to support the wall itself.

As each of the holes in the wall and floor were drilled and filled with steel, it was packed with cement grout to join the steel to the masonry: another messy task for Julian and Matt.

The third major project was attaching three heavy five-eighths-inch-thick wire ropes to the top of each diagonal. Each rope ran from the diagonal to the inner wall of the box-room, where it was attached to a large anchor bolt drilled deep into the raw stone. These fifty-foot-long ropes were relatively easy to install, once the anchors were placed in the wall with drilling, water, muck, and grout. The difficulty was tightening each rope with a large turnbuckle in such a way that all the ropes carried the same load. Almost every day part of the soft rock under the house fell away, slightly changing the loading on the installed steel and necessitating adjustment of most of the ropes.

In early October, there was a particularly beautiful sunset as a storm cleared. Matthew went up to the roof-top platform and looked out over the sea with Floris at his side. As they scanned the countryside and enjoyed the spectacular view, Floris commented softly, "You haven't been looking at yourself, but I have. You're changing, growing from a boy into a man, from an insecure child into a self-confident adult. You're succeeding in the grown-up world, and all your friends can see it and are welcoming the transition."

"You're exaggerating, but you're right about some things. I had an email from my old girlfriend at school, telling about an academic award she had won, and somehow it just seemed so distant, so unimportant. Although I've only been away from school a few months, it seems like years ago that I worried about grades and homework. Life in the outer world is so different, so much more challenging."

"And look at your foot. You don't watch yourself walking, but I do, and your limp is much less pronounced. You still favor the other foot, perhaps from habit, but that is changing too," Floris continued.

"Floris, am I becoming a ghost? Take my foot for instance, that isn't normal, and I can really feel inside rocks and machines and walls. Normal people don't do that kind of thing."

"Some of them do. Marti could do that, perhaps even better than you, but she practiced much longer. Don't worry about it now, you have a wonderful life ahead. Look around the country. Through Rick's old treasure you are probably the richest living person in all directions, and maybe the smartest, and I know you will have the nicest house eventually. The time is coming for you to take your place in the world, to help others instead of worrying about your own problems. We all have much to look forward to."

"I wish I could share it with Azur, I miss her so much, even though I know she is far from perfect. She has taken my heart and I cannot get it back. I can't let go of her memory. I almost cry when I think of her. It's not logical, but it's true."

"When you think of her, envision her return, how it will be. Imagine that she is here with you. Your psychic energy is not very strong, but perhaps by sending it often toward her, you will slowly gain her attention and pull her to us."

"I know you and I like her, but Rick is so negative. What if she did return, I mean, he might kill her."

"Let me worry about that. I never should have gone off and left you and Rick alone with her, you two don't have a clue about girls."

They watched the slowly setting sun in silence, each with thoughts of the future. Matthew knew that he was supposed to be off the property a week from today, but had no intention of moving an inch.

Every day, things stopped at noon, when Julian's cook and chauffeur arrived with a carload of goodies for the entire crew, enough for breakfast, lunch and dinner in one glorious pile. Today they had quite a surprise. The Range Rover contained Etienette as well as the food.

"Etienette, what a lovely surprise. When did you return," Julian asked.

"Just as soon as I read your letter."

"Look at all the progress we're making: Julian's a wonderful help. We do everything together. He's becoming younger and I'm becoming older," Matthew said.

"You're all such a mess, but so healthy and happy and strong, just bursting with energy. It reminds me of a dig I went on last year," she said.

"Why don't you come work here. We can use all the help we can get, and I miss your happy face and Jeane's sarcastic French comments," Matthew said.

"I spend all my time here. We have so much to do, and the

bottom is falling away a bit more every day," Julian said.

"You can have your choice among twenty or thirty bedrooms, but plumbing is a bit of a problem," Matthew joked.

"Before I arrived, I had so many questions, but I can see that they are not important now. Yes, I will join your project, but I think I will go home to my nice bathtub in the evening, and take Julian with me. You must share him now that I am back."

Later, after the extra workers had left, they were sitting on the terrace watching the sunset over the ocean.

"Tell me about Azur. Your letter from France, to Julian, made it sound like she isn't doing well. Was she sick?" Matthew asked Etienette.

"She sees you on television, walking with the architect, and all of you working furiously to save the house. Then she cries, and wishes she were here helping, with her father and with you. She records the television whenever she sees news about you and the house, then plays it over and over. I don't understand her. When I ask why she is wasting her time in school when there is a life and death struggle here, she just cries and stares off into the distance. And her clothes! She is wearing dreadful, old dark colors that match her mood perfectly. She has aged from inside and I warn her that no one will look at her unless she starts smiling and dressing like the attractive young woman I know she can be."

"Have you seen her friend Dexter? Is he all right," Matthew asked.

"Azur mentioned something about him. He was in a psychiatric hospital for awhile. Maybe a nervous breakdown or I don't know what. Why do you ask?"

"Oh, just curiosity. I met him a few times and he gave me a good tip about contacting an architectural library. When you next write to Azur or see her, please give her my warmest regards. I wish she were here, and in bright happy clothes. She never writes to me, but I would love to hear from her."

"I will write tonight. Now, whatever happened to that nice friend of yours, Rick," Etienette asked.

"The three of us have formed a boy's club, with absolutely no secrets among us. We all need help defending ourselves against women," Julian laughed.

"Yes, Etienette, much has happened since you and Azur left us to cry alone," Rick's invisible voice said, startling Etienette greatly.

Chapter 17
Much Planning Trouble

When Matthew awoke a few days later, on October 10th, the date of the sixty-day Power Plant Deadline, he was startled to see a police car by his front gate, and wide yellow tape blocking the entrance. Etienette discovered the blockage when she drove Julian over for the day's work. She talked out her window to the policeman.

"What's the meaning of this: what are you doing in front of this house," Etienette said.

"This place is sealed until the courts decide about the power plant," the policeman said.

"Young man, if you don't get out of the way immediately, I will drive this car over your body," she said.

"You can't do that. Who do you think you are!"

"I'm the French revolution, and you're about to get the guillotine if you don't move smartly!"

Etienette gunned the engine, honked and started forward through the yellow tape. The policeman moved just in time to avoid the car, as it drove to the house, dropped Julian off, then left. Fortunately, Etienette's imperious manner, coupled with the imposing Bently which she was driving, prevented her arrest this time. As she drove away, the policemen blocked the gate with their car, stopping any repetition of her stunt.

The power plant bureaucrats were furious. They had staked their reputations on their design for a large new plant which would re-invigorate the local economy, or so they thought. Julian's lawyers had been battling them on legal issues, while Matthew's TV appearances were slowly rousing public opinion against the plant. The bureaucrats wanted to know what had happened to their survey truck, but most of all, they wanted Matthew to immediately cease work on the house and vacate the premises. Their first attack, the police barricade, now made it impossible for the workmen and food deliveries to enter.

Matthew called the Antiquities Board, and explained to them that his beautiful, and historically significant, house was about to be trashed by stupid bureaucrats. He invited them to come immediately with a TV crew before it was too late. He enticed them with a vague description of the library and the old rooms of the house, and explained that he was trying to restore everything properly, for the benefit of the public. He invited them, and a cameraman, to come by helicopter, at his expense, so as to avoid problems with the local police who were interfering with the driveway. Matthew asked the historians if they had read "NO VOICE FROM THE HALL", in hopes that it would resonate with his story of greedy short-sighted bureaucrats.

The helicopter landed in the early afternoon, with two historians, a TV cameraman, and a box of food that Julian had requested. Outside the gates, the police were furious.

"Welcome, let me give you a quick tour from top to bottom, then you and your cameraman can wander wherever you want while I get back to work on the foundations," Matthew said to the arrivals.

"We couldn't bring John Harris, the author of 'No Voice', but your point was well-taken. His stories of beautiful houses being trashed by fools from the government is certainly appropriate here," a historian said.

"Let's start on the roof. I'm sure that you have heard stories about ghosts and that perhaps this place is haunted. Let me set you straight on those issues," Matthew said.

They went up through the servants rooms to the roof platform. The historians and cameraman couldn't wait to begin filming their story. Already they had seen enough to cover an hour long TV program.

On the roof platform, Matthew said, "look at the lines cut into the stone we're standing on. The lines show the Ley lines that meet here. That one runs straight all the way to Stonehenge, and that one runs perfectly straight to Glastonbury. This very spot is one of the most exciting confluences of spirit energy in the whole country.

Psychics love to come here and experience the earth energy. Now, I don't expect you to believe in all that, but some people do believe, and that is why this is a key site to them. Much like parliament is to government people, or the British Museum to historians. When outsiders, like police, bureaucrats and detectorists try to interfere with this place, the spirits become upset. That is the source of the haunted house rumors. The spirits won't bother you, or people who respect the site."

The cameraman was looking in all directions, and exclaimed, "this view is fantastic, can I get back up here for the sunset?"

"It's all yours and you can stay for sunrise if you want. Now, let's go down quickly," Matthew replied.

Matthew showed them some of the servants' rooms, then the ancient bedrooms, and finally they went down to the long gallery, with its partially-restored beautiful floor and columns.

"I can't wait to redo the rest of the windows. The view from the balcony is magnificent, and these floors and columns will be beautiful with a little spit and polish: we'll have people dancing the night away by next summer if we're lucky. But see that crack in the floor. That comes from the foundation collapse many feet below. Lets go down to the kitchens: there are so many rooms down there, and so much stuff from the past. You probably know much more about it than I do," Matthew said.

They walked past seemingly endless little rooms with wash tubs, ancient heaters and rusty appliances and a giant kitchen, then to a very well-traveled stairway, with electric construction lighting amidst the wires and hoses.

"Now let's go down to the most interesting parts," Matthew said.

They went down into the library. Matthew pointed out things along the way, "Look at all these books and old things. I haven't touched one percent of them, since I've been so busy with the foundation work. Here's a drawing of the structure and what we are doing. See all this bit here (points on drawing) is crumbling away, so we are putting in diagonal and vertical steel to hold the house in position. I wish we could save it all, but at least we'll preserve this room and above. Look out the window here, down below. There's a lovely island with the ruins of an old castle in the little bay. Some day we'll have the path rebuilt and visitors could go down there."

Matthew opened the secret passageway by the fireplace, to the amazement of the men.

"Please don't photograph the entrances to the hidden passages. You never know when their secrecy might be useful," Matthew requested.

They went down to the box rooms, where Julian was welding steel braces into position.

"Julian, these men are from the Antiquities Board, and I'm just giving them a quick tour," Matthew said.

Julian stopped work and removed his face mask. "Why Julian, I didn't recognize you with your welding helmet. Do you remember me? We met at a banquet, after your wife sponsored a restoration project last year. How exciting to see you saving this beautiful old house. (to cameraman) This is Sir Julian Lowther, a prominent supporter of historic restorations. You must get footage of him working with his own hands to save this house. I can't believe our luck," the historian exclaimed.

"Let's go down to the trouble zone. Be careful. We've made steel steps to replace the stone that's fallen away," Matthew said.

They went down to the bottom level. A large hole had opened in the wall. Billowing noisy plastic sheets covered it to keep most of the wind and spray outside. Bright red steel beams ran from the floor up through the ceiling. Tools, air hoses, rubble, and steel were lying everywhere.

"The floor on the ocean side is falling away, a bit more every day. We're trying to install thirty-eight diagonal and vertical braces to take the strain. As you can see we have six diagonals installed so far, but we've got the technique down, and are working as fast as we can, given the few hands we have to do the work," Matthew explained.

"Will you finish in time? The winter storms can be ferocious in winter on this coast, and you have a very exposed position," a historian asked.

"We were going faster when we had outside help, but the police have blocked the gate. Julian and I work twelve hours a day, every day. We're giving it our best shot, starting with the weakest point and moving outwards," Matthew said.

"There is so much to see here: what a beautiful house," the historian said.

"Stay as long as you like. Crash in an empty bedroom if you want to stay the night. We sleep in the east wing, as it has a semi-modern kitchen and plumbing. You can go out onto the Library balcony through the east window, but be careful. Don't go near the middle. Julian and I are anxious to get our story onto TV and to block those power plant creeps, by using the court of public opinion," Matthew said.

"Yes, you might win in a court of law, but by the time the solicitors were through, your house would have fallen into the sea. We'll do our best to show the promise and prospects of this old house. Maybe we will start the film with some old footage of houses and stories from "NO VOICE FROM THE HALL". Get people interested in saving this place before it disappears. And I'm sure the BBC will run short bits as interesting news items," the cameraman said.

"One last question, who designed all this steel support. I want to talk to the engineering firm and get supporting data," the historian asked.

"Sorry, wasn't time for all that, so I did it myself. After we get it stabilized, I'll hire a firm of restoration architects and do the upper floors properly, and clean-up the holes down here. Right now we're fighting for our lives, so I'd better get back on the drill and keep making holes so that Julian can fill them with steel," Matthew said.

Matthew, Rick, Floris and Julian had found that by working efficiently together, with no interruptions or problems, that they could drill the rock, assemble, and weld a complete diagonal and install its wire ropes in a bit over two days. At this rate, a straight seventy-five day effort would complete the thirty-two remaining supports, ending just before Christmas Day. They focused on that goal to the exclusion of everything else. Every few days a helicopter arrived with food and additional supplies. Otherwise, they ignored the gate, the policemen, the calendar, and the weather. Shaving had stopped.

Floris moved all the weight that she could carry, materializing for each visit of the helicopter. Whenever she wasn't helping with the work, she patrolled the grounds looking for trouble, and giving it a bad scare if it arrived. Floris was a very busy one-woman haunted house, driving curious reporters and photographers away. To Floris, this was a life-or-death struggle, for she understood the spiritual situation well. The living people could walk away, and Rick could find a new site, but she had to remain near this spirit well or fade into nothingness. This was her final stand and she gave it a 110% effort.

Etienette, living at her own home, wanted to run to Azur's side to try to help her, but Etienette realized that her effort as the "support team" was essential. She could not leave Julian, Matthew, Floris and Rick without a solid outside backup. Several times a day she pestered the lawyers and solicitors about the situation. When she wasn't busy with that, she called every friend in high places that she could contact. She called TV stations, gave interviews, wrote letters to newspapers, and worked tirelessly to squelch the power plant. Fighting the government was like punching cotton candy. It offered little resistance, but it made your hands dirty, and never seemed to shrink or go away.

Once a day, Etienette called Azur and told her about recent events, but the end result was always the same. Azur would not come home. Slowly Etienette began to suspect that there was something that Azur feared about coming back. Some reason that she felt that she could never come home. However Etienette also noticed that Azur always asked for news of Matthew. A promising sign in a sea of gloom.

Halloween and Guy Fawkes Day passed with no bonfires or costumes as the autumn rains fell and the weather turned cold and blustery. Most of the leaves had fallen leaving gray tree trunks against a gray sky. On a chilly mid-November day, Matthew was startled to hear Azur's voice when his cell-phone rang. "I just saw your film with the Antiquities Board. It was wonderful, and the house looked beautiful," she said.

"Thank you. I wish you were here to share it with me. We have twenty of the thirty-eight supports installed, but the house is slipping quickly. The loading on the steel is so uneven, I worry about it all the time. If only the house would stop moving, it would be so much easier to do our work . . . I care so much for you."

"I can never come back. Once or twice a day, I inadvertently think of Rick, and my muscles tense so hard that I double over in pain at the thought of him. Mother made me visit physicians but it was a waste of time."

"It's wonderful hearing your voice again but I do need to get back to work. By the way, I think your father has become my best friend: he treats me like an equal instead of like a child."

"I am glad that you are growing up so quickly. In the video, I saw you walking. You were not limping as much as before."

"Rick and I work on my foot every day, but it is far from perfect. Now I really must go."

"Good bye. It was very nice talking with you."

Later, Matthew told Floris about the call, choosing a moment when he knew Rick and Julian were far away. Floris smiled and replied that perhaps some of his thoughts of Azur were reaching her and having a good effect.

Less than a week later, a convoy of bulldozers and heavy construction equipment arrived at night outside Redcliffs Hall. Their mission was to clear the land in preparation for the construction of the power plant. They would demolish the house and push all the rubble into the sea. In the process they would remove extraneous gardens, trees and other obstacles. Soon the site would be flat and ready for the new power plant's construction. The court of public opinion was not proving effective at saving the house.

Floris was on guard and saw them arrive. She went into the cab of the first truck, a huge flat-bed carrying a Caterpillar D-9 bulldozer. The driver was startled as his door opened. He was more startled when he was yanked to the ground by invisible hands, then stomped by her shoes as she screamed curses. As soon as he could struggle to his feet, he ran in fright. Floris had a vague idea how to drive such a rig, and climbed up to the driver's seat. The engine was running, the gearshift was clearly labeled. She found the clutch, put it in gear, and slowly drove down the road, taking up the full width. Another big truck was headed straight at her. As the crash neared, she opened the door, shoving the hand throttle to full speed ahead as she jumped.

What a collision! She ran to the two huge mangled vehicles, found the fuel tank on one, and set it on fire, giving a blast of ghostly screams at the driver from the other truck as he staggered away. Floris ran back to the gate, opened the door of another truck, then drove it down the road toward the burning wreckage, smashing it into the mess, then setting it on fire. As workmen arrived to put out the fires, Floris took a CO-2 fire extinguisher and squirted it at the men's faces, making them run away in fear.

Rick sensed the problems and rushed to her side, proud of the damage that she had already caused. Together they trashed the entire convoy, vehicle by vehicle, making a huge bonfire with the expensive equipment, puncturing and lighting every fuel tank. Otherwise undamaged vehicles joined the survey truck at the bottom of the cliff.

Fear spread through the workers and they refused to touch the haunted equipment. Most left the area after giving frightened interviews. Millions of dollars in equipment had been wrecked in a single night. (Rick and Floris were pooped!). One TV camera had captured clear footage of a huge Caterpillar D-9 running toward the cliff with no driver. The last thing on the film was a shot of the underside of the machine as it disappeared over the edge. (Rick had jumped clear, but was sad to see such a wonderful machine put to death.)

TV commentators, referring to the Antiquities Board film, said that clearly the spirits were angry, just like Matthew had said. Nobody had expected that the spirits could cause this much trouble however.

Etienette called Matthew to report on a call she had just had from her sister Marie about Azur. "Marie had been with Azur as she watched the news coverage of the construction equipment fire. She laughed for the first time in ages. She said that she clearly could see the part that Rick and Floris were playing, and knew that if anything, both were growing stronger every day. Marie said that Azur smiled one of her rare and beautiful smiles as she watched the triumph of the spirit world over the bureaucrats. But then she doubled over in terrible pain. It passed as she gained control of herself, but Marie could do little but hug her and cry. Azur sits sometimes for it seems hours, and watches the Antiquities Board film over and over again. She cries each time that the film wanders about the house describing the various rooms, and then the little island with the ruined castle. She plays the ending, with Julian and you working away furiously in the basements, welding, drilling, and hammering as the waves crash outside, over and over. When asked how she feels about you, she said only that she could feel that you are growing very strong, spiritually as well as physically. She bitterly regrets her mistakes, caused I think by too much pride. She is a sad young woman."

To everyone's surprise, the next morning a few members of the Power Plant Siting Commission arrived at Redcliffs Hall, accompanied by spiritual experts from Glastonbury, who proposed to clear the site of its evil influences. Floris was on duty, and looked with contempt at the group of weirdoes wandering down her driveway, scattering garlic and incense. Smelly creeps with long hair, beads, and robes. They had no more spiritual knowledge than Marti's cat, probably less.

Floris approached one of the beaded experts, a woman, and goosed her. Quite a surprise as she grabbed her rear end, then her front side. Floris kicked a spiritual expert in the rear end, then tripped another as he ran to help her. Floris snatched the beads from one and tied it in a knot, almost strangling the unfortunate soul. Child's play for Floris. How to make them go away for good?

Floris found that one of them had a knife, which Floris snatched away. She pressed it to a commission member's throat, and said, "If you ever touch one blade of grass on this land, I'll cut your body to pieces bit by bit while you sleep, then feed it to the hounds of hell. You're going to die a horrible and painful death soon, today may be your last day on earth." Then Floris jabbed the knife lightly into the lady's fat rear end, where it wouldn't do much damage and stepped back to watch them run. Floris didn't know whether to laugh or to cry at their antics.

That afternoon, the petrified bureaucrat resigned her position on the Commission and went abroad for an extended absence. When she heard the news, Floris sensed victory and eagerly awaited the next visitor: one down, eleven to go.

Not everything was going badly. There was much excitement

at Christie's in London. The publicity about Redcliffs Hall had raised interest in the house and in the coming sale of old photographs. Matthew had invited their photo expert to assemble a collection of the 100 most interesting of Rick's old negatives then make one computer-processed duplicate 4x5 negative of each of the hundred. Already experts were offering close to two hundred thousand pounds for this set of duplicates, even though Matthew retained the originals. The catalog was beautiful. It showed pieces of some of the negatives, and commented on their rarity, the artistic value, and most of all, on the unusual vantage points of the unknown photographer. Although the catalog didn't flatly state that the pictures had been taken by a spirit, it implied that some of the pictures were so unusual, that they could only have been taken by something from the spirit world.

Chapter 18
Curses! Jail!

In London the people in charge of the power plant were furious. The commission now consisted of eleven people, all prominent bureaucrats, Sir this and Lady that. They were accustomed to giving orders and seeing them obeyed. How could obscure spirits near a remote coastal village cause so much trouble. The site was perfect for the new power plant, and the plant would be a great blessing to the whole country. It would boost the economy and bring jobs and prosperity to the region. It had never occurred to these fools that the people concerned hadn't requested the plant, didn't need it, and didn't want it.

The eleven voted to get tough with the spirits and stop being nice. Their first step was to order the arrest of Etienette and the helicopter pilot. These two were blatantly violating the law almost every day.

Etienette was not easy to arrest. Her solicitors blocked the move, leading to a compromise where she would remain under voluntary house arrest at The Chateau. However the helicopter flights stopped, and the pilot would be arrested if he tried another flight.

Matthew had another way of resisting the Commission. He, Rick, and Floris went to the front gate. He had called a TV crew with news of an important announcement. On a dark cold rainy night, he talked to the TV camera through the closed iron bars. Matthew held a wet piece of paper in his hand.

"I hold a list with the names and home addresses of each of the remaining eleven members of the Plant Commission, all of which I found on the internet. I won't bore you by reading this trash. Each of these people is about to learn first hand of the misery his or her selfish actions is causing."

A blue glow appeared on each side of Matthew. The glows

wavered and shimmered in the fog and misty rain. They almost appeared to be smoking and looked wonderfully scary on TV. Rick and Floris growled and laughed as Matthew continued.

"The spirits are fed-up with these eleven people. These people deserve a bit of pain, a chance to feel physically what it's like to annoy the spirits. One by one they are going to fear the dark. They will fear going to bed. They will be afraid to turn out the lights at night. And for good reason, because the spirits will make their nights horrible. Scrooge was visited by only three ghosts, and those were friendly, like Jacob Marley. These eleven people are going to meet unfriendly ghosts, spirits who are coming to punish, not to enlighten."

Rick and Floris gave their best "growls and howls". The camera man jumped in fright.

"Who will be first to feel the pain? Then who will be next? Will they be burned, or torn to bits, or stabbed, or just die of fright? There's a heavy curse on eleven heads tonight, and on anyone who tries to replace them or carry out their orders," Matthew concluded.

Matthew turned and slowly walked up the driveway as Rick and Floris faded to invisibility. The astonished TV people in London didn't waste a minute scurrying about to find the eleven and interview them. Those of the eleven who hadn't seen the broadcast were treated to instant replay, with every threatening detail, as well as endless commentary from spiritual experts which the media brought to the fore.

Two of the eleven resigned their positions that night and left the country for extended vacations. One of the others was not afraid and didn't believe that anything would happen, and said so publicly. All the others were scared stiff and demanded police protection.

The next day, Julian, Matthew, and Floris continued the construction work, aware that without helicopter flights of food and supplies, they would soon be in trouble. Invisible Rick took the afternoon train to London, armed with the list and maps, but without definite plans. After watching televised interviews with the cursed, he had a strong interest in attacking one person in particular. A man who said that spirits didn't exist, and that they were just figments of the imagination. Rick thought that this person would make a lovely target.

He found the man's posh house on a quiet street in Saint John's Wood, just a few stops on the Bakerloo Line north of Paddington Station. How convenient for Rick, who had just arrived by rail. He rang the doorbell, and a policeman answered, and seeing no one about, closed it. Rick rang again. The policeman returned, quite annoyed. The policeman stepped out for a good look around, while Rick entered and slammed the door shut, locking it.

Inside, Rick wandered around looking to see what opportunities for mischief might be present. He found the man taking a shower. This was too good to resist. Rick reached in and turned the faucet to full hot. The man swore and reached for the faucet, but Rick grabbed his hand and maintained the flow of hot water, as the man screamed in pain.

Rick yelled at him, "Stop screaming, the heat is just a figment of your imagination, like the spirit world."

Then Rick turned out the bathroom lights and gave a ghostly howl. When the man tried to turn on the lights, Rick grabbed his hand, then spun him around and stuffed his head in the toilet, and flushed it. He wasn't trying to drown the man, just give him something to think about.

Rick pulled his head from the toilet and yelled in his ear, "Leave my country tonight if you want to see the sunrise tomorrow."

Rick opened the door, so that the startled policeman, who was coming up the stairs, could minister to the victim. As Rick walked away, he turned out the lights in most of the house.

Rick thought that this had been much too easy, and wondered how he could extend the effect. Perhaps a fire would be good for publicity? While the men stumbled about upstairs, Rick went into the basement where he found a lawnmower and a can of gasoline. After spreading the gasoline around the living room furniture and drapes, Rick moved to the front door and opened it, then tossed a match. Rick had set enough fires to be careful to duck as a fireball engulfed the living room.

He loved the excitement as the fire brigade, police, and TV people arrived. What a good night's work. One down and eight to go. Rick suspected that there would be a few more resignations in the morning, as the excited TV people speculated on "who would be next".

Etienette watched the television with fascination. It occurred to her that her comfortable house arrest might end soon if people became mad. She and Jeane put on dark makeup and old clothes, then slipped away into the night. By morning they were in France at her sister Marie's house, making endless telephone calls to television and bureaucratic people. She had no fear of arrest in France and gave interviews and generated as much publicity as possible. Her message was simple, "Cancel the power plant so that the spirits can go back to sleep".

In London, Rick watched television and considered how he could have the best effect with the least effort. It was time to strike again then get back to the steel work at home. Hopefully one more good scare would finish the job. Last night's victim was in Germany, judging by a TV interview he had just given, and there were two fresh resignations today. Down to six targets, each with heavy police protection.

From curiosity as much as anything else, he went to the government building where they held their meetings. An old gray building in Whitehall with a guard at the entrance. Entering the building and finding their offices was not hard though he had to fool several guards and ride two elevators. Rick wished more than once that he could read better.

It was the middle of the afternoon when Rick arrived, and the six were busily preparing the text of a TV interview they were about to give. Rick could tell that they were continuing their hard line in spite of his work. There were three men and three women left. Various assistants scurried about with much deference and formality. It would be easy to poison the whole lot or kill them outright, but that would be a bit harsh at this stage of the game.

Rick was fascinated to watch them cooperatively enter the text of their statement into a computer. Each person had a keyboard and was helping edit simultaneously. Rick could read and write a little, and he was fascinated by computers. He had already started learning so that he could use Azur's photo processing software.

Rick realized, by pressing a few keys on someone's keyboard, that he could enter gibberish and cause a fair amount of confusion. And it was fun to pretend that he knew what he was doing. He started to help each of the six to edit, and soon the screams and shouts from one to another, as each blamed the others for the mess on their screens were fun to observe. This went on for several minutes until the document was completely trashed. Rick loved the delete key and held it down as long as he could, on each of the keyboards. The six swore at the computer and at each other, with no idea of what was actually happening.

Rick followed the wires from their workstations to a single computer in a deserted back room. This machine held all their documents. What a find. He could sense the innards of the computer and saw the magnetic discs spinning as the heads moved back and forth reading and writing. This was the only moving part inside the computer, so naturally it fascinated Rick. Rick, with no knowledge of electronics, correctly deduced that this piece of machinery must be the heart of the box. He found a screwdriver and opened the computer. No problem at all. Without bothering to unplug the computer, he undid the screws retaining the hard drive, unplugged its cables, and threw it through the nearest window, which happened to be closed. The people ran about after hearing the window break: they didn't know what had happened, but knew something was seriously wrong as their screens went dead.

Rick wanted them to know that spirits were here, so he gave his best bone-chilling laugh. As several ran to the phones to call for help, he trashed each phone in turn, ripping its wires from the wall. He blocked the door so that they couldn't get out. When one tried her cell phone, he threw it against the wall with such force that it shattered. Then he started to remove their clothes, jumping from one person to the next. Neckties were wonderful. He could tighten them easily, nearly strangling the owner: belts came off, zippers opened. Six against one. Good odds for Rick. The best approach was to push them into each other, so that much of the pain was self inflicted by the victims.

Rick knew it was time to go home, so he threw a few keyboards around the room, poured tea and coffee over the desks.

and tossed anything that he could lift at the petrified six. Their big conference table was heavy, but not impossible to move. He shoved it across the room, pinning five of the six against the wall. Then he turned out the lights, gave another good scream and left the room. Other people had heard the screams and a TV crew was rushing to the room. Rick assisted the crew, by tripping them. He noticed that one of the cameras seemed to be live, with a blinking red light on the front. Rick grabbed it and ran into a bathroom, sending shots of a lady on a toilet to the surprised viewers. He zoomed in on her frightened face, then flushed the toilet and headed for the door. He tossed the camera through a window: who knows what sort of picture it transmitted back to the station. Rick headed for the train.

Rick was well-pleased with his work and headed home in a first class compartment. When he arrived at Redcliffs Hall the next morning he was shocked to find that Matthew had been arrested and placed in a maximum security prison whose location was not disclosed. He had been taken by surprise while he slept, and Floris had not been able to save him in time. Fortunately, Julian had been working below, with the secret doorway closed.

The government announced that the spirit attacks were over: they had arrested the person behind them. Rick and Floris were furious but didn't know what to do.

Julian suggested that they do something to the Prime Minister at 10 Downing Street if they wanted to publicize the fact that they were very much alive and active. While they did that he, Julian, would carry on the work alone, as best as he could. He had twenty-four of the thirty-eight supports installed, and wanted to at least paint and preserve them before going further. Rick and Floris took train to London, and promised to return in a day or two.

Although the Prime Minister had many guards he was a public person, making numerous speeches and attending many meetings and impromptu gatherings. It was quite easy to locate him the next morning, especially since Floris could read and understand the newspapers and announcements.

They wanted to remind him that the spirits were still very active, and to embarrass him in some way. After a bit of work, they found him giving a hasty TV interview in front of his house. Rick was prepared. While Floris grabbed the PM's hands, Rick opened a bag of soft fresh dog poop and smeared it over the PM's hair on live television. As he did this, Rick shouted, "You're full of shit". Cameras flashed with close-ups of the PM's face. Then Rick yanked the PM's tie, knocking him to the ground. Floris kicked the nearest guard, and shoved another into the TV camera.

Rick ended the escapade by shouting into the nearest microphone. "We could have easily killed you. This is the last warning. Cancel that power plant and leave us alone."

Rick and Floris jumped out of the way as guards and police scurried about.

Back at Redcliffs Hall, Julian was very busy. Just by looking at the sky, he could tell that the weather was becoming worse, and then by listening to the radio, he found that a major storm was due in a day. Time to work as fast as possible before bad weather attacked the remaining foundations.

He was down at the bottom, painting a piece of freshly-welded steel with marine protective paint, when the floor on which he was standing collapsed. Julian just managed to grab the edge of the rock as his feet fell out from under him. Very slowly he crawled back up as stone rumbled over his body. When he regained the floor, he lay face-down breathing heavily, glad to be alive.

He slowly stood up, then fell in pain. Something was wrong, and he was completely alone. It appeared that the fall had damaged one leg, and blood was coming from his head. He could crawl slowly, but not easily. Damn, what a fool he had been for working without a safety harness and hard hat, especially when all alone.

Julian slowly worked his way up the first set of stairs, to the box rooms. Here was a first aid kit and a mirror. He bandaged his head and stopped the bleeding, but he was still on the floor, unable to walk, but he could crawl. He continued up the stairs, through the library, through the kitchens, and out the service entrance and onto the grass. Julian was operating purely on adrenaline, crawling down the long drive toward the policemen guarding the gate.

He didn't remember how he made it down the drive when he awoke in the local hospital. Although his will to live was strong, he had multiple broken bones, a concussion, and severe loss of blood.

A friendly and compassionate TV crew interviewed him, with much commentary about this famous friend of the arts who had almost given his life to save a beautiful old building. Julian was then quickly helicoptered to a hospital with better facilities.

Chapter 19
Royal Preserve

Rick and Floris wandered over to Buckingham Palace to see if the Royal Flag was flying. If so, perhaps they might pay a quick visit to the Queen before going home. When they saw the flag, they looked for a way to get inside.

They watched a side entrance where cars were driving through, then walked in, beside a car, past various guards and metal detectors. Now that they were inside, how to find the Queen in the maze of buildings and rooms? They wandered about listening to conversations and looking for concentrations of guards and important-looking people. Finally they deduced that she was behind a door at the end of a long hall whose walls were covered with portraits, but the door was closed, and watched by armed guards.

Floris started working the light switches. The Guards were startled, and ran to the switches and turned them back on, but she turned them off again. Soon both guards were guarding the light switches and calling for an electrician. Rick opened the door and they walked into a beautiful blue room, where the Queen was at her desk.

The Queen saw the door open and close but no people entered. Her dogs ran to the ghosts and start sniffing and wagging their tails. The Queen was mystified, "Hello, is someone there?"

Prince Philip was seated, reading nearby.

"Please don't be alarmed, we're a couple of friendly ghosts who need help: this is really important to us," Floris said.

The Queen blinked and removed her glasses in alarm, but Rick said, "Please don't worry, everyone greets us with a bit of apprehension, but we're really quite normal. Here, we'll make ourselves slightly visible so you can see that we're OK. We're just here for a brief visit."

"We would never dream of treating you like those silly bureaucrats," Floris added.

"Is this some kind of trick or magic act," the Queen asked.

"I used to be a magician, Floris the Magnificent. Maybe you saw me when I played this very palace one night for your parents in the late thirties. I was killed in the war when a bomb hit near our home," Floris replied.

"I remember, you did amazing escapes. I was only ten, but I wanted so much to see your show."

"I think I need a cup of tea: this is difficult to believe," the Prince said.

"Tea would be great. We've had a long journey, first the train, then the tube, then reminding the PM that we aren't in jail, then fooling your guards outside," Floris added.

"Don't you just fly places and pass through walls and all that," Philip asked.

"Oh no, we move just like you do, but we're usually invisible. We do like a good cup of tea however," Rick said.

"Send in tea for four please," the Queen said into her telephone.

"If you don't mind, we'll go back to being invisible, as it's much easier for us, and probably better for your staff," Rick said.

"But the dogs can sense your presence. They give your position away. See how they follow you around even though you are invisible to us," Philip said.

"We could catch you by using the dogs, and stop all this foolishness," the Queen said.

"But I can sense that your foot is not pressing the red button on the floor yet, so perhaps you will hear us out," Rick said.

"I love animals. I wouldn't want Rick to kill your dogs just because you tried to catch us," Floris added.

"You're the ghosts from a house called Redcliffs Hall, aren't you? We've been following the story on television," Philip said.

"Yes, the stupid bureaucrats are trying to take over our house and turn it into a power plant. We own it free and clear and yet they've sealed it off and are being a real pain. Now they've arrested our grandson, Matthew, who's a living person like yourselves.

Imagine how you'd feel if some fools arrested one of your children, then tried to knock-down your palace," Floris said.

A servant entered with tea, then left as the Queen indicated that she would pour. The servant looked around the room, but saw only two people.

"We've tried to be easy, just giving those fools a bit of a scare in hopes that that would stop the plant. I don't think we've badly hurt anybody yet, but this is frustrating. Although it goes against my better nature, the only thing left is to kill a few people to make our point," Rick warned.

"We were working hard to keep the house from falling into the sea before Matthew was arrested. It's a beautiful old house, and parts of it are older than this palace. We have enough troubles without these idiots getting in our way," Floris added.

"From what I can tell this argument has gone on long enough. You have a strong case, but I don't know what I can do for you. I would certainly like to keep you from killing anyone if I can," the Queen said.

Philip reached for the phone, "Let's ask John if there is some legal thing we might try."

"Can't you just make a royal proclamation telling them to leave ghosts alone," Floris asked.

"I don't think that's in my limited powers. There are lots of things I'd like to do, but not too many that I actually can do," the Queen said.

"There must be some way, some ancient power that the creeps haven't taken away from you," Rick said.

At this suggestion, both the Queen and Philip had a good laugh. Then John, the Queen's personal Attorney and legal expert, entered and the situation was explained to him.

"You could proclaim their property a royal sanctuary: it hasn't been done in ages, but you have the power, at least I don't think it has ever been revoked," John volunteered.

"What's a royal sanctuary," the Queen asked.

"It's a special property. Queen Mary started it, to reward people who had sheltered her. She declared that several houses were Royal Sanctuaries, which means that they are free of government taxes and interference forever," John explained.

"There's one in Kent somewhere, isn't there," Philip asked.

"I believe so: it's just considered an ancient anomaly. If you were to make such a proclamation in a few very special cases, no one would complain, and from the little that I know, this is a perfect situation for a designation," John said.

"Actually we do use it as a sanctuary for tired ghosts who need a place to rest," Rick said.

"It sounds like a bit of fun: a chance to do a good dead by ourselves, without waiting for permission from some committee," the Queen added.

"Let me call my staff and gather the details," John said as he reached for a phone.

"How long have you been a spirit," Philip asked.

"We're ghosts, spirits are just little vapors," Rick replied.

"There're lots of odd creatures in the spirit world, but ghosts are at the top of the heap: they're kind of like the humans of the spirit world," Floris added.

"Yes, there're only a few dozen ghosts in England, and probably most of them are asleep," Rick explained.

"But there are spirits and poltergeists and other odd things wandering around all the time, just like there are cats and dogs and other creatures in the living world," Floris said.

Floris was petting the dogs who rolled over, enjoying the attention. The Queen looked at the dogs, "You can't be too scary or they wouldn't be so friendly."

"My assistant has found a sanctuary proclamation from 1842. It sounds perfect: we could just copy it and change a few words," John said as he held a phone.

"Could you do it tomorrow," Floris asked.

"Tomorrow? Is the situation that critical," the Queen asked.

"No, it's my birthday," Floris replied.

The Queen laughed, "If it's just copying an old document it might be possible.

"You've been so helpful, is there anything we can do for you," Floris asked.

"Can you tell if a place is haunted," Philip asked.

"Sure, that is, we can walk around and see the other spirits," Rick replied.

"How would you like to spend a few days at Windsor and let us know who else is living there? We've heard rather unusual noises," the Queen asked.

"We'd love to, and that would be fun for us. There are lots of odd sleeping places in a castle that big, so there could be a few ghosts sleeping there, but spirits are probably more of a nuisance," Rick replied.

The phone rang and John answered, "Thank you, I'll tell them right away." John turned to the others, "It's just been on the news, your helper, Sir Julian, has fallen and been hurt badly. He's in critical condition, alone in hospital."

"We must leave. Where's the hospital? Please get Matthew out of jail and send him to Julian right away. I'm sorry. This is a disaster for us," Rick said.

"I'll take you both to the hospital. It's not far and I'd like to thank Julian for his hard work," Philip said.

"And your grandson won't be far behind," the Queen said as she picked up the telephone. "This has gone on long enough. John get busy. Print that proclamation and bring it here for me to sign. I'll read it myself into a TV camera. People are going to be surprised when they see that I'm not just a pleasant old figurehead."

It turned out to be a very exciting day for the media and especially for royal watchers. First, people were astonished by the poop attack on the PM. If ghosts could do that, in broad daylight, then they could do anything. No sooner was that news out, when Prince Phillip paid a surprise visit to the hospital where Julian was recovering. What's this? A royal endorsement of the ghostly side of the power plant argument, instead of criticism of the attack on the PM?

But, by far, the most astonishing news event was the Queen's appearance on live television, speaking in her own words without a prepared speech. She told people that she had met two pleasant ghosts, discussed the situation, and then decided that the matter had gone on long enough. The Queen made it clear that if action were not taken now, the whole business could change from a minor annoyance to a struggle where many people might be hurt or killed. Therefore, she was invoking an ancient power, for the first time since 1842, by declaring the ghosts' ancestral property off-limits to government interference. And furthermore, she had pardoned the owner of the property, and sent him to aid his injured co-worker. The matter was over, and peace had been restored. The power plant, if it were ever built, would be somewhere else. Then she read the proclamation and signed it as the cameras focused on her hands.

When the PM was interviewed later, he correctly sensed public opinion and offered to forgive and forget. He had been extricated from a tricky political situation, and was delighted to shift allegiance to the winning side. He didn't need a power plant, he needed votes.

That night at the hospital Matthew, Floris, and Rick sat by Julian's side talking about his injuries, the coming storms, and the demise of the power plant. Both of Matthew's hands were on Julian's injured leg.

"It's amazing, but I can sort of see inside your leg. I can't do anything about it, but I can see the problems, the broken bones, the leaking veins, the blood moving around," Matthew said.

"Here, let me see if I can do anything. This should be easier than working on your foot. I used to be able to fix simple problems, but I haven't tried anything like this in a long time. Perhaps I can make energy flow into the problem areas and speed the natural healing," Rick said.

Fortunately there was no nurse in the room as Rick materialized, then slowly worked on Julian's leg, "Yes, I can see the problems."

Rick gently ran his hands slowly over Julian's leg, which was in many bandages and a temporary cast. His eyes were closed.

"Perhaps things are beginning to change, but very slowly. Can you feel anything Julian," Rick asked.

"No, just a peaceful sort of warm glow. I'm still pretty well doped up from the operation."

"You're getting a little better every minute. Matthew, Floris, put your hands here and watch. Maybe the three of us together can do something grand."

"Look the bone is growing back together. You can almost see it moving," Floris whispered.

"The doctors will faint when they examine Julian tomorrow," Matthew said.

"We're just helping his body heal itself, giving it some of our strength and energy," Rick explained.

Chapter 20
The Storm

The doctors were indeed amazed in the morning, and finally allowed Matthew to take Julian with him, in a special ambulance, (with invisible Rick and Floris) back to the Chateau. Etienette had come home as soon as she had seen the Queen on TV. Julian dressed quickly in work clothes and they rushed to Redcliffs Hall in his Range Rover. They had difficulty reaching the house. A strong winter storm had already knocked several trees down, and the driveway was impassable. It was raining lightly as they walked to the servants' door. They could hear deep rumbles as ocean waves that had developed far away, rolled in and crashed into the shore far below. Some of the spray reached the top of the cliffs. The wind was strong.

Matthew flew out of his travel clothes and into his coveralls, gloves and heavy boots. In no time at all, he was measuring the tension on the sixty wire ropes that they had already placed. A few were completely slack, while others were dangerously overloaded. The central portion of the building had moved slightly as more of the foundation had collapsed.

The turnbuckles on the tight ropes were hard to turn, even with three-foot-long wrenches. If the tension weren't reduced in these ropes immediately, they could snap, sending a springing, thick coiled piece of heavy steel rope sailing through the air, cutting anything in its path to ribbons. As he eased the tension in some, others became tight as they picked up more of the load. In spite of the cold and wind, Matthew was sweating. He had once seen a safety film that showed a construction accident. A worker had been cut in half by a flying piece of steel rope as it snapped under strain. Not a pretty sight.

When the tension was balanced among the ropes, he, Floris, Etienette, and Rick started to place steel in the holes that had already been cut. The design called for thirty-eight supports, but only the middle twenty-four diagonals were in place. Holes had been drilled for six more, so these could be placed, bolted, and welded. Not all of the old masonry had collapsed, so the loading on the steel was not too bad yet.

Matthew was well-aware of the inaccuracies and estimations in his design. He had never calculated anything like this before and he knew that there was much room for error. The whole mess might crash about him if he were wrong. No one had checked his design for mistakes or omissions. This was no homework assignment. They worked as fast as possible through the day as the storm became stronger. The wind was now cold, and the temperature was dropping through the freezing point.

Into this furious rush of activity walked Azur, soft, vulnerable, and very much afraid. She held her head high and walked directly to Rick. Everyone stopped work and stared. "Rick, I will trouble you only a moment. I have come to ask Matthew a single question, then I will be gone." She turned to Matthew, her voice trembling as she held her fear in check, "I am sorry for the way I treated you, very sorry. You said once that you loved me. Do you still, for I will kill myself if we cannot be together, forever?"

Her parents were in shock, and Matthew, who had been strongly willing her to return, could not speak, he was so surprised. His desire for her return had been intense, perhaps much too intense. Matthew hugged Azur, lifted her and spun her around in the air. There wasn't time for anything else as a crash down below indicated that more of the foundation had collapsed. Everyone rushed back to work.

Floris removed her work gloves and handed them to Azur, "Welcome back, we can use your help." Rick was strangely silent as he stared at Azur.

Rick installed new wire ropes. He could feel the strain in the existing ropes and worked frantically to install the remaining thirty strands so that the load would be divided across the one hundred rope anchors they had installed.

Julian had taught Matthew the basics of heavy arc welding, but Matthew hadn't had much time to practice. Julian was still too weak to work hard, so Matthew was the only available welder. There was much to be done. He put on Julian's cotton cap, helmet, fireproof jacket and long fireproof gloves. He started to carefully weld braces across the new supports, beginning with the easiest joints. By focusing very carefully on what he was doing, he could feel the welds forming beneath the white hot glowing surface of the molten steel. He was sensing what experienced master welders knew instinctively from years of practice. He could see the molten steel penetrate into the hard steel. When it was just deep enough, he stopped and moved to the next joint. He knew that much skill is required to make a strong weld. The operator must melt enough to solidly join the two, or more, pieces, but not so much that the steel deforms and changes shape or slips out of position.

As Matthew worked, with sparks flying in all directions, Azur, in protective construction clothing, and a welding helmet to protect her eyes, was never far away. After a particularly loud crash from the rocks below, he stopped and asked her to go upstairs to a safer location, but Azur replied, "If you die, I want to die with you. I will never be far from your side". Upstairs, Floris felt, with her heart, these few words between Azur and Matthew and focused any spare energy that she could muster onto their efforts. She wanted them to be strong and to survive. She wanted her great-grandchildren to play in this house.

As they worked, the storm became intense. The wind was growing and was now at gale force. It was raining hard, with lightning flashes and thunder. The main noise however, came from the surf, which was pounding against the base of the cliff, sending spray as high as the chimney tops. The bottom level, where they were working, though far above the beach, was almost awash as the spray and freezing rain blew in, then ran back out.

Julian felt each steel column. By tapping each lightly with a hammer, he could roughly gauge the load each was carrying by the sound of the ping the hammer made. A few of the diagonal columns on one side were carrying far more than their fair share of the load. He quickly warned the others to stand clear of these two, for they might buckle soon unless the strain could be relieved by more steel columns.

Matthew didn't dare weld braces to the two overloaded supports. The heat might weaken them just enough to cause their collapse. Instead, they rushed to install two more columns on that side of the building, while Rick eased the tension on the ropes connected to the two over-loaded diagonals.

Fortunately they were all at the lowest level, amidst the spray and wind, installing bases for the new columns, when a large piece of the foundation gave way. This shifted the pattern of loading on the steel, and there was a very loud snap from above as one of the cables broke under the new strain. Bits of rock and dust floated down as one of the steel beams started to buckle outward, pushing against the hole where it passed through the ceiling. Strange deep rumbles, groans, and squeaks came from the structure as it twisted, adjusting to the new load distribution. Matthew had never seen steel bend like rubber. The floor where they had been standing earlier was gone. The steel structure as a whole twisted slightly, but was still rigid.

"Quick, escape while you can. Don't stay down here: it's too dangerous," Matthew shouted to the others.

"Let's get these last two columns finished first. If we work like mad they'll be solid in an hour," Julian argued.

"Let me go up alone and adjust the ropes. You finish these foundations," Rick said.

"No, everyone leave now, while you can," Matthew commanded.

"But you calculated that the steel will hold up the house, so why should we worry," Etienette asked.

"But that's only math, it could be wrong, or I could have forgotten something, or made a mistake."

Rick focused his energy on the small group, then ordered, "You must believe, all of you, you must believe intensely that he did not make mistakes and that this will work. The house is settling into a new position. Get busy, move!"

Rick scampered up the steps to work on the ropes, as the others struggled to force the new columns into position, bolting them together quickly.

Then Matthew chased all but Azur up the stairs as he started to weld supporting braces onto columns 29 and 30. As he finished they heard a loud low frequency rumbling sound. A huge wave was approaching the cliff. They stood flat against the inner wall, alone together in the sub-basement, as the giant wave tore the last of the outer floor and the old wall away, into the sea far below. Only the steel stood between them and the black void outside.

Matthew collapsed, falling toward the gap between two columns into the void. In a flash, he saw a vision of the future, like a movie running too quickly through his head. If was hard to see the details, but so frightening. A vague, cloudy, dark spirit was attacking Azur, and Matthew was loosing his life as he struggled against it trying to save her. As the brief dream faded, Azur was holding him tightly.

"What happened, you fainted and nearly fell into the sea," Azur asked in fear.

"I saw something, or imagined it. It was like a flash of memories of things that haven't happened yet. It was so terrible."

"What was it, what did you see?"

"Not now, some day, but not now. Let's go up to the others." He was soaked in a cold sweat and shaking from the experience. Scenes from the terrible vision overlaid his sight, as he blinked, trying to make them go away. He and Azur looked out though a forest of steel braces into the stormy night, as wind and water blew through the room soaking their clothes. Matthew could see the newly-exposed limestone of the cliff. Rick had been exactly right about the geology. All the soft rock and ancient masonry was now down on the rocks below, while the steel footings were on solid limestone, holding the house against the storm. The wind, singing through the steel braces, was so strong that they could hardly climb the steps to help the busy workers above.

After they tightened the last cable, they stepped back exhausted and looked at their work. The house was stable, with no creaks or groans. Although the old foundation was completely gone, the new steel was supporting the house well. The three exhausted couples stared at the work that they had done with much pleasure and satisfaction.

Matthew excused himself, and went up to the library, then

returned holding something. He walked to Azur, who was standing with her parents and Rick and Floris. Conversation stopped. Matthew looked straight into her eyes. "Azur, will you stay with me for the rest of your life, no matter what happens?"

She answered instantly, "Yes, always and forever."

Matthew removed the very old gold and diamond ring from its box, the valuable ring from the treasure chest that Rick had given him months ago, with a heart-shaped diamond, sparkling alone on an old, scratched and dented, golden band.

"You need fear no more: I will always be close to you. Rick and Floris know that your vow is true, and that we will never part. Please wear this ancient ring as a symbol of our enduring love."

Matthew placed the ring on her finger as tears came to Azur's eyes. They embraced and Etienette hugged them both. As Matthew looked into Azur's beautiful eyes, he still could not see clearly. Vague amorphous scenes from his vision of the future were confused with the reality in front of him.

Floris asked, "Rick, would you tell us about this ancient ring and where you found it?"

Rick was very serious, worried, not at all his old playful self. Tension built as he stared hard at Azur: the others sensed that he was thinking long before he spoke slowly and carefully. "I had planned to tell about it on Matthew's wedding day, but I will tell you a little now, as this is a very important moment for each one of us. I have guarded that ring since 1539, when Glastonbury was destroyed."

"The ring feels so old. I can sense that it must have seen much and that it is special," Azur said quietly.

"It is special, very special, in both good and evil ways, for its story is one of a great love that ended in tragedy. Legends describe a ring like this one, as having been worn by Queen Guinevere. According to the legends, Merlin made a ring by using his magical powers, then King Arthur gave it to her on their wedding day. Those are just old stories, from fourteen hundred years ago, but perhaps they're true. Arthur and Guinevere are buried at Glastonbury and the monk who gave me this ring was there, just after the cathedral was burned. After I saved his life, he gave me this and asked me to guard it forever. Now I am entrusting it to the two of you, and you must protect it during your lives. You are drawn to each other like moths to a flame; you can never separate. This ring symbolizes your total commitment, there is no turning back."

No one spoke as they stared at the ring and recalled the legends of Arthur and Guinevere's romantic, but heartbreaking story. There was no reply to Rick's enigmatic words, and he offered no explanation of their deeper meaning. Floris sensed that Rick knew much that he was not saying, and worried what it might portend. When she focused on Azur, she sensed something, something odd about her aura, her psychic personality. She was almost a part of Matthew, not a separate being.

Although they were cold, wet, and very tired, Matthew and Azur walked up the stairs to the roof, and looked out to sea from the old stone platform. A light snow had fallen, dusting the roof, and throwing the engraved Ley Line orientations into relief. The cold wind blew through their hair, but the storm was subsiding. The black sky overhead was slowly lightening into a cold watery gray dawn. The house was standing solid against the sea, as faint sunlight peeped over the horizon. The ring was almost glowing as it sparkled in the faint light. They hugged each other tightly and watched the sun grow in size, bringing a bright new day.

Rick and Floris were invisible, but not far away, watching over them, protecting them, as they looked to the future.

Epilog
Christmas Party

Matthew and Azur had much to be thankful for and wanted to do something in return, to find a way to partially repay the world for their good fortune and happiness together. They both had the idea at the same moment. They would stage a Christmas party for everyone in the village.

When Azur and Matthew announced their intention, the others were just as excited. Etienette had given many large parties and took charge of the arrangements. Quickly the guest list expanded to include everyone who had helped in the work, including the Christie's people and Etienette's staff. Floris and Rick started planning a magic show, as it would have been in 1939. They had only three weeks before the party, so time to start practicing. Hand-written notices were posted in the church and the pub. The entire village of around one hundred souls was invited.

While party preparations occupied Etienette, the others finished the construction project. They installed the remaining braces, then painted everything with marine paint to protect it from the spray. Heavy plastic sheeting was placed over the steel to block most of the spray and wind from the basements until material for a fiberglass wall could be delivered.

Meanwhile the window contractor replaced more of the glass in the ocean-side windows of the Long Gallery restoring a beautiful view of the sea. Cleaners washed a century of dust from the public rooms. Activity everywhere as the night of the party approached.

Guests arrived at dusk as a light snow began to fall. A beautiful sight. The rooms were illuminated by hundreds of candles, just as they had been originally. Heat came from roaring fireplaces. However, the plumbing was not authentic: porta-potties provided tacky but functional temporary facilities near the entrance. The catering company had been working all day, operating from the old kitchens downstairs.

Conversation stopped as people heard the sound of a helicopter outside. Only Julian knew who had arrived.

Smartly-dressed guards marched into the room, followed by the Queen and Prince Philip. Astonishment, then many bows and curtseys, as Julian introduced everyone. Rick and Floris were fully visible, and were elated at the surprise.

Floris greeted the Queen, "You're just in time for the magic show. I'm going to try to do my escape and a few other old tricks from the thirties. I hope that they do justice your childhood memories."

A stage was at the far end of the Long Gallery. Floris and Rick left the group and prepared for the show, as Julian arranged everyone in seats. The performance went well and all had a good time. Invisible Rick tickled people in the audience and helped Floris do amazing things on stage.

As they sang 'God Save The Queen' Matthew stood at Azur's side, tightly holding her hand. He was crying slightly, overcome with happiness, as he thought of everything that had happened since he had come to this house. He felt a powerful emotion as everyone sang the old anthem. As the tribute ended, he hugged Azur tightly. He could find no words to express the joy he felt surging through their hearts.

APPENDIX
Details Of House Stabilization

An appreciation for the design and installation of the steel under the house can be obtained with a little high school math and a few practical approximations. The following material describes how Matthew analyzed the situation then designed a workable solution. The problems are presented first, then his design and the logic behind it, and finally the implementation details. In order to make this presentation complete, relevant details from the main text are repeated and summarized below.

Redcliffs Hall: Dimensions
Main House, total exterior width, 112'
Wings, each, total exterior width, 50'
Total frontal width is therefore 212'
Central pediment and columns:
       -columns 30' high, 3' diameter at base
       -steps and pediment 37' wide
       -base of pediment 3' high
       -peak of pediment above base 6'
       -clock diameter 4'
Roof (all areas):
       -slope 60 degrees, slate, on visible portions
       -balustrade railing 3' high
       -chimneys project 5' above flat roof
Windows, 12 stacks in main house, 4' space between
       -windows, public rooms, 4' x 11'
       -windows, bedroom floor, 4' x 9'
       -windows, dormers, 4' x 4'
       -windows, servants' halls, 6' x 4'
Front door is 6' wide
Windows in the wings, 7 columns, 3-1/2' between
       -public rooms, 3' x 8', dormers, 3' x 3'
       -main house is 70' thick, front to back

-wings are 40' thick, front to back

INTERIOR DIMENSIONS, MAIN HOUSE
-exterior walls 3' thick: interior walls 5' or more thick
-spiral stairs, 6" rise, 16 steps = 360 degrees, 22-1/2 degrees each step
-staircase inside dimensions 5' x 5', 4" dia iron post in center

The Situation

Matthew's first step was to define the problem. He started at the bottom of the house, thinking about the structure which supported it. Geologically, most of the cliffs on which the house was sitting were a form of very hard and stable Limestone, an excellent durable building material. However, the central portion of the house, on the ocean side, was supported by a wedge or intrusion of softer shale, which was washing away. The soft area was seventy feet wide, and extended twenty-five feet under the house. Originally the soft stone had extended further out to the sea but erosion over the centuries had removed much of the exterior shale. Looking at the situation from the outside, an old painting of the house, dating back to the beginning of Victorian times, ca 1840, showed a stairway down to the beach. Photographs made in the 1930's showed a slightly-different stairway to the beach, and the beginnings of the foundation's collapse. Today the stairway was washed out in the middle, where it had once sat on the soft shale.

The machine shop rested directly on the stone. Its floor was brick, overlaying the shale and limestone. From cracks and fissures in the brick, he could see the approximate geology. The ocean-side wall was a mixture of stones and cement, varying between two and three feet thick, and it had three arched windows. The glass in the windows had broken ages ago and now salt spray, wind, rain and seagulls entered the room at will. The wall was cracked irregularly and some of its stones had fallen to the sea leaving gaping holes. The ceiling was supported by arches, brick barrel vaults, running parallel to the outer wall. Matt measured the ceiling to be about one foot thick, stone, brick and cement, at the thinnest part, over

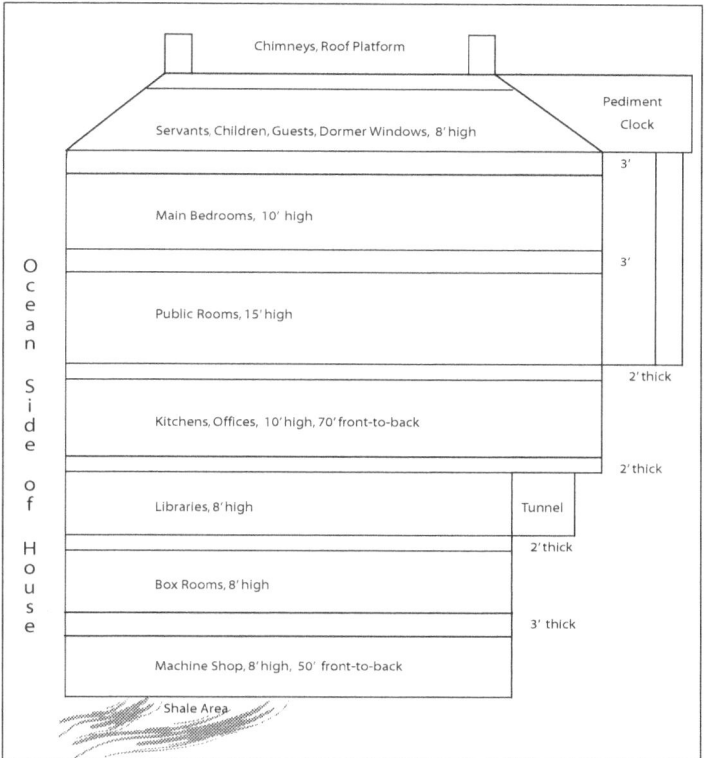

Chimneys, Roof Platform

Pediment
Clock

Servants, Children, Guests, Dormer Windows, 8' high

3'

Main Bedrooms, 10' high

3'

Public Rooms, 15' high

2' thick

Ocean Side of House

Kitchens, Offices, 10' high, 70' front-to-back

2' thick

Libraries, 8' high

Tunnel

2' thick

Box Rooms, 8' high

3' thick

Machine Shop, 8' high, 50' front-to-back

Shale Area

Side View of House and its Dimensions

the high point in the arches. The ceiling on the ocean side sagged in the middle with many uneven cracks. Bricks from the barrel vault on the ocean side were lying on the floor. A damaged and slippery stone staircase climbed against the back wall, on the east side of the room. The back wall, against the cliff, was bare natural stone, as were the side walls. The remains of a heavy door covered the top of the stairs, keeping the seagulls out of the box room above. Bird poop and the remains of nesting material were everywhere.

Matt reasoned that when Rick had equipped the machine shop the geology had been sound, or he wouldn't have installed so much gear in the room. He noticed that each machine had its own electric motor, so the machines were less than a hundred years old, since before about 1900 machines shared overhead power shafts and central steam or electric motors. Therefore, the collapse of the outer wall was a relatively recent event, perhaps in the past fifty years.

The <u>box room</u> just above was slightly bigger, cut deeper into the cliff. Masonry walls partitioned it into smaller rooms, and these walls gave support to the library above. Rick's darkroom as well as a wine cellar extended back into the cliff's rock. The ocean-side wall of the box room was concrete, though the outside was faced with local limestone to match the rest of the house. This wall was cracked in many places and Matt suspected from the wall's probable age that it contained no steel rebar to strengthen it. The outer wall had five windows which were covered with old boards to keep most of the wet and birds out of the rooms. The floor was concrete with many cracks on the ocean side. It hadn't sagged as much as the machine shop floor, yet. The ceiling on the ocean side had dropped perhaps half a foot at the center. A stone staircase led up the back wall to the Library and secret passages above.

In addition to the staircase, a large, five foot square trap door in the ceiling would have allowed things to be lowered from the library into the box room: a matching trap door in the box room floor allowed material to be lowered down to the machine shop. When he went upstairs, he noticed that the trap in the library floor was under an old carpet, so that is why he hadn't noticed it until he had explored the box room carefully. After discovering these traps, he saw that there was a matching opening in the Library ceiling that had been painted over. This series of three trap doors had probably allowed Rick to move equipment down to the machine shop sixty or seventy years ago. After Matt found the trap in the library ceiling, he spotted a strong hook on the kitchen ceiling above the traps: a big pulley or chain hoist could have been attached here to move things up and down to the machine shop floor, thirty feet below.

Unless something were done soon, the outer half of the machine shop floor would collapse as the soft rock under it gave way. The wall on this side had already dropped a foot on average, and there were holes where parts of the wall had fallen to the beach. Once the floor fell, it would take the load-bearing vaults and columns with it. This would cause a failure all the way up through the center of the ocean side of the house. After the house's walls above broke open, the marine air would invade the house leading to corrosion and decay: eventually the whole house would collapse, from the ocean side toward the land.

Possible Solutions

Matthew knew that the textbook solution was to bring in a large construction crane which could reach over the house and lower supplies and scaffolds down to the soft rock foundations below the machine shop. Horizontal steel could then be installed under the machine shop floor, wedged into the limestone on the sides of the soft slate valley, a project just like building a bridge over a narrow canyon. The soft stone under the floor would be replaced by steel and cement. Large hydraulic jacks would then lift the outer wall of the house up to its correct position, then steel and cement bracing would hold it there forever, solidly anchored into the limestone. This was not an impossible project, but it would be comparable to work done for major highways, not something he could do secretly in a few months without planning permissions.

The next best solution would be to try to do the same large-scale work from indoors, working from inside the machine shop to try to stabilize the house above. There were two major difficulties with this approach. The first was getting the heavy steel into this level without a large crane. The second was cutting into the thick outer wall in order to insert supporting steel brackets, while somehow holding up the rest of the house as the wall fell away. Once in position, the brackets would be raised by hydraulic pistons to move the outer wall up into its correct position. The brackets would be supported by complex beams wedged into the limestone walls. Eventually the floor would give-way, leaving the steel structure supporting the building above. The more he thought about this solution, the more he realized that it would be nearly impossible for him to do.

The least complex solution was to sacrifice most of the

machine shop and box room, filling them with a cobweb of steel. The focus would be on stabilizing the structure above which was the important part of the building. The key word was "stabilizing": with this approach there was no attempt to lift the outer wall back into position. The goal was to keep it from falling further. If he could do this, future construction projects could involve heavy equipment and attempt the lifting of the outer wall. The new steel web in the machine shop and box room would support the house until then. The two lowest rooms would be trashed by this plan but the rest of the house would survive.

Although the house was large with many problems on each floor, he decided to concentrate all his energy on the two lowest floors and the new steel web. The more he thought over the situation, the more he became convinced that in practical terms, he could not install anything under the whole house with the resources he could muster quickly. The soft slate valley under the house was almost inaccessible and was washing away into the ocean. Therefore his plan was the only option. If these two bottom layers could be replaced with steel, the rest of the house above would be stable until a more elaborate solution could be installed.

Outline of Chosen Solution:

Given the financial, time, and planning constraints, as much of the stabilization approach as was practical would be implemented.

The first part of the solution was to install diagonal steel under the library floor so as to stabilize it in its current position. The steel would take the weight of this floor, and everything above it, and transfer this weight diagonally onto the limestone portion of the machine shop floor two stories below. These long diagonals, at 59 degrees from vertical, would run from the outer wall down through holes in the box room floor and end in the solid limestone portion of the machine shop floor. All of this steel would be in compression.

The second part of the solution would be vertical steel, supporting the middle of the library floor, half way between cliff and ocean sides. These vertical steel posts would run from the machine shop's limestone floor, up through holes in the box room floor, thence to support some of the weight of the library. This would carry the weight of the middle portion of the house down to the limestone below.

The third major part of the solution consisted of wire rope in tension. This would run from the outer edge of box room ceiling, to the inner limestone wall. This would keep the diagonal steel from forcing the outer edge of the ceiling toward the sea.

Once the above was done, and if there was time before more collapsed, the outer quarter of the box room floor would be tied with steel and cable to the above-mentioned structures, so as to save the outer wall of the box room.

This solution used many small pieces of material, which could be bolted and welded together on-site, rather than large cumbersome pieces which would require a crane. Each piece would be carried, by just a few people, down staircases and through trapdoors inside the house. The underlying strategy was to substitute machinery and cleverness for large pieces and brawn.

Sizing the Chosen Solution

How much steel? What size? The goal was to take most of the load which the library floor represented and transfer it to the limestone two stories below. This would be done with many small pieces of steel, rather than a few large ones. Many adjacent diagonal steel columns, wedged at approximately 59 degrees between the box room ceiling and the machine shop floor would be used. As the distance between the box room ceiling and the machine room floor was nineteen feet, and the solid stone began twenty-five feet in from the wall, diagonal columns about 31 feet long were needed. Considering that two people would handle each column, even the smallest steel wide flange I-beam, which is 4"x4", would be heavy. (13 pounds per foot, or 403 pounds per thirty-one foot column). Therefore, each column would be divided into four pieces, one hundred pounds each, with bolted plate joints holding the assembled column together. This meant that four trips would be needed for each column, and each trip involved carrying a one hundred pound piece of steel, over seven feet long. Thinking this over, Matt put an electric winch at the top of his shopping list: he would hang the winch on the hook in the kitchen ceiling, then raise and lower material through the three trap doors, from the kitchen all the way down to the machine shop floor. The winch and much else would be run by a large diesel generator parked outside.

How much weight could one of these 4"x4" columns support? The load that a steel column can carry depends on its length. A short column can carry much more, safely, than a long column of the same material. This is due to the tendency of the long column to bend or bow, thereby breaking in the middle, as the load is increased. For example, an 11' 4x4 Wide flange column can carry 32,000 pounds, while a 6' column of the same material can safely carry 62,000 pounds (abbreviated 62 kips).

In order to take advantage of the strength of short columns, the structure would be arranged with horizontal bracing every six feet on each column. This would allow each column to act as though it was a group of six foot long columns, and support 62 kips instead of much less.

How many columns would be needed? Until the lower masonry collapsed, all the weight would be carried by the existing structure with no weight on the steel. However, as the soft stone and masonry gradually failed, the steel would pick up more of the loading. But the cross-linked box structures in higher levels of the house would divert some of this loading to the limestone side walls, so the steel would never carry the full weight of the structure above it. Given a full set of building plans, and extensive detail on the actual construction materials and their current condition, a computer model of the whole structure could be made and the exact forces calculated using finite element analysis. However, an approximate solution was needed immediately.

To start, he asked himself how much does the outer ocean-side wall of the house by itself weigh? The weight of the central portion of the wall, the portion over the soft stone, could be roughly calculated. This part of the wall is 70' wide, by 65' high. The average thickness, allowing for windows, balconies, hollow chimneys and passages, etc was perhaps one foot. This gave a volume of 4550 cubic feet (70 x 65 x 1). If the wall (stone, wood, glass, cement) was similar in average density to concrete, which weighs 150 pounds per cubic

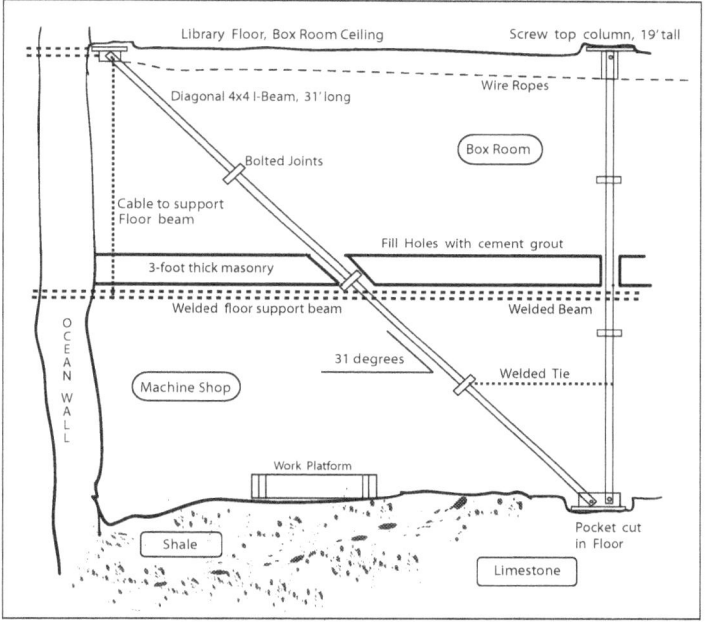

Library Floor, Box Room Ceiling — Screw top column, 19' tall

Wire Ropes

Diagonal 4x4 I-Beam, 31' long

Box Room

Bolted Joints

Cable to support
Floor beam

Fill Holes with cement grout

3-foot thick masonry

Welded floor support beam — Welded Beam

OCEAN WALL

31 degrees — Welded Tie

Machine Shop

Work Platform

Shale

Pocket cut
in Floor

Limestone

Steel Details

foot, then the outer wall over the sensitive area weighed 683,000 pounds, (683 kips) which is 340 tons.

But he didn't need to just support the wall, there were floors, furniture, interior walls, fireplaces, and much else to support as well. To simplify all this, he decided to just estimate the floors, and to consider that the outer half, perhaps 10' by 70' in area, of each floor would be on his steel. The five floors and ceilings above were various thicknesses, and some were wood and some hollow and some masonry. If the average of all this were similar to cement a foot thick, this would add 525 kips to the total weight he needed to support.

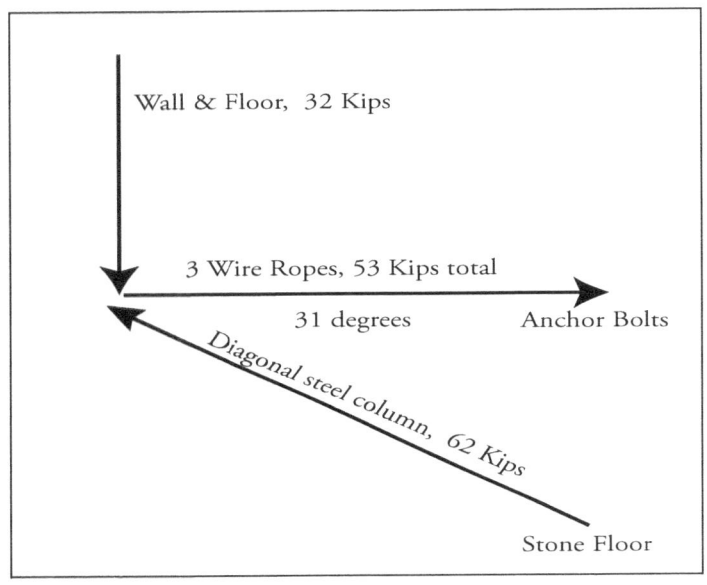

Stress Diagram, one of 38 supports

The total weight above the weak area was then 1208 kips.

The diagonals run at 59 degrees, so the compressive load in them, from the vertical weight of the structure above is (1208 / cos(59)), which is 2345 kips. If each diagonal took its full load of 62 kips, then 38 steel diagonal columns would do the job. These would be installed in a row seventy feet wide, so they would almost form a steel wall. With this arrangement, the centers of the columns would be twenty-two inches apart. The many horizontal braces among the columns would make the virtual wall almost complete.

Is this enough steel? The loading factor of 62kips per column is a "safe load" according to text books: in reality, twice as much weight could be carried before the steel actually became plastic and moved significantly. Corrosion could reduce the steel's size and strength, but many coats of thick marine paint could be sprayed on the steel to protect it. The load supported by the steel might be different from 1208kips, perhaps more, perhaps less. Some of the joints might be imperfect. The building might twist as the soft stone failed, placing heavy loads on just a few supports, overloading them, leading to a cascading failure as each of the other columns became overloaded. In the end Matthew decided to proceed with this design: it was a solution that would be possible to implement with just a few people, and there were enough redundant parts that the failure of any one column or joint would not be catastrophic. There was no more time for analysis: the house was slipping further every day.

The nineteen-foot-long vertical steel columns, behind the diagonal steel, would carry an unknown load. These columns would share some of the load that would have been carried by the outer wall, but the exact amount could not be estimated. Matthew decided that these would also consist of 38 vertical 4x4 wide-flange I-beams, built-up from three pieces, with suitable horizontal bracing. This vertical structure would be able to carry 2294 kips, which is 1147 tons. An additional and quite important purpose of these vertical steel columns was to solidly force their base plates into the limestone, so that the horizontal force from the adjoining diagonal beams did not have a chance to push the base plates toward the inner wall.

When he thought about the reality of installing these columns, he realized that factory-cut pieces would never tightly wedge into the space: they would never fit exactly: they would be too long or too short. He decided to have the steel fabricator make custom columns with a screw-jack on top. Each column would be delivered as three interlocking pieces with a total length under nineteen feet, and a big two-inch-diameter screw on top. Once the column was in position the screw would be tightened with a giant wrench so that the column was tightly wedged in position, carrying a load even before the floor failed.

The diagonal and vertical steel together would need 266 heavy pieces of steel. A lot to move around the site, and this didn't include the bolts, the horizontal braces, load-spreading plates at the top and bottom of each column, and the heavy tools which would be needed to do the work.

Matt ignored the weight of the heavy steel in his calculations because it was small compared to the weight of the house. For instance, he calculated that the 38 diagonals, at 300 pounds each, would weigh a total of only 11 kips.

Wire Ropes in tension

Consider the forces on the top of each of the diagonal columns. These forces must add to zero, or the columns will move. On each diagonal there is a vertical downward force of 32 kips from the weight of the walls. There is a diagonal upward force of 62 kips from the diagonal steel. To balance these, there must be a horizontal force of 53 kips, pulling toward the inner rock wall ((1208*tan(59))/38). The floor is mostly stone and cement. This is strong in compression, but it can easily pull apart in tension, so the floor could not provide the necessary horizontal tensile strength.

Wire ropes would supply the needed tension. These would pull the top of each diagonal column toward the cliff face. Looking at a table of 1x19 stainless steel wire rope, Matt saw that 14mm (5/8 inch) diameter rope would break at 31 kips. This material is relatively easy to handle, easy to cut, and easy to attach to fittings, but many pieces would be needed. If the rope were operated at slightly over half of its ultimate strength, 18 kips, three pieces of rope would be needed to create the tension for each column, or over one hundred ropes total (actually 114 ropes). This large number of ropes would provide redundancy in case one rope or attachment point should fail.

Each of the ropes would need two end fittings and a turnbuckle to adjust its tension, as well as an anchor bolt drilled into the inner limestone wall. The anchor bolt would be substantial, capable of supporting an axial load of 18 kips.

Once much of the above were in place, Matt would consider saving the outer wall of the box-room. To do this, horizontal beams perpendicular to the cliff face, with one end projecting through a hole in the outer wall, would be placed under the box-room floor to support its ocean side wall and floor. Each of these horizontal beams would need to be welded to a diagonal column on the inner end. The outer end would be supported by a wire rope in tension, through a hole in the box-room floor. The upper end of this rope would go to the top end of the diagonal column. This would provide additional attachment points between the actual wall and the steel structure and it would save the ocean-side portion of the box-room floor. However the installation of these horizontal beams might need to be done after part of the machine shop floor had fallen away, so the work would be dangerous, even if there were time to do it.

Implementation Details: Steel

Consider the reality of installing one of the diagonal braces. Let's start at the bottom, on the machine shop floor. A small pneumatic jack-hammer would be needed to clear away the brick floor, and to make a pocket in the limestone. An area 16" square by at least three inches deep for each of the thirty-eight columns had to be cut into the floor. A heavy steel plate, half an inch thick, would then be placed in the pocket. In advance, two vertical brackets, 4" apart, were welded to each plate. High strength cement grout would be placed between the limestone floor and the steel base plate to spread the load evenly under the plate.

The next step would be to install one of the custom-made vertical steel columns, after drilling a six-inch-diameter hole in the ceiling above the plate. The bottom of the column would attach to the welded brackets on the floor plate. The top of the column would have a similar sixteen-inch-square plate which would press against the box-room ceiling. The last step would be to tighten the screw jack at the top of the vertical column as much as possible so as to firmly wedge the column in place.

Then a carefully-marked diagonal hole would be cut in the masonry ceiling of the machine shop, which is one to two feet thick. This would be done from the box room above with a six inch diameter diamond core drill. These drill bits are long steel cylinders with diamond dust at the cutting edge. While drilling, water is forced into the cut to lubricate and cool the cutting surface as well as to remove the chips. Either an electric or pneumatic motor would power this kind of drill, but Matthew was partial to pneumatic motors because they run cooler and weigh much less. For this reason he used a Sunitek two horsepower motor which weighed only eighteen pounds to power the core drills: it consumed 77 CFM from the diesel compressor in the front yard, which was sized to easily deliver 300 CFM at 90psi. The main trick was drilling at the correct angle, 59 degrees, in the correct location. Matthew needed to measure the locations of these holes very carefully so that each diagonal steel column would fit perfectly through the hole. He estimated, from his limited experience at summer construction jobs, that drilling each hole would take three hours of concentrated very accurate work.

The upper end of each diagonal column would end at a steel plate, sixteen inches square. If it did not fit perfectly, smaller plates would be used to shim the gap so that each diagonal fit tightly.

After each diagonal floor hole was done, four of the 4x4 steel beams were bolted together in place through the hole. The bottom piece was attached to the floor plate with a large horizontal bolt, an inch in diameter. This would let the column pivot a little as loads developed. Same at the top end.

As each pair (a vertical and a diagonal) of columns was installed a small horizontal beam was welded to the columns, to support the machine shop ceiling (the box room floor). Cement grout was then poured into the floor holes from above, filling them, so that the ceiling was well-bonded to the columns. This arrangement provided the columns with excellent horizontal support, and sealed that part of the steel against marine corrosion. It was important to install each pair of columns completely (grout plus horizontal bracing) in case part of the soft rock gave way before the whole project was complete.

The top plates would press against the ceiling, next to the outer wall, under the library floor. In order to support the actual wall however, more was needed. Next to each ceiling plate a horizontal 6" diameter hole was drilled through the outer wall into the open sea air. A 4x4 I-beam was poked through this hole, then this I-beam was welded to the 16" plate at the top of the diagonal column. Matthew didn't know if this method of attachment to the actual wall structure would work, but it was the best solution he could envision. He did know that somehow he needed to get into and through the wall to support it: just supporting the edge of the ceiling with a steel plate was not sufficient. The main problem here would be supporting the heavy horizontal 6" core drill and getting water into the cutting surface, up near the box room ceiling. Scaffolding, ladders, and a brace arrangement for the drill would be needed for each of the 38 holes. This would take a fair amount of time. The 6" holes would be filled with grout after the steel was installed. As an aside, he imagined the view of these grouted holes from outside: a row of holes with long streamers of white glop dribbling down the wall, somewhat like cliff-side bird nests but on a large scale.

Implementation Details: Wire Rope

The hardest part of the rope work was drilling the anchor bolts into the wall. Matthew had worked with a highway construction crew and was familiar with rock drills. These are pneumatic drills that pound and rotate long hard steel bits into solid rock. During operation, water is fed into the holes to wash away cuttings, cool the bit, and make breathing safer: rock dust from similar drills had caused silicosis in miners before water lubrication was introduced. In textbook solutions the strength of the stone is measured then appropriate anchors are selected. Matthew had no way to analyze the rock's characteristics so he selected the strongest anchors he thought he could reasonably handle and planned to drill them as deep as possible into the rock. The strength of the steel in the anchors was over-kill, but he had no idea if the stone would support them, or if it would fracture and release the anchors. He reasoned that overly-large diameter anchors would grab more limestone, thereby providing a better chance of permanent adhesion.

Each anchor is a long steel screw with a hollow segmented cone on the far end. A conical steel sleeve fits over this cone. After a deep hole is drilled and washed clean, the anchor assembly is inserted. Then the screw is turned which pulls the cone into the expandable sleeve, pressing it against the sides of the hole. When tight, the screw anchor is deeply embedded in the rock and it can support huge loads. For example, Matthew calculated that the Williams "Spin-Lock" anchors, with one inch diameter screws and 1-3/4" holes, which he planned to use, would support a tension load of 90kips, or 45 kips with a safety factor of two. However, he didn't know if the limestone would support anything like this kind of loading, so he scattered the holes over the rock face, as far apart from each other as practical. After each anchor bolt was tight, he filled the hole with cement grout both to protect the anchor from marine corrosion as well as to improve adhesion between the anchor and the limestone. He hoped this arrangement would support his design load of 18kips for each anchor but had no way of knowing if it would work.

Even small rock drilling rigs, such as the Airrex-35 that Matthew used, are heavy and cumbersome. However Matthew had seen smart construction workers supporting drill motors with "air-legs". This are sloping legs that expand and contract, powered by compressed air. As the drill digs horizontally into the rock, the operator presses a button and makes the air-leg longer. The result is that the operator only needs to steer the drill, he doesn't need to hold its thirty-five pound weight in position all day. However, while drilling, the motor is pounding the drill bit hundreds of times a minute, making a horrendous noise, and shaking the operator vigorously, so the air-leg doesn't eliminate all discomfort.

The wire rope was cut to approximate size with a hydraulic shear before it entered the house. In addition, one of the end connectors was attached to each piece of rope while the rope was outside. Matthew used screw-on connectors, swageless terminals from S3i, because they are strong and one person can easily install them with a pair of big wrenches. After each diagonal steel was placed, three ropes were attached and trimmed to final length. A long turnbuckle then connected each rope to its anchor. The cables were tightened approximately, using the turnbuckle, then a tension meter was used to check each cable as the final tightening was done. Matthew knew that as the house settled, he would need to monitor the tension in all the cables and make many adjustments, so that none of the cables became too tight or too loose. The goal was to spread the loading evenly across many cables, so that no one cable became too tight and snapped. All the turnbuckles and connectors were covered with grease to prevent marine corrosion. The stainless cables were sprayed with marine paint to protect them from the salt air.

An Accident

An unforeseen accident occurred when a baseplate slipped out of its pocket, allowing the attached diagonal steel to bend. The force diagram shows that the baseplate, and the stone pocket in which it sets, must withstand a horizontal force of 53 kips. Matthew's plan was that a vertical steel column would press down hard on each baseplate, preventing the steel plate from moving. This accident happened when part of the soft stone collapsed rapidly, providing a dramatic change in loading on the relevant steel diagonal. Unfortunately, the six inch diameter holes in the box room floor had not been grouted, and the cross bracing was not welded in place either. This left each diagonal brace on its own to react to forces. The cure was to install additional steel on the machine shop floor, horizontally between the limestone wall and the baseplates so that they could never move again.

Implementation Details: Miscellaneous

Before anything could begin, much old machinery and junk needed to be removed or repositioned on both working levels. In addition, adequate and safe electric work lighting was installed everywhere to minimize the chance of accidents. Damaged steps in the staircases were rebuilt with steel plates bolted to the stone. A 20KW diesel generator, a large diesel arc welder, and a 300 CFM diesel air compressor were positioned near the house with many 50 gallon drums of diesel fuel.

When the steel was ordered, it was run through heavy galvanizing, and heavy painting for protection. Rust and corrosion were the main enemies of this solution once it was in place.

Matthew knew that the soft stone would eventually fall into the sea, so he wanted to build a temporary floor completely over the soft stone under the machine shop floor to support workers, in case the rock should fail unexpectedly. However, such a structure would require many long pieces of steel or aluminum to span the 70' wide by 25' deep soft area. In the end, it was just not possible given everything else that was needed. As a substitute two seventy-foot long steel beams were created by bolting together 4x4 I-beams, and these long pieces of steel were laid across the soft stone. Once these long straight beams were in place, the sag in the soft stone floor became obvious. Workers attached personal safety cables to these beams, and occasionally placed pieces of plywood and wood across the beams as temporary work flooring.

About one third of the steel was needed in the machine shop, and two thirds in the box room. It was delivered to these levels and neatly stacked as work began.

Endnotes

No Voice From The Hall (early memories of a country house snooper), John Harris, London, 1998.

A wonderful and very sad book describing the author's adventures in the 1940's and 1950's as he climbed over fences and wandered through abandoned old English country houses after the war. Eventually he became an Architectural Historian, so the book is a combination of memories as well as factual research into the same buildings. The book describes many houses that were torn down because the owners could not afford the necessary repairs due both to the government's socialist tax policies and to the miniscule reparations that were paid for the damage that the military had done to the houses that it had requisitioned during wartime. He describes the contrast to France, where most country houses survived, due to different government policies. In 1950's England a large old house or two was torn down every week. The author attended many of the demolitions with his friends who were antique dealers. Sometimes they would buy a whole room, paneling, fireplaces, chandeliers, for little more than the cost of hauling it away.

The Design Of The English Country House 1620-1920. John Harris. Trefoil Books, London, 1985. Many drawings and descriptions of country houses.

The Georgian Country House. Dana Arnold. Sutton Publishing 1998. Information and drawings about the design of English country houses as well as descriptions of daily life when these houses were built.

Jane Austin's Town and Country Style. Susan Watkins. Rizzoli 1991. Descriptions of what life was like in Jane Austin's time, with wanderings through country houses.

Creating Paradise. Wilson and Mackley. Hambledon & London 2000. The building of English country houses from 1660 to 1880.

Haunted Steel Adventures

Much detail, drawings, etc.

Discovering English Architecture. T.W. West. Shire Publications 1979. Paperback guide which can be carried while exploring houses today.

Palladian Architecture

(part of an internet article from Britain Express)

Palladianism is, loosely, a philosophy of design based on the writings and work of Andreas Palladio, an Italian architect of the 16th century who tried to recreate the style and proportions of the buildings of ancient Rome.

The first popularizer of Palladian style was Inigo Jones, Surveyor-General under James I. Jones, who was responsible for several very early classical buildings, notably Queen's House, Greenwich, and the Banqueting House at Whitehall. In many ways Jones was ahead of his time, for it was not until well into the 18th century that adherence to the classical ideals of Palladio became truly widespread in England.

The 18th century saw a huge growth in the number of ostentatious country houses such as Stowe and Stourhead. A whole new class of wealthy merchants and landed nobility vied to outdo one another in the building of lavish countryside estates and gardens. It is in the design of these country house estates that Palladian principles are most evident today. Palladian ideas and examples were widely disseminated through several influential books. Volumes such as Colen Campbell's Vitruvius Britannicus and William Kent's Designs of Inigo Jones were lavishly illustrated, and many Palladian architects took their inspiration from the detailed drawings in these "design manuals".

Simplified Engineering For Architects And Builders, Harry Parker, Wiley, 1975.

This describes, using high-school algebra, how to design basic structures in steel and wood. There is enough information to safely design simple buildings, and a grounding to allow the reader to understand more advanced techniques.

WWW.Williamsform.com,
   Extensive information on spin-lock anchors.

WWW.Jackhammer.com,
   Information on rock drills and bits.

The Old Straight Track, Alfred Watkins. Methuen & Co, 1925
   The original and definitive book on Ley Lines, by their discoverer in modern times. He wandered the English countryside as a traveling salesman and photographer on horseback around 1900, and observed long straight alignments in illogical places. His book, describing these alignments, was the basis of "The Old Straight Track Club", a group of people who went on to discover alignments across the whole country. The advent of airplanes and aerial photography did much to advance the recognition of these lines. Watkins did not attach psychic significance to the lines which he discovered. Modern research has shown that many of the lines pre-date the Romans, and that some of the straight Roman roads are on pre-existing alignments.

The Ley Hunter's Companion. Devereux and Thomson. Thames & Hudson 1979. Book about Watkins discoveries of Ley Lines and how to find them now.

Dowsing In Devon and Cornwall, Alan Neal, Bossiney Books, 2001. This book is about how to make and use dowsing rods. The author describes dowsing for water as well as for metal and old spirits. He believes that anyone can dowse, and that developing the skill just takes lots of time, patience, and practice. This is a textbook for people who want to learn how to dowse.

Radiocarbon Dating, Sheridan Bowman, British Museum Press, 1990.

A small book with all the basic information on how carbon dating works in theory and in practice.

Famous Five (series of 25 books), for example Five Fall Into Adventure, Five Go Down to the Sea, Five on a Treasure Island. Enid Blyton. Hodder & Stoughton. Ca 1953.

The Emperor of scent. Chandler Burr. Random House. 2002.
      "'The Dreamer' by Versace startles you. It is absolutely mouthwatering. It is walking through a French pastry shop next to a spice market in southern Thailand. Then there's ice cream, gun powder, fruit candy, hot cocoa,. . . It is the most mesmeric fragrance I know." (P 327)
      "'Happy For Men' by Clinique. A guy who smells like this is sunshine and cool, summer beach and intelligence, snowboarding and sexiness. Damn, this stuff is nice." (P 328)

Fortean Times,
      Each issue is filled with semi-believable stories of the paranormal. SHC is only one of their favorite 'weird' subjects. Others include sea monsters, people with multiple heads, space visitors, etc.

Ghost Hunters. Deborah Blum. Penguin Press 2006.
      Contains detailed accounts of many psychic occurrences covering a wide range of subjects. Much about the investigation of these events and possible explanations.

Parapsychology. Jane Henry (Ed). Routledge, NY, 2005.
      Research papers organized into: Parapsychology, Paranormal Cognition, Paranormal Action, Anomalous Experience, After-life Associations.

A Brief manual For Work In Parapsychology. Parapsychology Foundation. New York 1999.

Best Evidence. Michael Schmicker. Writers Club Press 2002. Many examples of paranormal phenomena documented and described.

Kirlian Photography (www.ufoseek.com)

In 1939, Semyon Kirlian discovered by accident that if an object on a photographic plate is subjected to a high-voltage electric field, an image is created on the plate. The image looks like a colored halo or coronal discharge. This image is said to be a physical manifestation of the spiritual aura or "life force" which allegedly surrounds each living thing. Allegedly, this special method of "photographing" objects is a gateway to the paranormal world of auras. Actually, what is recorded is due to quite natural phenomena such as pressure, electrical grounding, humidity and temperature. Changes in moisture (which may reflect changes in emotions), barometric pressure, and voltage, among other things, will produce different 'auras'.

Living things are moist. When the electricity enters the living object, it produces an area of gas ionization around the photographed object, assuming moisture is present on the object. This moisture is transferred from the subject to the emulsion surface of the photographic film and causes an alternation of the electric charge pattern on the film. If a photograph is taken in a vacuum, where no ionized gas is present, no Kirlian image appears. If the Kirlian image were due to some paranormal fundamental living energy field, it should not disappear in a simple vacuum (Hines).

There have even been claims of Kirlian photography being able to capture "phantom limbs," e.g., when a leaf is placed on the plate and then torn in half and "photographed," the whole leaf shows up in the picture. This is not due to paranormal forces, however, but to fraud or to residues left from the initial impression of the whole leaf.